On This Christmas, I Thee Wed

by

Virginia Barlow

Christmas in the Castle Series

On This Christmas, I Thee Wed

Cover Art by *Teddi Black*

The Wild Rose Press, Inc.
PO Box 708
Adams Basin, NY 14410-0708
Visit us at www.thewildrosepress.com

Publishing History
First Edition, 2024
Trade Paperback ISBN 978-1-5092-5908-3
Digital ISBN 978-1-5092-5909-0

Christmas in the Castle Series
Published in the United States of America

Dedication

For Varie, because you've always been there.

Chapter One

Sheffield, England
November 1, 1784
Only one person alive could save her now.

"Thank goodness you're here." Lady Lavinia Holbrook flung open the heavy oak door of the cathedral antechamber and kicked the train of her satin wedding gown aside so her friend could enter. "Your timing could not be better. Margret just left."

"That old dragon. She has a nose for mischief and spoiled many a grand lark." Victoria Beaumont's strawberry mouth tilted down at the corners before her humor returned. "Good morning, Lavinia. You are looking very…pre-wed." She strolled inside with one eyebrow quirked as she took in her friend's ivory dress, stocking feet, and bare head.

"Good morning," Lavinia returned as emotion welled in her eyes. "How I've missed you."

Emerald eyes met hers in an assessing glance before Victoria drew her in for a much-needed hug.

Although months went by since they last spoke, it felt as if no time had passed at all. Hope fluttered in Lavinia's chest for the first time in weeks. Together, they would find a solution like they always did.

"Your mother will have a fit of apoplexy if she discovers me here. She is convinced I led your brother astray and holds me responsible for his death. I must confess your cryptic note inviting me to your antechamber before the wedding ceremony surprised me, and I came straight away. A loose chignon is all the time I allowed for my hair, and I walked out the door of my chamber as my maid tied the back of my gown. No doubt, Matilda will give me a tongue-lashing when I return." Her friend's dancing eyes said the maid's irritation amused her. Tilting her head, she sobered. "I must say, you are too pale by half. The Lavinia I remember had mischievous eyes and a ready smile. What brought about the change? Am I summoned here as your knight in shining armor, I wonder? Had I known, I would have worn my plumed hat."

Lavinia pictured her slender friend in a metal suit holding a drawn sword while her flaming red hair fanned out behind her in the breeze and smiled. "I had no one else to turn to. I spent the entire night contemplating my options, and your face kept popping up as the answer."

"I should hope so. No one else has my experience getting you out of trouble." Victoria untied the ribbons of her cape and nudged her chin toward the tea trolley. "Do we have time for tea before the battle? Or should I ready my steed?"

Before Lavinia could reply, heavy footsteps approached with a determined ring.

"Quick, in here." With a cry of terror, she shoved Victoria behind the changing screen and turned to face her executioner.

The heavy inner door to the chapel swung open with a bang, and the Earl of Holbrook stepped inside her sanctuary. Her father's wide smile and sparkling eyes disappeared the second he closed the door.

A rock formed in her belly.

His gaze swept over her and darkened with anger. "Your future husband grows impatient. We cannot delay the ceremony longer." His lips thinned, and his gray eyes narrowed as he inspected her from the top of her bare head piled high with curls to the bottom of her stocking feet, peeking from beneath the hem of her white gown. "Where the hell are your veil and shoes? And where is Margret? Really, Lavinia. You try my patience past my ability to endure. I commanded you to be ready at ten thirty. The time is now a quarter past, and you are not prepared. I will not allow you to insult the viscount further." Tall and handsome with peppered black hair, her father wore his finest black linen suit, which consisted of satin breeches, a matching velvet overcoat trimmed with gold embroidery, a pristine white shirt beneath an intricately folded neckcloth, and high-heeled buckle shoes that caught the morning light. Despite being dressed in the height of fashion, his foul disposition ruined the effect.

"Every bride in the Ton arrives five minutes late as is fashionable. The ceremony is not scheduled until the eleventh hour." Her chin rose in defiance as she stared at her father. "Even the condemned are executed on the stroke of the clock and not a moment before. I deserve no less and have given the viscount no insult." Not yet, she amended. "'Twas not me parading my lover for all and sundry to see."

The earl shot her a furious gaze. "Mind your tongue, girl." His words cracked like a whip, and for a fleeting moment, she feared he would strike her. A heavy silence hung between them before his fists relaxed at his sides, and a cold mask of indifference settled over his face. "I have had enough of this nonsense. Your husband's actions and who he associates with are none of your affair. Know your place, or you will learn it the hard way. Hudson is not a man to trifle with."

Withdrawing a watch from the pocket of his gold silk vest, he checked the time, and his lips tightened. "You are lucky the viscount favors you at all, such as you are. For reasons known to him alone, he wants you. This extravagant spectacle, with all its unnecessary pomp, was his idea. As for me, I would see you wed on the street in rags in exchange for the title to the hundred acres my wastrel uncle gambled away." Snapping his watch closed, he replaced the article in his vest pocket. "I dare say I am getting the superior bargain."

His icy words hit her like a runaway carriage. They were meant to hurt and found their target with remarkable accuracy.

"I want no more excuses. You have ten minutes before I drag you into the church barefoot and bareheaded if I must. Find your worthless maid and finish your preparations. I want this done. My patience is at an end. Do not anger me further, or you will rue the moment you were born."

The door clicked with the solid thud of a cell door in Newgate prison, and Lavinia rushed forward to slide the bolt behind him with shaky fingers. *I would see you wed on the street in rags*...Damn them all to hell.

She refused to be treated like a worthless beast whose purpose in life was to procreate and pander to the whims of some man. Her heart surged with defiance as she took a swipe at her cheeks. She *had* worth, dammit. She could speak five languages, do sums in her head, and run a household of sixty servants. Despite what society believed, women deserved respect, and their voices should be heard and valued.

"Out of curiosity, are we whisking you away to an undisclosed location, burying Hudson so deep no one will ever find him, or shooting your father between his cold, black eyes?" Her friend's dry tone lightened the tension. "You have yet to tell me the reason for my summons, but from what I witnessed a moment ago, I can guess."

Lavinia met the deviltry in Victoria's eyes with a weak smile as her friend stepped from her hiding place.

She grimaced. "We are whisking me away. I refuse to live the life my mother and sisters lead. It dawned on me last night that unless I take action, my fate will be the same as theirs. Quick. Unlace me." Turning, she presented her back to her friend. She could not wait to be rid of the lot of them.

Victoria stepped closer and tugged on her laces. "Leaving the most eligible viscount in England at the altar will be an unparalleled scandal. Even bigger than mine."

"Indeed, but nothing short of death or a bolt of lightning will sway Papa's resolve. Or Hudson's, either. And you're well aware of society's views on women. Papa has been obsessed with reclaiming the land between Holbrook Manor and Waterdown Castle for years. And after the duke stripped Hudson of his funding, you can imagine how reluctant the viscount will be to relinquish my hundred-thousand-pound dowry when his debauchery is at stake." She shook her head. "Even if I were to have a sudden attack of smallpox, they would both prop my body up before the priest and carry on with the ceremony." She sighed, shaking her head again. "No. To put an end to this, I must leave. Margret will return soon with my things, and I must not be here when she does."

Victoria sighed while she worked on the laces. "You left precious little time to make your escape. Why did you wait until now to run away? You could have escaped in the night weeks ago."

"And risk the servants' betrayal and weeks of Papa's cruel punishments? I think not." Lavinia declared, holding her breath to aid Victoria's efforts. "Besides, Papa has locked me in my room every night since the moment Hudson returned with the coveted title and they finalized the marriage contract."

"The earl will have an episode when he discovers your absence," Victoria remarked, loosening the strings down Lavinia's back.

"I couldn't care less. Papa put me in this predicament, and neither he nor my mother care a fig how I feel." Lavinia's bodice slipped down her shoulders and over her slim hips. She stepped out of the white satin gown bearing hundreds of seed pearls, a tight-fitting bodice, long-fitted sleeves, and a small, elegant train. She flung it across one of the brocade settees with a careless gesture. "Now, my skirts."

Victoria untied them with practiced fingers, ignoring Lavinia's frantic attempts to help. "So where are we going? You know I enjoy a good adventure. When we were in school, you were much more organized."

Lavinia shook her head. "Back then, we were concerned about Sister Fran, and things were simpler." She stepped out of her underskirts with a shudder as if they were infected with the Black Death and left them in a pile on the gray flagstone floor. Darting over to the corner, she retrieved a valise from beneath her cloak. "I prepared a dark gown and a change of clothes. I packed them after Margret retired last night and stashed them in the boot of the carriage this morning after she collected my breakfast tray."

Victoria chuckled. "You must have been quite a sight in your bedrail and dressing gown. What if someone saw you?"

Lavinia shrugged. "I have been sneaking out of the castle since I learned to walk. I know where all the secret passages are."

"How did you get the valise into the antechamber? You must have slipped it into the church like a thief carrying the Crown Jewels to escape Margret's notice."

Lavinia laughed as she drew a navy walking gown over her head and turned for Victoria to lace her up. "She does have an uncanny talent for such things. I suspect that's why Papa assigned her to me."

"I have no doubt you're right." Her friend's voice grew thoughtful. "You did not answer my question. Where we are going."

"To my godmother's near Falstone. My parents will go to Miryam's first and then to Anabel's. Both of my sisters will tease our parents to stay. When they do not discover me with either sister, they will travel to my grandparents to search for me. I calculate in pleasant weather, I have until the middle of December before they find me. With any luck, there will be a snowstorm, and I'll be safe until the New Year." In any ordinary situation, her older sister, Miryam, would be her first destination. But in this dire circumstance, she could not trust her sister to support her. Miryam had been married off to a man twice her age during her first season and grew fat with his child.

"Falstone? We shall travel close to a fortnight to get there." Victoria finished lacing her into the gown and tied the strings.

"I am aware," Lavinia murmured. "The further away, the better."

"How long before Margret returns?" Victoria walked around to face her.

"I left my wedding slippers and veil at home on purpose so she would have to fetch them. I calculate the time she takes to gather them, and return will be sufficient to set my plan into action."

Her friend chuckled, and then she sobered. "It is doubtful your father or the viscount will ever forgive you. Your mother and sisters will follow the earl's lead."

Lavinia nodded. "What they think is not important." She lied, and they both knew it. "I plan to move on with my life like you did."

Neither one mentioned the scandal Lady Victoria had been involved in a year ago. Much of the Ton refused to acknowledge her to this very day because of the uproar. Yet, Lavinia remained steadfast in their friendship as if nothing of import occurred.

"Shall we go?" Victoria turned toward the door.

Lavinia lifted her valise and broached a delicate subject. "You do not have to accompany me, Victoria. I will pay for the use of your carriage. I could not take Papa's because the servants will inform him of my whereabouts. That's why I requested yours. At the same time, I do not wish to bring further condemnation upon your head."

Victoria gripped her shoulders and gazed into her eyes. "I have known you since we were four years old, and I recognize the look in your eye. Did you plan to leave me behind all along?"

"Yes, that's why I asked for both of your carriages. One to whisk me away and the other for you to return home with." Her confession came out with a sigh. "Using your carriage will get you in enough trouble. If you come, you will be involved in another scandal, and I cannot risk it."

Her friend fixed her with a long, penetrating stare. "I suspected as much. That's why I rode in my old carriage and left a driver with instructions in the second one. If someone asks, they will assume I am in the newer one since I never go anywhere in the old one anymore." Victoria's gaze narrowed in defiance. "I'm coming. Like it or nay. You cannot go alone and unchaperoned."

Lavinia wanted to weep. "I will not add to your misery." She searched her friend's face. "I have considered the danger and packed a pistol in my valise. I will be careful."

Victoria gave a snort. "The gun will do you no good if it's tucked away in your valise when trouble arises. Nay. We will take my carriage and travel together. I had the foresight to pack a trunk. So you cannot use my lack of clothing against me. Your brother left me with enough coin to travel in style despite your father's attempts to stop the funds, and I insist we make use of it. My outriders will see to our protection."

"Are you certain?" Lavinia stared hard into Victoria's green eyes. "I do not wish to tarnish your reputation further."

"We shall argue on the way. If you're certain you're running away, I am just as certain I am coming with you. So *we* ride for Falstone and Chauncy Castle." Biting her lip, she shot an assessing glance toward the oak doors. "I hear organ music."

They exchanged a quick glance and hastened toward the exit.

Lavinia clutched her valise against her chest and stepped out the side door with Victoria right behind her. They tugged their hoods forward, moving toward the waiting carriage with the same nonchalant stride they used to escape drawing attention in their youth.

The nuns at the convent used to call them the terrible duo because of their antics, and none of the good women would be surprised to see their charges' current activities.

Victoria's footmen assisted them into her carriage, and they took their seats.

The door closed, and the carriage surged into motion.

Leaning forward, Victoria gave her a small smile. "We'll rendezvous with my men at arms and my lady's maid at the fork in the road."

Lavinia's lips twisted. "Am I so transparent? You knew I intended to run away before you arrived at the cathedral."

"Lavinia, you requested me *and* my two carriages. Most brides plan to leave their wedding with their new husband. I didn't need to be a genius to figure out you had no such plans."

No. She didn't, and she came anyway. Gratitude filled Lavinia's heart as she studied her friend.

Victoria stood an inch shorter than Lavinia's stately five-foot-seven stature, possessed long red hair and wicked green eyes that caught men off guard, and then filled them with delight. Her curvaceous figure and infectious smile had her admirers tripping over their polished boots to make her acquaintance.

Lavinia's brother had been no different. But where others failed, he succeeded.

Victoria crossed her long, elegant legs, adjusted the skirt of her emerald green day gown, and removed her gloves. "Thank goodness Cook packed a hamper so we wouldn't have to stop." Leaning forward, she inspected the basket of food sitting beside her. "How delightful. Finger sandwiches *and* lemon cake. It's not the most substantial breakfast, but it will suffice. I will never let Adeline go. She knows what I like and packed plenty. Are you hungry? I am. I haven't had a single morsel to eat yet this morning."

Lavinia smiled as her best friend prepared food on two plates. "Yes, but one sandwich will do. I haven't been able to keep much food down these last few days."

"You cannot run if you do not eat." Handing her a plate, Victoria leaned back. "I do not mean to make light of the situation, but things tend to look better after a meal. You will see. Let's talk while we eat. I want to hear every tiny detail."

Lavinia stared out the window. "You have not asked me why I wish to run or what I hope to accomplish. And I love you for your support. The truth is simple. I refuse to wed Viscount Becker despite Mama's insistence he is the best catch of the season." She swallowed hard. "You may think me silly or fanciful, but I can't abide a loveless marriage." She took a tiny bite of her sandwich. "I thought I could fulfill my family's expectations, wed as they demand, and produce the obligatory heir. But after last eve, I no longer believe Hudson will treat me with anything but indifference." Licking her dry lips, she tightened her grip on the porcelain plate on her lap. "When I saw the viscount and his mistress together, it struck me. I will live the same miserable life my mother and sisters do unless I do something drastic. I am not made of the same malleable fabric as they and shall never submit to any man's tyranny. My instinct tells me to escape while I can. There is something…unsettling about Hudson that I cannot explain." She cast her friend a pleading glance. "Do you remember when we ran away from the convent and got lost in the woods?"

Lady Beaumont nodded as she placed another sandwich on her plate. "We heard wolves and climbed the nearest tree, afraid to let go of each other for fear we'd fall and get eaten."

"Yes, and when morning came, we discovered the fearful black shapes beneath us were just berry bushes and not ferocious predators hoping for an easy meal." A small smile graced Lavinia's lips before the weight of her current situation returned. "To me, Hudson is a wolf disguised as a berry bush. He is the opposite of what everyone perceives. The Ton worships him for his impeccable bloodlines and does not see the evil lurking in his eyes." She took a deep breath and lifted her chin. "But I do."

Victoria set her plate on the linen covering her knees and pinned Lavinia in place with a ferocious frown. "Has he hurt you?" Her narrowed eyes said she would slice him from nose to ankle if he dared.

A sigh escaped, and Lavinia's chin dropped. "Not hurt, exactly. And therein lies the problem. I ceased to believe in love long ago, but I did expect to receive respect as befitting my station. First as an earl's daughter and second as the viscount's wife. Yet, he humiliated me in front of the entire village mere hours before the ceremony. If he does this now, what will he be like later when I am his legal wife, and no one can say nay against him? There is a darkness about our future together that terrifies me. But no one will heed my protests. My heart tells me to run, but my duty is to wed. I have wrestled with my conscience and find self-preservation wins. I refuse to be a sacrificial lamb for the family's honor. But in rejecting the viscount, not only do I incur my parents' wrath but society's haughty judgment as well."

Victoria grimaced and gave a delicate shudder.

Lavinia nodded. "Just so. I knew you would understand, given everything you've endured. Papa thinks I've gone daft, and when I confided in Mama, she dismissed my concerns as premarital jitter." Dropping her chin, she stared at the delicate cucumber sandwich on her plate with unseeing eyes. "But 'tis more. The knot in my stomach is the same as the one I had that night in the woods. As if a predator lurks in the shadows, waiting to devour me." Her chin lifted. "I must be true to my own inner guidance, and my parents leave me no choice but to take the matter in hand." She cast another gaze at the rolling countryside. "And so, here I am."

Chapter Two

"Tell me of his humiliation." Victoria's voice softened as she made her request. "I wish to know every detail."

They lapsed into silence for a few moments until Lavinia leaned back.

"Hudson brought his new mistress with him from London."

Victoria nodded. "I know of this atrocity, and although a small consolation, the whole village is aghast on your behalf. My maid spoke of nothing else all day yesterday." She paused and leaned forward to nibble on a slice of lemon cake. "Who is the woman? Do you know?"

Lavinia's expression darkened as she glanced out the carriage window. "Her name is Miss Constance Fairchild. She is an actress performing in Convent Garden." She handed her plate back to Victoria with a wrinkled nose. "I cannot bear another bite, or I fear I shall be ill."

"Understandable given the circumstances." Sympathy warmed her gaze, and she curved her lips in a gentle smile.

"Can you imagine Hudson's audacity inviting her to my wedding? We crossed paths with them on our way home from Lord Darby's dinner soiree last evening." Lavinia rolled her eyes in exasperation. "My dear fiancé sent his regrets for not joining us citing a sudden headache as the cause." She snorted. "Yet as Papa's carriage turned onto the main road, there they were as bold as brass, strolling along arm in arm for all the world to see."

Shaking her head, she met Victoria's understanding gaze. "I refuse to be silenced by the man I marry and afraid to speak my mind as my mother is. Can you fathom smiling from the sidelines at whatever function you are attending while your husband flirts and fawns over every other woman there to entice them to his bed? The mere thought makes me queasy."

She stared out at the autumn leaves swirling over the cobblestone road with unseeing eyes. Her voice dropped to a whisper. "My father would do anything to reclaim the Holbrook lands. When Hudson returned from France with the deed, the hasty wedding arrangements came as no surprise. I would be wed and no doubt withering away at Becker country estates big with child if not for the sudden death of Hudson's grandfather, the duke." She released a shaky breath. "Thank God"

Victoria gathered up the plates and repacked them in the basket. Shaking crumbs from her linen napkin across her knees, she nodded. "I agree. I could not bear it if you were unhappy, dear friend. A six-month reprieve, even for mourning, can be welcome at times."

"I will not be a meal for the wolf, nor will I be a bargaining chip passed from man to man." Lavinia's chin came up. "Hudson thinks no more of me than a poker marker. I wonder if he plans to include this woman on our wedding trip. If he invited her to our wedding why not there, too?" she mused. A shiver raced down her spine at the thought.

"Are you feeling chilled? I have warm tea." Victoria leaned toward the hamper and lifted the wicker lid again.

"I am not cold, but a warm cup of tea would be most welcome. Margret said Hudson is rumored to have unusual appetites. I thought she referred to eating habits, but now I suspect she meant something else."

"Do you mean in the marriage bed?" Lady Victoria's eyebrows rose, and she paused as she poured a small amount of steaming tea into a tall mug.

"Yes. It is maddening how my parents avoid the subject altogether. My mother will not speak to me, and Papa informed me my wedding shall take place today despite my aversion to the groom and his, er, appetites." Lavinia held her arms wide. "The price of my life and body equals one hundred acres of land in exchange for a hundred thousand pounds." Her lips twisted with bitterness. "*Quid pro quo* from one man to another." Anger and frustration burned in her bosom. "Despite what my parents say, I am worth so much more, Victoria, and in my heart, I believe the right man will agree."

Accepting the steaming cup, she took a sip as the carriage slowed down.

"How could he not see your worth? You are not only a dear friend but a wonderful companion. Any man would be fortunate to have you." She paused with her mug halfway to her mouth. "I cannot say I am surprised the viscount brought his actress to Sheffield. He has quite a reputation. And even if what you say about his…preferences is true, the Ton will not care. The *Beau Monde* ignores his indiscretions because his father is a duke, and his mother is the daughter of the Count of Gifford." Glancing out the window, she nodded. "We are at the fork in the road. My other driver has been instructed to drive through town to divert attention. We will be safe here while we wait for my men."

"I wish I could be a speck of dust in the cathedral right now. With my beloved fiancé making no effort to conceal the presence of his lover, our distinguished guests will draw their own conclusions about my disappearance. While to Papa and Hudson, this may be a mere transaction, to me, it's *my entire life*." She swallowed hard. "Truth be told, I desire more than either of my sisters have or nothing at all. I am determined to remain unwed rather than suffer a similar fate."

Victoria nodded. "Then you're making the right choice. One would think after the ultimatum the viscount's father gave him; he would be cautious not to bring dishonor upon your family." Victoria shrugged her delicate shoulders. "But alas, once the ceremony is complete, he has met the terms. The Duke of Becker will unloose his purse strings, and Hudson can do with you as he pleases."

"Not quite." Lavinia pursed her lips. "He releases a meager stipend. Hudson must produce an heir within a year of marriage for the duke to restore his full allowance." She grimaced in distaste and shuddered. "An heir…God help me. They came about in one way, and I have no intention of sharing anything with Hudson, least of all a bed.

"With your dowry at his disposal, he can afford to keep a wife, both mistresses, and his extravagant lifestyle until an heir is born. How cunning of him to scoop up a wealthy bride to ease the discomfort of his father's disapproval. And how unfortunate he set his sights on you." Victoria tilted her head in Lavinia's direction. "I *am* surprised your mother did not support you when you voiced your concerns. Everyone knows the earl dallies with a new mistress every season, despite the sadness etched in his wife's eyes. I cannot believe she thinks such misery is normal. While she may resent the earl, her love for her children should outweigh any loyalty toward him. As for her feelings toward me, they're nothing short of obsessive. Even though I had no hand in Arthur's death, I am convinced she would run me through if she had evidence to the contrary." Victoria paused to give her a thoughtful glance. "Speaking of certain demise, why wasn't your mother in the antechamber fussing over you? It is your wedding day, after all. My mother would not miss the occasion if things were…different."

They both knew she referred to Lady Beaumont's refusal to utter her daughter's name since the scandal involving Lavinia's brother became known. Dressing in black as if mourning her daughter's death did nothing to help the tension between them, and Lavinia hurried to change the subject before Victoria had time to dwell on the matter.

"Mama announced she would sit beside the Duchess of Waterdown and downplay Hudson's indiscretion rather than attend me in the antechamber. She believes keeping the gossip to a minimum is paramount." Her dislike of *that woman*, as she referred to Victoria, kept her from sending her an invitation to the wedding. And if she were aware of her daughter's presence in Victoria's carriage, she would be furious. "She substitutes the Ton's attention for Papa's. And today, her lack of empathy towards my plight served me well." Her voice softened. "But you are here, and I *am* grateful. Thank you for responding to my note with such haste. If you hadn't, I would either be dodging bushes and trees in my haste to escape or be *married*. At this point, a band of bloodthirsty bandits would be more welcome than being Hudson Becker's wife."

Victoria nodded. "Indeed. My head groom thinks I have gone daft. You should have seen his expression when I insisted, I take my older coach to go to your wedding. I never use it anymore."

Riders approached, and Lavinia cast a frantic glance out the window. Relief flooded her when she recognized their green and gold livery-her brother's colors.

A knock interrupted their conversation, and Victoria leaned forward to give her instructions. "Send Timothy home. If anyone enquires about me, inform them I have a dreadful disease that is very contagious, and I cannot be disturbed. Inform Chadwick I will return within six weeks' time and to tell no one of my absence."

"Very good, m'lady." The footman touched his cap.

She turned to the driver. "Chauncy Castle and make haste. Take the backroads."

"Yes, m'lady." If her driver wondered about their destination, he gave no indication and closed the door behind him.

Trust Victoria to think of everything. If Papa asked for her at Lady Beaumont's estate, he would find her carriage and her butler, Chadwick. The man would inform her father of Victoria's fabricated illness, ensuring her father would not return for fear he would catch it, too.

Lavinia sighed. Now they were on their way, she should relax, but found she could not. Her mind kept wandering to the scene in the cathedral. What did it matter what Papa thought of her? Soon she would be at Chauncy Castle with the duchess, and until then, she had

Victoria. And her brother's men for protection.

Arthor's outriders took up positions in front and behind the carriage, and the road rumbled beneath the wooden wheels in a soothing, steady rhythm.

Tension eased out of Lavinia's neck and shoulders with each step the horses took north.

Although Victoria referred to the conveyance as old, they were far from uncomfortable. The well-crafted carriage boasted luxurious red velvet seats and ornate interior, complete with embossed door handles and full-plated lamps. Equipped with a folding top for fair weather, the landau provided both comfort and style.

Lavinia remembered driving down the road in this very carriage with her brother Arthur when he informed her of his intent to court Victoria.

"I purchased this landau with her in mind. Do you think she will like it?" His blue eyes sought hers in her seventeen-year-old face. "Do you think she will like me?"

"She speaks of nothing but you. I am sure she will." Rolling her eyes to let him know how silly she thought they both were, she shook her head over their sorry state.

Arthur thought both girls a plague until they made their debut in society.

And then something about Victoria's lush figure, red hair, and almond-shaped eyes drew his attention like flies to honey.

Her brother hadn't been able to tear his gaze away from her dearest friend. Or her him. He courted her until the day she turned eighteen and then asked for her hand in marriage, planning their wedding for the spring.

However, everything changed when disaster struck, and Arthur never came home again. That day remained etched in Lavinia's memory, a day of profound grief and the shattering of her hopes and dreams, all brought about by the tragic loss of her beloved brother.

And the arrival of Viscount Hudson Becker.

A bump in the road jolted her back to the present. Her gaze shifted to a polished cane wedged between the velvet seat and the padded side of the carriage. The carved head depicted an eagle with splayed talons. Arthur's cane.

A bittersweet smile touched Victoria's lips as pain filled her beautiful eyes. "He placed it there on his way to the docks the day he left for France. I haven't had the heart to move it. Having a reminder of him here is like having a piece of him close to me, even now."

Lavinia nodded, unsure of what to say.

Victoria lost more than anyone. She lost Arthur, her baby, her reputation, her family, and her good name. If Arthur hadn't opened a bank account in her name and deposited funds there before his fateful trip to France, her dearest friend would have been homeless. His solicitor had specific instructions to see to Victoria's welfare, and although the earl fought to stem the flow of funds into her account, he could do nothing. The money came from Arthur's private investments and, therefore, out of the earl's reach. Victoria lived in Arthur's elegant home, rode his thoroughbred horses, enjoyed the protection of his men, and lived a life of luxury few could attain.

Who would have thought their lives would take such a turn? Victoria lost her fiancé to a dagger in the back, and Lavinia left hers at the altar.

Sliding the red velvet curtains across the tiny window beside her to block the midday sun, Lavinia closed her eyes and let the rumble of carriage wheels lull the worry from her mind. Every rotation of the well-greased wheels took her further away from a life she refused to live.

Victoria did make a valid point. When Papa discovered she left the church and Sheffield, he would have an episode. The mere idea sent a shiver down her spine. Although he had never resorted to physical violence, his methods of punishment were cruel and relentless. Locking her away in her chamber without light, warmth, or even blankets to shield her from the biting cold, he would ignore her pleas for mercy, leaving her to endure hunger and isolation until she submitted to his will.

But he couldn't do a thing if he didn't know where to find her.

Her glance slid to her companion.

How had she gotten so lucky as to have a friend like Lady Victoria Beaumont? Memories flooded her mind as the carriage rumbled north.

Victoria lived two estates down from Lavinia's country home in Watford. They met when Lavinia's mother called on Victoria's family, and the little girl wandered up to the nursery while the ladies took their tea.

Lavinia walked into the room and came to a stop as she took in the sight of Victoria crying while her nanny put a plaster across her skinned knee.

This new friend ignored her mother's warnings and climbed over the garden railing, only to tumble down and scrape her knee on the walkway below.

Victoria's pitiful wails made Lavinia's chest hurt, and she hurried over to see the extent of her new friend's injury. Water-filled green eyes met hers when she knelt beside her and took her hand.

"Hold onto me," she whispered as she surveyed the nanny's administration. "I hold my nanna's hand when I get hurt."

Her new friend nodded and when her nanny released her announcing she would live, Lavinia lifted her skirt and showed the other little girl her own plaster. She fell the day before doing the exact same thing in her garden, and *her* Papa made her stand in the corner for not obeying.

"I do not like the corner." She announced when Victoria's eyes rounded at the news. "There is nothing to do and nothing to see. And I get in trouble if I wiggle." She nodded to emphasize her point.

"I do not think I would like the corner, either," Victoria announced. "I would want to wiggle. You must have something to do and see."

Lavina agreed, and the two had been inseparable ever since.

But no one felt the true weight of the girls' combined shenanigans until their parents sent them to the same convent to learn deportment and ladylike behavior the year they turned twelve.

Lady Madelaine later gave Lavinia Mother Superior's letters when her second season failed to produce an acceptable marriage proposal. "You are old enough to understand what a trail you are, darling. These dear nuns prayed for you to go home every single day you were there. They are the sweetest, most forgiving women on earth, and yet they couldn't wait to be rid of you. No man will want you either, Lavinia, unless you learn to temper your words and actions. Men do not want an intelligent wife; they want an obedient one."

Lavinia scoffed. More fool them. But she opened the letters and read them anyway.

Mother Superior's letters confirmed her mother's opinion.

The devout woman believed she offended heaven to receive two such devious girls into her care and spent hours in supplication, repenting of everything she could think of.

According to her letters, she could never finish her prayers the entire four years the girls lived with her. For each time she bent in supplication, another sister would come to her for assistance with yet another situation involving the terrible duo.

By the time the girls departed, there was not a window they had not replaced or a door they had not rehung. A new bell adorned the tower after a disastrous fire caused by a misplaced lantern burned the previous bell tower to the ground. Another fire destroyed the entire south wing, leaving Sister Agnes haunted by feverish nightmares of hellfire for a good year after their departure.

The girls had not meant to cause harm, she knew. They were both cursed with vivid imaginations. Sister Francis abandoned bible study when the two imps recreated the plagues of Egypt. She had been the first to discover the red coloring the girls put in the water bucket, and her screams were forever imprinted in Mother Superior's memory.

Sister Edna and Sister Myrtle discovered the frogs and neither one climbed into bed since that night without checking every inch of their room with meticulous care.

Mother Superior did not give either girl a free minute for weeks. She had no idea where the two imps would find lice for the next plague, but she did not wish to find out.

When that upset died down, they used honey, plaster, and a bolt of fabric the nuns had in storage for new habits to recreate their version of Jonah inside the belly of a whale.

Mother Superior could not eat fish to this day after stumbling into their project in the dark. She could still smell the fishy scent and feel the honey on her hands and feet. When she tripped over a plaster tooth and landed face first in the gooey red honey mess supposed to be the whale's tongue, she sent them to clean the entire prayer room with a scrub brush.

When the letters arrived informing Mother Superior of the girls' imminent departure, the entire convent breathed a sigh of relief. And subsequent letters expressed gratitude for their absence. Now, three years and two scandals later, the two women reminisced about their wonderful years with the sisters as they traveled northwest of Sheffield, leaving behind a cursing, scowling fiancé, an irate, determined father, and a socially embarrassed mother.

Lavinia figured the only person who retired the night of the almost wedding with a smile was Viscount Hudson Becker's new mistress, Miss Constance Fairchild.

But that would change, she mused, when Miss Fairchild discovered Hudson's pockets were to let without her dowry. He would be forced to find another heiress to marry or set his extravagant lifestyle aside. Beginning with the actress.

She shrugged. Whatever Hudson and his mistress did no longer concerned her, and as mile after mile slipped away beneath the rumbling carriage wheels, the knot in her stomach relaxed. She had twelve days of traveling time to produce a new life plan before she arrived at her godmother's castle and asked for refuge.

Chapter Three

"She travels to Miryam. I am sure of it," Lady Madelaine stated as she stared at the pile of delicate silk underskirts in the middle of the antechamber floor. Her lips thinned with anger as she picked up the exquisite pearl wedding gown carelessly draped across the cream brocade settee. "I know Lavinia had…misgivings after we returned home last evening, but I assured her she would adjust. Everyone does." Madelaine handed the gown to Margret and motioned for her to collect the underskirts. Twenty-five years of marriage had not dimmed her resentment over her husband's infidelity, but she had learned to hide her feelings. With a sigh, she turned to face him. "What excuse did you give Viscount Becker?"

The Earl of Holbrook shook his head. "I requested a private moment alone with my daughter. He is unaware of her absence."

Madelaine's eyes widened in disbelief. "He did not inquire why I summoned you to this room? The ceremony should have started ten minutes ago. I assumed he would hear Margret's commotion and draw the same conclusion I did."

The earl frowned at her. "No man envisions his bride abandoning him at the altar to face the Ton alone." His gaze narrowed. "Especially not one of the viscount's social standing. I cannot fathom what Lavinia hopes to achieve by such inappropriate, unbecoming behavior."

Madelaine shrugged, a mixture of frustration and anger in her voice. "She had *that woman* with her. Margret witnessed her carriage waiting in the churchyard. This is her fault. *She* convinced our daughter to participate in some reckless scheme to disgrace us and seek revenge."

The earl's face flushed with indignation. "Regardless of the reason, we must concoct a plausible excuse for your daughter's absence. I will not allow her foolish actions to jeopardize my chance to acquire the land."

His wife halted, her gaze piercing. "Are you more concerned about the land than the safety of *your* daughter?"

"Of course! This is a travesty, Madelaine. I searched for that piece of property for years, and I refuse to let Lavinia's absurd conduct ruin everything."

The Countess of Holbrook squared her shoulders and glared at her husband. "Well, Mortimer, without a daughter, what chance have you?"

Lavinia's fears were very real, as Madelaine knew too well. Her heart clenched as she regarded the cold, indifferent man before her. She, too, had tasted the bitter sting of abandonment, left to languish at the country estate while her husband enjoyed the vices of society. If given the opportunity to escape the whispers, the anguish, and the betrayal of her husband's infidelity, she would seize it without hesitation. The last thing she desired for her daughter, any of them, was to endure a similar fate.

The earl gave a grunt of annoyance and turned to stare at the chapel door. "What shall we tell them,

Madelaine?"

She dropped comments about the viscount's unsuitability in her earlier conversation with the Duchess of Waterdown once Margret informed her of Lady Victoria's presence. If *that* woman were here, some mischief was afoot, and Madelaine understood the importance of safeguarding one's reputation. In the delicate dance of high society, one could never be too cautious.

"Say what you will, but the truth will surface regardless. The Ton's two most notorious gossips, the Duchess of Carding and Lady Haversham, occupy the front pews. And with Hudson flaunting his mistress all over town, the majority of the guests are here to see if Lavina proceeds with the wedding. The Duchess of Waterdown mentioned as much to me earlier." Her lips curved in distaste as she observed her husband's mounting fury.

The earl paced with his hands clasped behind his back. "We will say Lavinia has fallen ill, and we must postpone the wedding to a more appropriate time."

Madelaine rolled her eyes. "You issue the same excuse for everything. We dined with both the duchess and Lady Haversham last evening. They will know something is amiss. If they departed soon after we did, they spotted Hudson and his actress as well. Think what—"

Her speech fell short when Viscount Hudson Becker burst into the room unannounced, leaving both doors wide open.

"Why do you make me wait out there like a trussed-up goose before the entire Ton?" He glanced around the room, and a red flush rose to his handsome face. "What goes on here? Where is she, my lord? Where is my bride?"

Madelaine's gaze flitted to the guests seated closest to the doors. They repeated what they could see and hear from their prime positions to those in less auspicious seats.

Ripples of whispers started at the back of the church and grew in volume until Madalaine could not hear either man in front of her, though they hurled their accusations at each other at the top of their voices.

"If you had kept your paramour in London, Lavina would not have run away!" The earl's angry voice rang out in the small antechamber. His dark eyes glimmered with anger as he faced the younger man. "Were it not for what you offer in return, I would show you the door."

Viscount Becker's eyes narrowed. "What I do is of no consequence. The fault lies with you. If you wanted the land, you would make sure your daughter attended her own wedding. Instead, I am left a fool." Both men were red in the face, and neither one realized the church behind them grew silent as the guests strained to hear more of their conversation.

Madelaine placed a hand on her husband's arm to get his attention. "Mortimer, we should have this discussion in private."

His scowl swung to her. "Do not interrupt me." But then his gaze drifted past her and focused on the straining guests vying to get a better view of the scene in the antechamber. His color dropped as he rushed forward to close the heavy double doors.

But his action came too late to stop the scandal.

"Lady Lavinia left him at the altar. She has run away!" The murmurs grew as he shut the doors with a sound click.

The two men stared at each other.

Running a hand through his hair, the earl glared at Hudson. "I will get her back. Give me a fortnight. At which time the wedding will go forward as planned. I want the land, and I know you are anxious for her dowry."

"The damage is irreparable. Listen to them." The viscount's eye twitched as voices rose in the other room.

The earl harrumphed. "I refuse to concede defeat. This wedding will go forward per our agreement. By spring, the Ton will have forgotten this debacle. Think man. Lavinia's dowry is unmatched in size."

Madelaine observed Hudson as he contemplated Mortimer's proposal.

Close to her husband in height he stood five foot nine inches with dark brown windswept hair, brown eyes, and full lips. Wearing black trousers, a royal purple waistcoat, and a black fitted jacket with gold buttons, he cut quite an attractive figure. His starched white cravat had been tied in an impossible knot and held in place with an amethyst pin, adding a touch of elegance.

Her gaze trailed down his slim figure to the glimmering golden buckles on his polished black heels, reflecting the light of the chandelier overhead. Her eyes rose back to his square jaw and mocking eyes. Labeled a dandy by the Ton, he fit the image to perfection.

She clicked her tongue in disapproval.

Hudson's gaze narrowed, his tone dripping with ice. "Our bargain is off unless Lavinia returns before Christmas with a profuse apology." He paused, letting the weight of his words sink in before continuing. "I require an additional ten thousand pounds for my damaged reputation." Brushing an imaginary speck from his jacket, his demeanor turned calculating, and a greedy glint entered his eyes, adding years to his youthful appearance. "If my terms are not met, I will entertain offers from other interested parties." His lips curled in a satisfied smirk. "I do have another buyer anxious to purchase your hundred acres, complete with an unwed daughter."

The earl froze. "The Duke of Waterdown offered for the land?"

The viscount's smile did not reach his eyes. "Yes."

"You cannot mean to make the same arrangement with him. His daughter is fifteen years old, at most, for God's sake. It's indecent. And Waterdown cannot afford such a healthy dowry." The earl's voice crackled like thunder, and his hands made fists at his side.

"Lady Abby is…more pliable and, at this moment, more appealing than Lady Lavinia." Hudson's words were soft, but his lustful grin contained a sinister undertone, causing Madelaine to draw in a sharp breath.

Drawing a lace-edged kerchief from his pocket, Hudson dabbed at the corner of his mouth as if to hide his predatorial smirk.

Madelaine's heart pounded with concern.

The shadow in Viscount Becker's eyes sent a chill down her spine. She heard whispers of men with unusual tastes and dismissed them as exaggerated gossip. Now, she questioned her previous certainty.

Viscount Becker's expression made her skin crawl, yet her husband remained oblivious to the malice lurking behind the viscount's smile.

Lavinia said as much, and she didn't listen. Sickened, she took a step back and waited for the men to finish their conversation.

"It is regrettable my uncle gambled the property away during his tenure as earl, or we would not be having this conversation. Arthur assured me he could regain the land before he left for France last year." A dark shadow passed over the earl's face as if remembering the notoriety of his son's death. "And if Lavinia is the price for restoring my family's estate, so be it. She shall be here in her wedding gown before Christmas. You have my word."

The two men locked gazes, the weight of their agreement heavy in the air.

"I require the ten thousand pounds in advance." Delivered in an icy, ruthless voice, Hudson's lip curled with disdain.

The earl offered a stiff nod. "You will have it by the end of the day."

The viscount made a mock bow and disappeared out the antechamber door, avoiding the cathedral.

Madelaine held a hand to her chest to ease the tightness. Once the man left, she could breathe again. Losing her son almost took her will to live, and the ensuing scandal involving *that woman* made attending any social function unbearable. Thinning her lips with determination, she vowed to find her daughter before any further embarrassment occurred.

Her husband stared after the viscount. "I confess I harbor suspicions about the way Viscount Becker came by the title, and Arthur's demise." He gave a deep sigh and held up a hand when Madelaine opened her mouth to comment. "Yes, I know. We've been over the matter countless times. But something is off about the whole affair. Every instinct I possess tells me so."

Turning, he held his arm toward Madelaine. "Come along, my dear. We will make our apologies to our guests and then depart. I have arrangements to attend to."

Arm in arm, they entered the church, their presence commanding a hushed silence from the congregation.

The Earl of Holbrook walked with a ramrod-straight spine to the front of the church, where he apologized for the delay. "After an unfortunate event, we have decided to postpone Lady Lavinia's wedding until the week of Christmas. We shall send out new invitations at the appropriate date and time. Thank you all for coming."

Holding Madelaine's arm, he walked from the church with his head high.

His dignified demeanor lasted until they stepped into their carriage. Then, his lordship cursed like a dock worker. "When I find *your* daughter, Madelaine, I will demand an explanation. She will pay penance for embarrassing me today, and you will not interfere." His cold, clipped voice fell into the silence between them.

She murmured her agreement and set about making her own plans to rescue Lavinia. For she refused to be tarnished by the scandal sure to arise from her daughter's association with *that woman.* "No good can come of this. Of that, you can be sure."

Chapter Four

The Duchess of Chauncy stared into the crackling fire as she stoked her white Persian cat, Princess. Her thin hands slid across the silky fur in long, thoughtful strokes, oblivious to the opulent surroundings of her sitting room. A high-arched plaster ceiling adorned with gold detailing, ice-blue silk walls, and a gray marble hearth on the east wall added to the room's elegance. The warmth and light from the fire contrasted with the golden glow of the magnificent chandelier overhead, illuminating the white brocade settees, marble coffee table, and ice-blue Persian rug beneath her feet. Large paned windows facing north gave a sweeping view of the duchess's rose gardens. On sweltering summer days, she opened the windows and allowed the heady scent of the blossoms to fill the room as she wandered the haven of delicate trails winding between the flowers toward a three-tiered fountain with plaster cupids pouring water from golden vases.

With a sigh, she rubbed Princess' ears. "How do I persuade Oliver to take a bride? He refuses to do his duty to the family and produce an heir. When I introduce the subject into the conversation, he is most vehement his younger brother can continue the Chauncy line. 'I already have an heir in Algernon,' is his usual rejoinder." She stroked the cat's back in thoughtfulness. "I have hosted countless parties, inviting all the young ladies of the Ton, and he takes no notice of them. I even extended invitations to widows and second-season debutantes in hopes of piquing his interest. But alas, he liked none of them either. I am at my wit's end, my dear. I desire to hold my grandchild in my arms before I take leave of this life, and if he continues to delay, I may never have that joy."

Several long minutes passed as she stroked her cat in contemplative silence. A log settled in the hearth, sending a shower of sparks into the air, startling her.

"I know he cannot resist a good wager with family, so I have decided to resort to trickery."

Princess turned her head and gave the duchess a doleful stare.

"My intentions are honorable, my dear, with the ultimate goal of securing an heir for Chauncy and a grandchild for me. If I happen to make a few gold coins on the side, who will be the wiser?" She chuckled. "Now, if only I knew who to use as bait. There is Miss Myrtle Marshal from the local gentry, Lady Priscilla Covington from Covington Manor, and Lady Elspeth Perth from Bath, who is visiting with her cousin this winter. Tea today proved a disaster. Oliver walked in, took one look at my company, and fled. He made some excuse about having to check on his horse, but I know he deserted me for fear I planned to throw the poor girls at him. I did, but that is of no consequence. If he refuses to do his duty to his family, I have no choice but to force his hand. But how?"

"Meow." Princess stretched and arched her spine against the duchess's hand.

"Of course. You are right, but he will not be pleased. In fact, such a course of action may well make him angry." The Duchess of Chauncy smiled in satisfaction. "Nevertheless, it is a splendid plan, my dear. I knew I could rely on you for assistance." With a final pat, she placed Princess on the ice-blue rug at her feet, ready to set her scheme in motion.

Taking hold of the delicate woven coverlet in shades of blue and silver, she draped it back over her legs and settled back against the settee with a contended smile.

The tall, thin door behind her opened, and her butler, Cecil, stepped into the room.

"Your Grace, there is a young woman here asking to see you. She claims she is your goddaughter, Lady Lavinia Holbrook. I informed her you have retired for the night, but she is most insistent."

The duchess waved him over with a graceful gesture. "Show her in."

Cecil hesitated. "She is not alone, madam."

Arabella's eyebrows rose with curiosity. "Who is with her?"

His tone dripped with icy disdain. "Lady Victoria Beaumont, Your Grace."

The duchess smiled. Cecil could not be more condescending if he tried. She knew about the rumors, of course. Who had not heard the lady dallied with Lord Arthur Holbrook and conceived a child out of wedlock? The heir to the Earl of Holbrook disappeared following their indiscretion, and a month later, the authorities declared him dead.

Such a tragedy for his parents. And for her. She could not fathom what the poor girl must have gone through being pregnant, unwed, and alone.

"Show them both in." Compassion tugged at her heart for her goddaughter's companion. She, too, remembered all too well the challenges of youth, love, and societal expectations.

"As you wish, madam." His disapproving sniff and retreating footsteps made her smile widen. Poor Cecil. But he would get over his judgmental attitude in a day or two. He always did.

A moment later, his stiff footsteps approached, followed by the click of two pairs of slippers on the marble floors and the swish of silk skirts.

Cecil strolled around her settee to bow. "Madam, this is Lady Lavinia Holbrook and Lady Victoria Beaumont." His nose rose in the air as he addressed the two beautiful women standing off to his right. "Allow me to present Her Grace, the Duchess of Chauncy."

Both ladies dipped a deep curtsy, and Arabella waved them to the seating opposite her. "Thank you, Cecil. Have one of the footmen bring us a tray of refreshments."

"Very good, madam." His silver head dipped a bow, and he left, closing the door behind him.

Arabella smiled as the girls settled on the opposite settee, and Princess jumped back into her lap. "Welcome to Chauncy Castle, ladies. To what do I owe the pleasure of your visit?"

Her gaze drifted over her goddaughter. Blonde-haired and petite, Lady Lavinia had a slim build and a dimple on her cheek. At first glance, she appeared to be the typical English Rose until one gazed into her unusual violet eyes. Fringed with thick black lashes, Lavinia's eyes gave her an exotic, delicate beauty.

Lady Beaumont's red-haired beauty, flashing emerald eyes, and lush figure would have the same reaction.

Together, the two ladies made a formidable pair, drawing admiration and envy alike.

Lavinia shot her friend a glance and met Arabella's gaze head-on. "I need your help, Godmother." In short, precise sentences, she related the details of her marriage contract with Viscount Hudson Becker and the events leading up to her wedding.

"At which point, I left the church and came here."

Arabella's lips twitched with amusement. She grew fonder of the girl with each passing moment, though as her godmother, she refrained from expressing such sentiments outright. "Your mother will come here searching for you."

Lavinia sighed. "I calculate I have until Christmas before I am discovered. Possibly until the new year if luck is on my side."

"Ahh," Arabella murmured. "And what do you hope to accomplish? There will be a scandal, of course. Although with most of society at their country estates, the whispers will not begin in earnest until the new season begins. By then, perhaps, some newer and more scandalous affair will capture the Ton's attention. Tell me, my dear, are you searching for another suitor? Or do you hope to put some distance between the two of you in anticipation of Viscount Becker finding another bride?"

"The latter would certainly provide a solution to my problems. But I do not think Papa will like it. He wants the land." Discouragement laced her words, and the duchess frowned.

"Do not be so down in your feelings, Lavinia. I am sure a solution will present itself before long." Arabella reassured, offering them both a warm smile. "I must say, I am delighted you came to me with your problems. Your father has always been rather obstinate when it comes to matters of property. I do wonder what Madelaine's thoughts are on all of this." Her voice trailed off when Cecil knocked, and a footman carried in a tray of tea and finger sandwiches.

As the footman set the tray before them and left the room, the duchess turned her attention to Lady Victoria. "And what role do you play in this dilemma?"

Lady Victoria met her gaze with steady regard. "I am Lady Lavinia's closest friend and her means of escape. If it pleases Your Grace, I would like to stay the night until I am rested enough to return home."

Arabella waved her hand in a sweeping gesture. "Stay as long as you wish. I am not one to adhere to the rigid standards of society. I am aware of the scandal surrounding your child, and I do not care a whit. In any event, I am certain the rumors have misconstrued the truth, and you are most welcome here. In the countryside, such matters hold far less significance than they do in London."

Victoria flushed crimson when she mentioned the scandal and then paled when Arabella mentioned the child. Her gaze dropped, and her hands shook so hard she set her sandwich down. "Thank you, Your Grace."

Arabella had to lean forward to hear her whispered words. "Do you travel with the child, as well? I should like to meet the infant."

A heavy silence filled the chamber, and then Victoria raised her eyes. "He died nine weeks after his birth. I rose in the night to check on him, and he was…gone."

Terror, pain, and grief filled the girl's eyes as tears ran down her cheeks.

"I am sorry, my dear. Forgive an old woman for causing you pain. I would not have done so with prior knowledge of your loss. I shall inform the staff of your presence and ensure your needs are met. For now, I shall leave you in Cecil's capable hands. He will have Mrs. Whittle show you to your chambers."

Ringing the bell at her elbow, Arabella gave Cecil her instructions and rose to her feet. "We will speak more tomorrow. For now, have a pleasant sleep."

With Princess trailing behind, she ascended the stairs to her chamber. Once she closed the door and her maid helped her undress for the night, she sank into her feather bed and lifted the fine silk bedclothes to her chin. Turning her head, she smiled at the cat curled in front of the fire. "It seems the gods have sent us more bait. Do you not agree, Princess?"

"Meow."Princess agreed, and the room lapsed into silence as Arabella drifted off to sleep, thoughts swirling with the new developments.

Chapter Five

"I knew my godmother would welcome you with open arms. What do you think of the castle?" Lavinia picked up another sandwich and nibbled on the corner.

"From what little I saw out the carriage window in the dark, it is magnificent." Victoria's shoulders relaxed as she poured a cup of tea. "The duchess is not at all what I expected. Everyone speaks of her as though she were a dragon, but I quite like her. She did not turn a hair at the mention of my name, and I believe if Charles were still with us, I would have brought him to visit her. She had such a gleam of longing in her eyes when she inquired about my child."

Lavinia chuckled. "The duchess can be formidable when she chooses, but she is quite loveable. I adored visiting her when I was a young girl. She is one of the few people in my life who never got annoyed with me."

As the door opened, a tall, elegant woman in a high-necked black dress entered the chamber. With the air of an upper-class servant, she dipped a small curtsy. "Good evening, my ladies. I am Mrs. Whittle, the duchess's housekeeper."

Her dark hair, touched with hints of gray, gleamed in the light as she tilted her head, and her brown eyes met Lavinia's. "Welcome back, my lady. I offer my congratulations on your marriage."

Heat rushed to her cheeks. "Thank you, Mrs.

Whittle, but I did not wed."

The housekeeper's eyebrow rose, but she made no further comment on the subject.

Lavinia knew by breakfast tomorrow everyone in the castle would be privy to her story, but she saw no need to elaborate further now.

"If you will both follow me." The housekeeper led them out of the blue and silver salon and down a wide, elegant corridor with gold-etched plaster and gray marble flooring. The walls were adorned with gilt-edged pictures, along with colorful portraits, while golden candelabras hung between the frames, casting a warm glow and lending a cozy atmosphere to the opulent surroundings. Above them, a pale blue ceiling depicted cherubs playing the lute in various scenes and positions.

Mrs. Whittle stopped at the bottom of a curved wooden staircase. "I have placed you in your old room on the second floor, Miss Lavinia, and Lady Beaumont in the west wing."

Lavinia nodded. The second floor housed the family's sleeping quarters, and she had been given a chamber there years ago as the duchess's goddaughter.

Visitors and guests stayed in the west wing.

"I will accompany you to Lady Victoria's chamber, Mrs. Whittle, and then you may retire. There's no need for you to show me to mine. I am quite familiar with the way." Cecil no doubt woke Mrs. Whittle when they arrived because of the lateness of the hour, and she noted the housekeeper's lack of argument to the contrary.

"Very good, my lady." The housekeeper turned right when they arrived on the third floor, and they followed her halfway down the next corridor before she stopped and opened the door.

"This is the Queen Anne room, my lady. She is reported to have stayed here on one occasion, and the duchess changed the décor to shades of yellow when she and her husband inherited the castle. I thought you would find it comfortable."

The room looked inviting indeed. A white marble fireplace adorned one wall, while a large bed with a floral coverlet occupied the opposite wall. Two white satin chairs faced the fireplace, and tall paned windows were draped with golden velvet curtains. In one corner stood a white gilded wardrobe, complimented by a matching chest at the foot of the bed.

"It's perfect. Thank you, Mrs. Whittle, for seeing to our comfort. We shall be quite all right now, and you may retire."

"You are most welcome, my lady. I bid you good night."

Once the housekeeper walked away, Lavinia followed her friend inside and closed the door behind them. A sense of relief settled over her as she turned to Victoria.

"Thank you for coming with me. The drive is long, and I would have gone mad without someone to talk to. Thank goodness we arrived, for I do not think I could spend another minute bumping over country roads."

Victoria nodded, her fingers tracing the delicate coverlet on the bed. "I have never stayed in a yellow room before. I am amazed at how airy and clean it feels."

"Her Grace maintains yellow was the queen's favorite color, and she speaks with such authority that very few want to argue. But she has other rooms more interesting than this. I cannot wait to show you the whole of them tomorrow following breakfast. The duke keeps the best stable in the country, and the gardens are spectacular. I confess, now I am here. I wonder why I did not think to come weeks ago." She kissed her friend on the cheek. "Sleep well, my friend. I am one floor down and five doors away should you require anything."

"Or I could pull the rope beside the bed." Victoria grinned. "I will be fine, Lavinia. I have slept in strange places before and will see you at breakfast."

Lavinia returned her smile and bid her good night before closing the door and wandering down the corridor, deep in thought. She wondered what Hudson thought when he discovered his bride missing. How she wished she could be a spider on the wall and witness the scene. She gave a wistful sigh as she ran her fingers along the cream silk-covered walls of the corridor.

The man had to know flaunting his mistress in the village before his wedding was simply not done, didn't he? Or did he presume she would tolerate his indiscretions like her mother, always wearing a placid smile despite her agony within? Being the son of a powerful duke should not grant him immunity from proper behavior.

Her gaze narrowed as she considered the matter. She detested the pomp of Parliament's opening and the onset of a new social season as much as she despised her father's infidelity and the anguish he caused her mother. Though she maintained a composed façade in polite society, enduring sympathetic glances and incessant gossip, her mother's red eyes and miserable face filled her with resentment. Not that her father paid any attention to his wife's suffering.

But she did.

With her older sisters in much the same

predicament, it appeared Lady Holbrook's daughters were destined to share the same miserable fate unless Lavinia took decisive action.

Overhearing Lady Haversham mention the fact to her closest friend when Lavinia's engagement became known at the end of the previous season gave her much to consider.

Papa set the wedding date for the middle of April, but when news of Hudson's grandfather's passing arrived, the viscount retreated into mourning for six months, acquiring yet another actress and a new house in Convent Gardens.

Lavinia shook her head, knowing she would never be the submissive wife he desired.

Who could love a man who spent more time on his dress and hair than she did? Considered a dandy by the Ton, Hudson had been known to return home to change if a sprinkle of rain fell on his immaculately tailored shoulders.

The image of her fastidious groom standing alone before London's elite, anticipating a bride who never arrived, filled her with a sense of satisfaction.

Did he shrink with displeasure when their guests gawked at him in anticipation? Lord, she hoped so. A wide grin spread across her face as she paused to gaze out a long paned window into the dark. Many marriages in the Ton were for convenience's sake, and once an heir came forth, both parties went their separate ways until social etiquette required them to attend together.

Unlike Mama.

On one occasion, Lavinia crossed the foyer in time to overhear her parents arguing. She cast a glance at the two footmen standing in the hall and took pity on them.

As she crossed the entry to close the library door, her mother's voice floated to her ears, expressing her desire for the dowager house and a stipend to sustain her needs.

"I shall depart for there tomorrow, Mortimer. I do not wish to live here anymore. I cannot abide another season of whispered rumors and scrutinizing stares."

Lavinia paused as she clasped the handle. Her heart leaped into her throat as she waited for his answer. Her mother had finally had enough.

But Papa only laughed. "And give those old cronies more to talk about? I think not, Madelaine. I will not be labeled as a fool who cannot control his wife. You will stay by my side and do your part, or everyone in England will know of my displeasure. And if you insist on this foolishness, I will cut you off without a penny. Your high-handed attitude will do little to keep you warm or put food into your mouth."

His harshness made Lavinia gasp in outrage. Making fists with her hands, she waited for her mother's response and swallowed against the tightness in her throat.

"Very well, Mortimer. But I refuse to do more than appear in public with you. Do not cross the threshold of my bedchamber again. You are the reason for the gossip, not me. If you are not more discreet, I will take a lover, as well. We both know no one will blame me for doing so. I think the Ton may well applaud me for it."

A long silence followed, and as Lavinia closed the door, her father answered. "If you do, I will kill you both. I will not be cuckolded."

She retired that night sick to her stomach and turned the conversation over in her head. Why could men do as they please and not women? Lord Emory paraded his wife around the year before with a halter around her neck and then sold her a week later, and all because the poor woman refused to accept his advances when he came home drunk.

How could such treatment be overlooked and accepted? Or legal?

And her impending marriage would be no different from her parents' tumultuous union. A shiver coursed down her spine as she gazed at the sliver of silver moon hanging high in the sky. In her heart, she yearned for strong arms to hold her, a sharp mind to challenge her, a sense of humor to rival her own, and a loving heart to catch her when she didn't have the strength to stand. A man quick to defend but wise enough to let her fight if she so desired.

Lavinia sighed and pressed her nose to the cold glass. Did such a man exist? Or were they folklore like unicorns and dragons?

A footman walked past, making his rounds, shaking her from her moment of reflection.

Such questions would have to wait until she had some sleep. Weary to the bone from her travels and the post-excitement of her momentous escape, she blew out a deep breath. For the first time in more than a year, she could sleep without fear of what tomorrow would bring.

Viscount Becker and Papa could both go to the devil for she would never submit to being bought or sold. Not for a hundred thousand pounds or a hundred acres of prime woodland once part of a century old family estate. They would just have to find someone else.

She counted the stairs as she made her way to the second floor and then the doors as she walked along the corridor containing the family's chambers.

The door to her chamber opened with a rush of warm air. A hearty fire crackled on the hearth as she strolled inside and sank onto the bed. Her tight bodice would be too uncomfortable to sleep in and she sat up with a groan to work the lacing of her gown. She must mention to the duchess she would require a lady's maid since she abandoned Margret in Waterdown with her veil and wedding slippers. Her mood lightened at the thought, and her bodice came off with a tug. Her petticoats followed, and Lavinia removed her slippers and stockings with a loud yawn. Her stays followed, and then, with a shrug, she removed her garter and slipped into bed in her chemise and pantalets.

The crisp, clean sheets were magic against her tired flesh, and with another lusty yawn, she closed her eyes and received the fright of her life.

"I am, of course, delighted with your unexpected presence in my chamber, and although you cannot stay, you may offer my gratitude to my mother for sending you."

Lavinia froze and turned her head toward the deep voice coming from the direction of the hearth. Panic surged through her as she grappled with the realization that a man occupied her chamber.

"What?" Her eyes widened as they settled on the imposing figure of the Duke of Chauncy reclining in a brocade chair clad in nothing but a pair of form-fitting black trousers.

Oh God, what had she done? Her heart rose to her throat and threatened to choke her. "This is my chamber. It always has been. What are you doing here?" Unable to tear her gaze away from him, she lifted the coverlet up to her chin and stared.

Dark curly hair spread across his wide chest, disappearing beneath the waistband of his pants.

Lavinia's gaze followed the line down until it formed a V and then flushed as he gave a small chuckle.

His black hair gleamed in the light of the fire, and a dangerous glint shimmered from the depths of his dark eyes. "No, my dear. This is my chamber, as I'm sure you're aware. I thought the night quite boring until you entered and shed your garments." Crossing one bare foot over the opposite knee, he gave her a sardonic smile. The sleek muscle in his arm bulged as he leaned an elbow on his bent knee and studied her.

She swallowed hard and shook her head. "But—"

"I must say your performance could use a little work with the timing. I came close to losing interest while you struggled with the strings on your stays. But then off it came, and your bounty sprang free with the correct amount of allure. I felt quite compelled to stroke your bosom and taste you, although I must complain about your lack of a display. A man must know what he purchases, should he not? You gave me no peek of eager naked flesh as an added enticement to offer for your hand. But then, I thought for one moment you intended to remove your undergarments and waited expectantly while you teased me with your garter, but alas, my hopes were dashed, and you slipped into my bed without further ado."

She didn't know whether to be offended or flattered. "But I didn't...I mean...I never expected—" Frowning, she swallowed hard.

"Although you entice me more than any woman my mother has sent thus far, I must decline your appealing offer and ask you to convey my regrets for not cooperating with her little scheme." He paused as he studied her flushed face. "You would be quite irresistible if you put your mind to it. You should practice before you enter another potential husband's chamber."

Lavinia's mouth dropped open. Her body hummed, and her mind could not form an entire sentence. "Husband?" She shook her head to clear her shock and surprise away.

"But I counted the doors. This is my chamber." Her voice trailed off when the duke rose to his feet and strolled toward her as if he were a panther circling his prey.

"Did you?" His gaze drifted to her heaving chest, and he gave her another insatiable grin.

She clutched the coverlet tight and stared, unable to break free from his predatory gaze.

"Who could mistake the grandeur of the ducal suite for a guest chamber? If nothing else, my great grandfather's carved headboard with the family crest is a dead giveaway." He reached the bed, pinning her in place with the intensity of his gaze.

"What? I didn't check the bed. It was dark…" She faltered, her breath catching as the duke leaned closer, surrounding her with his presence.

"And yet you had to climb to slip beneath my covers. Are there many beds this size in all of England, I ask you?" His warm breath blew against her cheek, smelling of brandy, mint, and potent mature male.

She swallowed to ease the dryness in her mouth and met the anger in his. He had a point.

"I do not know. I am tired, you see…" Her tongue wouldn't form the words she wished to say, and she gripped the bedclothes tighter to her chest.

"Ah. Then I recommend you retire to your *own* chamber with all possible speed and in the same condition you entered mine, chaste and empty-handed." Before she could blink, he leaned forward and tossed the bedclothes back.

Lavinia's mouth dropped open. Her body hummed with alarm and a strange excitement. Licking her dry lips, she hoped for a clever retort to ease her embarrassment, but her mind remained blank.

He chuckled at her expression and scooped her from the bed.

Before she could protest, the duke bundled her clothes into her arms and set her outside the door. "Thank you for an entertaining evening."

Then he closed the door and slid the bolt into place with a resounding thud.

She gaped and glanced down at her bundle. How the hell did she get in this mess? Boots thumped down the corridor, and she tensed. The footmen could not see her in her present state or anyone else. Her reputation would be irreparable-perhaps even worse than it already was.

If these were Oliver's rooms, her door would be two more down on the right.

She hurried in that direction, wondering how she could have miscounted and ended up in the duke's bed.

A minute later, she swung another door open and stared inside. Her gaze flew to the chairs before the hearth, and she blew out a breath of relief when she discovered them empty. Never again would she venture into a chamber after dark without checking the entire area for inhabitants.

After inspecting every corner and patting down the red velvet drapes, Lavinia hurried to bed and slipped beneath the covers. Her feet were frozen, and her heart thumped loudly in her chest. Her hands shook when she tucked the coverlet beneath her chin and let out a deep sigh.

What a colossal mess she made of her life. Her parents would be livid over her defection, The scandal would be all over the Ton, and she may not ever have another offer of marriage. Not that she cared what they thought. But she did want a husband and children. And just when she thought of the perfect place to hide until it all blew over, she ended up in the duke's bedchamber. Sitting up, she punched her pillow and laid back down. "Now what?" She asked the ceiling as if the angels frolicking over her bed had an answer.

Chapter Six

The duchess sipped her morning coffee and studied her eldest son over the rim as she considered how to put her plan into action. To her utter delight and surprise, he did it for her.

"Good morning, Mother. You are looking quite well this morning. Radiant, in fact." He paused. "I imagine you are quite pleased with last night's activities. And since you tend to shine in the evening rather than the morning, I shall wait to disillusion you about our new houseguest's performance until you finish your coffee."

He took a slice of lamb and added bacon, cheese, and coddled eggs before taking his seat beside her.

Her eyebrow rose. "Houseguest?"

He gave her a sardonic look. "Yes, Mother. A small woman with blonde hair and unusual eyes. She gave the impression of innocence. Quite a difference from your usual applicants for the position of duchess. But sweet nonetheless. I would have been drawn in except for the fact I do not wish to marry. And although I have been straightforward about the subject and most vehement in my decision to remain a bachelor, you persist in throwing women at me. When will it stop, I wonder?'

Lavinia. How delightful. She must still mix her numbers and letters up like she did in her youth. If she were told to go two leagues to the north and one to the south, Lavina would go one league to the north and two to the south.

Arabella could not mask her fascination or her curiosity. "What happened?"

He grimaced. "Nothing I will admit to, and your timing is off. The footmen or whoever you planned to catch us did not appear before I tossed the woman out. If you have sent for the priest, I'm afraid you will be disappointed."

Her eyes widened, and satisfaction hovered at the corners of her mouth. "Threw her out of…where?"

He shot her a glance of disapproval. "You know very well where, and I refuse to say it aloud."

Her goddaughter must have entered the wrong chamber by mistake. Arabella had the most insatiable wish to know what happened. "Did you compromise her reputation?"

"I can feel you drooling at the possibility from across the table, Mother. And no, I did not. She is as chaste as she was before we met—wherever we were."

Arabella chuckled. "You sound like you did when I caught you sneaking into the Christmas tarts when you were five."

"I do not find the situation humorous." His blue eyes snapped with anger as he took a violent bite of his bacon.

"My dear, our houseguest is my goddaughter, Lady Lavinia Holbrook, and her friend, Lady Victoria Beaumont. I did not send either one of them to your chamber. You can cease your glaring. Whatever you did with whomever you did it with, you did it on your own. I had no hand in it."

When he gave her a dark, suspicious look, she chuckled again and added, "Wherever you were."

He ate his eggs in silence. "You swear you did not

orchestrate the situation?"

"I did not." She could not contain her satisfaction. Lavinia and Oliver were perfect for one another. Why had she not thought of this before? "What did happen, exactly?" She studied his face with care as he took another bite of breakfast.

"Nothing untoward, thank God. Had I not been suspicious, things may have gotten out of hand." He frowned when her grin widened.

A wise woman plays her cards close to her chest and keeps her ace hidden until the proper time. The duchess sat lost in thought for several long minutes before she smiled and tilted her head, keeping her keen gaze on her son's face. "I would like to place a wager on your marriage, Oliver."

His head came up, and he glared. "There will not be one, Madam."

She nodded to soothe his anger before answering him. "I wager ten thousand pounds you will be wed by Christmas. I will have Cecil hold the money."

His glare could have melted solid stone. "And if I refuse to take this wager? I will not marry, Mother. That is my final answer."

She shrugged. "If you are so insecure in your conviction, you do not wish to place a paltry ten-thousand-pound wager. It is just as well. I would have won without much effort, anyway."

He leaned back in his chair and stared at her. "You forget for a wedding to be legally binding, both parties must consent to certain terms. And since I have no such intention, I will accept your wager and give Cecil my money to hold, as well. But rest assured, you will not be the victor. "He rose to his feet and threw his napkin on his empty plate.

"Your Graces, Lady Lavinia Holbrook and Lady Victoria Beaumont." Cecil stepped aside and allowed the two women to enter the room.

Lavinia wore a pale blue muslin day gown that drew out the unusual shade of her eyes. Her curly blonde hair was plaited and tied behind her back with a matching ribbon. She strolled into the room beside Lady Victoria dressed in an emerald-green muslin gown with her fiery red hair in a similar plait. They were stunning.

Arabella shot a discreet glance at her son. He stood as if turned to stone with his gaze on Lavinia. He appeared bored, but the pulse in the side of his neck beating at an accelerated rate betrayed his interest in Lavinia.

The two women dipped curtsies and approached the table. They took a seat on either side when Cecil and a waiting footman held their chairs out for them.

Arabella noted Oliver had not stirred.

"I apologize for our tardiness. I fear we overslept." Her goddaughter's soft, husky voice filled the silence. She kept her gaze downcast as if avoiding Oliver's eyes.

Her son gave them a charming smile. "Good morning."

Arabella made the appropriate introductions, and she studied Oliver when he bent over Lavinia's hand. Did his lips linger a little longer than usual? The unfolding drama promised to be most entertaining. And to think she anticipated this holiday season with dread, fearing it would be as dull as the last one.

Now, to set the rest of her plan into action. Oliver was an astute man, and tricking him into matrimony would take skill and finesse. She gave him a sweet smile when he kissed her on the cheek.

"Have a pleasant day, Mother. I will see you tonight. Now, if you ladies will excuse me, I'm off for my ride."

"Good day, Oliver."

Had he bothered to turn around as he left the breakfast room, he would have seen a victorious smile hovering at the corners of her mouth.

****

Earlier, Lavinia woke to a timid knock on her door, and a thin maid bustled in.

She had long blonde hair, brown eyes, and a thin body. Wearing a stiff navy uniform with a crisp white apron, she approached the bed and bobbed a curtsy.

"I am Annie. Lady Arabella sent me to help you. I will be your maid while you're here."

"I am pleased to meet you." Lavinia sat up and brushed her hair from her eyes.

"Now then, where is your trunk so we can get you dressed?" Annie circled the room with her hands on her hips.

Lavinia pointed to her valise. "The footmen carried it up last night while I had tea with the duchess."

Annie placed the valise on the trunk at the foot of the bed and lifted out her pale blue muslin day dress. She wrinkled her nose at the creases and rang for a footman. "Take this to the kitchen and have Amy get the wrinkles out. Bring it back to me when she's done."

Turning, she smiled. "Would you like a bath this morning, your ladyship?"

Lavinia smiled. "Yes, please. And you may call me Miss Lavinia. All the older servants know me as such."

"Yes, Miss Lavinia."

The girl worked her miracle, and an hour later,

Lavinia strolled down the stairs with Victoria to find something to eat.

When Cecil announced them, she entered the breakfast room, her gaze drawn to the duke. Her chest tightened, and her mouth went dry at the sight.

Dressed in black riding breeches, a white shirt, knee-length riding boots, and a dark gray riding jacket with black trim, he exuded athleticism, handsomeness, and masculinity that left her breathless.

He glanced her way, and for a moment, their eyes met. The world faded away, and time stood still. She couldn't move, and her knees knocked together beneath her blue muslin skirt.

The spell broke when Victoria slipped her arm through hers, and they approached the table.

Conscious of his size and proximity, she swallowed and shifted her gaze away from the duke to Arabella.

The duchess smiled when the duke bent over her hand.

Lavinia sucked in a breath as his warm lips brushed her skin, hoping he couldn't feel her tremble.

And then he was gone.

Lavinia leaned back in her chair and stared down at the table as Victoria and the duchess talked. She had a stern talk with her heart the night before after she lay awake for hours reliving the scene in the duke's bedchamber. Between them, they decided to keep their distance from the duke. She came to escape a marriage, not rush into the next one. And despite the intoxicating effect his nearness had on her, she would pretend indifference. After all, didn't he set her outside his door as if she were nothing more than an inconvenience the night before?

Squaring her shoulders, she lifted her chin and joined the conversation. When the duchess learned Lavinia arrived with a small valise and two gowns to her name, she sent a footman to the village to collect the seamstress and any fabrics she had on hand.

Victoria wanted to leave by luncheon, but Lavinia convinced her to stay one more night.

"I want to show you the castle."

"You may stay as long as you like, Victoria, and rest." The duchess rose to her feet. "Make sure you show our guest the stables, Lavinia. If you tour the library, salons, and kitchens, Oliver will be back. And he can instruct you on which horse he will allow you to ride while you are here." She waved her hand toward the corridor. "I will be in the blue and silver saloon if you need anything. Cecil or one of the footmen will show you the way."

The girls had a marvelous time exploring the castle.

Lavinia introduced Victoria to all her favorite hiding places, including the window seat in the library.

Four salons, the breakfast room, dining room, ballroom, and kitchens were located along the corridor on the lower floor. The two girls explored them all before exiting the back door of the castle and walking along the frosty cobblestone path to the now-empty vegetable and herb gardens.

"The orchards are beyond the wall, and the flower gardens are to the left, directly behind the salons. We can go there later. First, I want to go to the stables and see His Grace's horses. Come on." Lavinia had taken her time showing Victoria the ground floor as the duchess suggested, giving the duke time to return.

Victoria cast her a side glance as they strolled along

the walkway. "How long has it been since you visited your godmother?"

Lavinia frowned. "I haven't been here since I turned thirteen. I calculate six years. Why do you ask?"

She shrugged. "The duke stared at you so hard when we came into the breakfast room. I worried you would turn into a pillar of salt."

"Did he?" Lavinia smiled and hoped her fluttering heart didn't give her away. "He may not have known we were here. I would stare, too, if two ladies appeared in our breakfast room."

Victoria snorted. "With your father's reputation, who wouldn't?" She tucked her arm into Lavinia's. "What happens now? We have whisked you away to safety for the time being, but you don't have long before your parents find you. Have you given any thought to your future?"

Lavinia stopped and turned to her dearest friend. Victoria would not like her plan, and she tensed for the argument sure to follow. "I thought I would send word to Mama's cousin who lives in the lowlands in Scotland and inquire if she will allow me to live with them." When her companion frowned, she hurried to explain. "Cousin Gwendolyn is a kind, loving soul, and I'll be protected. If I am in Scotland, neither Papa nor the viscount will have any authority over me. It is my only option. With the scandal I've caused, there will be no more marriage proposals, and I find I do not care. I refuse to be some man's broodmare, impregnated and discarded like a…settee in the parlor. Forgotten until the lord requires someplace to sit." She folded her arms over her chest and lifted her chin in defiance as she waited for Victoria's response.

Her friend tilted her head, her expression thoughtful. "I believed you wanted a husband and children. Has Hudson soured you on the idea, and so you've given up?"

Lavinia scoffed. "Nay. My parents did. I will never allow a man to control and dishonor me." She shot a sarcastic smile at her companion. "I do not believe the idea of marrying has merit now, anyway. A spinster I shall be unless some handsome Scot carries me off to his highland home to ravish me, far away from English lords, the Ton, and polite society. I have no use for the lot."

Victoria chuckled. "And if he did? Would you accept his proposal?"

Lavinia stared at the clear gray sky streaked with wisps of white clouds. "If he treated me as an intelligent, capable woman and respected my decisions, then yes."

"And would you bear him children? You've always spoken of having them."

Lavinia had a vision of Oliver's steel blue eyes gazing into hers and the breathless excitement she felt the night before. Gulping back the memory, she nodded, unsure if she would bear children for her imaginary Scottish hero or not. "Yes."

"Then I approve. Now your future is settled, shall we visit the stables?"

They strolled along the last remaining feet to the stables and entered through the open doors only to meet the duke on his way out.

His gaze lingered on Lavinia's lips and dropped to her breasts. His eyes were as cold and gray as the sky. When he glanced back at her, his lips tightened, and she had the most peculiar feeling she angered him.

"Your Grace." Squaring her shoulders, she met his gaze head-on. "I would like to request your permission to ride one of your horses while I am here."

He glanced at one of the grooms to his right brushing a black stallion a good seventeen hands high. "Tom, show Lady Lavinia and Lady Victoria Grace and Belle."

"Yes, Your Grace." The man had red hair and a deep voice. He wore a red and black livery with polished boots. Setting his brush down, he led the stallion toward a stall fifteen feet in front of them.

Oliver's gaze returned to her face. "Grace and Belle are three-year-old mares and quite spirited. If they prove too much for you, Tom can saddle two older mares. Do not venture north past the outer fence. I would hate to have you captured by…marauders during your stay here."

He gave a mock bow. "If you will excuse me, I have estate matters to attend to."

When he disappeared along the path to the castle, Victoria raised an eyebrow. "Did he hear our conversation?"

Lavinia gazed after him, furrowing her brow. "I fancied we were too far away." She cast a glance at the castle and frowned. But had he?

Chapter Seven

Oliver stormed up the stairs, slamming the door to his study closed with a bang. He hadn't been able to sleep, thinking of the way Lavinia disrobed the night before. She had the grace of a queen and the body of a Courtesan. Her soft lips and wide eyes tormented his dreams, while her soft curves, rounded in all the right places, made him toss and turn all night.

When she strolled into the breakfast room looking for all the world like an angel with her golden curls and lavender eyes, he couldn't tear his gaze away, to his mother's delight.

He cast one glance at her smug expression and rose to his feet. If she thought her goddaughter would capture his interest where so many others failed, she would soon learn her mistake. He avoided afflictions of the heart with as much care as he would a debilitating disease.

A cold, crisp ride along the north road to the forest would cool his blood and clear his head for the battle ahead. Despite his mother's delicate façade, he knew her true nature all too well.

Her wager took him by surprise, and he gritted his teeth in frustration.

His mother planned his downfall into marriage with meticulous care or she wouldn't have goaded him with her bet. And he didn't believe her innocent of sending Lavinia to the wrong chamber last night, despite her feigned innocence.

Nay. His mother had nothing to do but plot his matrimonial demise and design a nursery for his progeny.

God. Though he loved her with all his heart, why wouldn't she accept his decision to remain a bachelor?

Lavinia's voice played in his head.

There, neither Papa nor the viscount can order me to do anything I don't want to do.

He understood her frustration, but even Scotland wouldn't save him from his mother. The woman had a tenacious streak to rival Satan's.

And who the hell was the viscount? He knew of no scandal involving Lavinia.

Her voice continued.

I refuse to be some man's broodmare, impregnated and discarded...

Snorting, he wanted to add his discontent to being a...What would a man forced to sire a child be called, anyway? A brood sire?

He chuckled. *Discarded like a settee in the parlor. Forgotten until the lord required someplace to sit.* The girl used amusing analogies, he thought. But if she were his, he wouldn't be sitting on her. Nay, she would be atop him. The memory of her soft body in his arms made him rigid.

Shifting in his seat to ease his ardor, he remembered her mentioning being abducted by a Scot and taken to the highlands to ravish. Then her voice went all dreamy and soft as if ravishment by a highlander were every girl's fantasy.

His lips tightened as he swung his chair around to stare out the window, steepling his fingers in thought.

English lords were much better lovers and far superior in every other avenue. What the devil did she have against them?

Perhaps her parents were the answer. The Earl of Holbrook and his wife were the epitome of a marriage of convenience, and with their history, he could understand her reluctance to join the marital throng. He avoided the marriage noose for much the same reason. Thoughts of being tied to some of the ladies his mother paraded through the castle made him shudder with revulsion. Good god, what a dreadful thought.

Lavinia would be different. His chest tightened, and for a moment, he envisioned her riding away in her Scotsman's arms. The notion irritated him, and he clenched his fists in frustration. Why would she entertain the idea of bearing a child for a Highlander, yet not an English lord? A baffling silence enveloped his mind, followed by astonishment at the direction his musings had taken. God, just listen to him. And why did he care?

If he treated me as an intelligent, capable woman and did not interfere with my decisions, yes.

And therein lay the answer. What did the unknown viscount do to make Lavinia so cynical and bitter? Or did her ire spring from her parents' tumultuous relationship?

His gaze caught on two white mares bearing the two ladies racing across the field north toward the forest.

Their carefree, laughing faces made him smile. They should ride while they had the chance, for soon glistening snow would cover the countryside and riding would be difficult.

The ladies turned east and disappeared into the forest.

Oliver sat for another moment, staring after them.

Everyone knew of the scandal involving Lady Victoria and Viscount Holbrook but what happened with Lavinia? He would swear she hadn't been kissed properly, judging from her shy response the night before. If another man hurt her or compromised her in any way, he'd beat the bastard to within an inch of his life. He owed his mother that much. Lavinia *was* her goddaughter, making her family of sorts.

He rang for Cecil,

The door opened, and his butler appeared. "Find out everything you can about Lady Lavinia. There is a scandal involved, and I want all the details."

Cecil gave no indication of his thoughts and inclined his head. "Very good, Your Grace. Is there anything else?"

He hesitated as his mother's wager crossed his mind. "Yes. I want you to move all my belongings to the Duchess's chamber. You may trade places with the furnishings if you must."

Cecil raised an eyebrow. "Of course, Your Grace. But may I ask why?"

He spoke with the familiarity of a lifetime of service, and Oliver allowed his impertinence.

"My mother wagered ten thousand pounds she would see me wed by Christmas. We are both acquainted with my mother's tenacity when it comes to getting her own way. She will not play fair. If I am to prevail in my bachelorhood, I must remain vigilant and cunning. Moving my bedchamber to discourage surprise night visitors is paramount to my protection." He followed the direction the mares took with his eyes and cleared his throat to ease the sudden dryness created by last night's visitor. He couldn't keep his mind off her flushed face and soft pink lips.

"I understand, Your Grace. And if I may be so bold as to make a suggestion?" His old blue eyes twinkled.

Oliver sighed. Every servant in the castle knew of his mother's relentless scheming to see him married, and while most of them were quite amused by her antics, he was not.

"There may be a bit of inconvenience for you, Your Grace. But if we were to relocate your belongings to a different chamber at random, Her Grace would not be able to pin you down, as it were." He paused. "I understand Her Grace has invited three young ladies to a house party next weekend. If they do not know where you sleep, they cannot be found in a compromising situation and therefore end your bachelorhood."

Oliver's frustration simmered in his chest. "Bloody hell! Of course, my mother did. You have my permission to move my things, but this must remain confidential. Batty can be trusted to inform me where I am to sleep each night."

His valet would find the situation as amusing as Cecil, but they were both loyal, thank God. Otherwise, he would be in a position of perpetual marital bliss at this very moment with babes toddling all over the nursery.

Oliver shuddered as the image paraded before his mind's eye. As a duke and master of the castle, he should have the liberty to sleep wherever he pleased. But whoever wrote the rules on etiquette and entitlement forgot to take his mother into account.

Cecil smiled. "Now then, Your Grace. If you're that worried, I can have Ivan make ye a chastity belt. No one could doubt yer word if ye were…locked away."

Their smithy possessed the skill to make anything

he desired, and Oliver rolled his eyes at the suggestion. Casting Cecil a dark glance, he frowned to discourage any further pursuit of the subject. "Very amusing, Cecil. Changing bed chambers should suffice. Now, if you have any more practical suggestions, please voice them or go about your duties."

Cecil's face split into a wide grin. "I'm done, Your Grace."

"Fine." He leaned over his desk and pretended to read his overseer's report until the door closed behind him. He didn't get any real work done, however, until he caught sight of the two ladies returning, with no Scots trailing behind, intent on ravishment.

With a self-derisive smile, he bent to the task of reading and answering the correspondence before him.

****

The next day, Lavinia stood beside Victoria's carriage following tea as her friend prepared for the tedious journey home. She gave her a tight squeeze and begged her to be careful. "Write to me when you arrive home, or I'll worry."

Her friend returned her hug with equal ferocity. "I shall. If I hear anything about the situation, I'll send word."

Understanding her friend's unspoken concern about Lavinia's parents or Hudson finding her, she nodded. "Thank you, dearest friend. Until we meet in happier times."

Victoria chuckled. "Indeed, until then. But if I receive a letter from the highlands proclaiming you are with child, I'm coming to investigate with my gun loaded. The father better be besotted with you, or he will face my wrath."

Lavinia laughed. "He would have to be. I would never bear his child unless he gave me my heart's desire."

"And what is your heart's desire?"

She jumped in alarm when the duke's voice rumbled behind her.

For two mad seconds, she entertained the notion he asked because he cared, and without thinking, she blurted out her response. "Love and respect. I require both to remain at any man's side."

"I see." One eyebrow rose as he studied her face. "What makes you so certain a Northman would honor your terms? Many men take what they desire without considering the consequences, regardless of their nationality. Be it wealth or circumstance, there is nothing a Scotsman can offer you a good English nobleman cannot." His words carried weight as his steely gaze pinned Lavinia to the ground. After a moment, he turned to kiss Victoria's hand.

"I bid you a safe journey, my lady."

"Thank you, Your Grace." She gave Lavinia a wide smile and allowed the footman to help her alight.

As Victoria's carriage disappeared into the distance, surrounded by her outriders, Lavinia stood still, gripped by a sense of trepidation over her uncertain future. She had no idea what happened after she fled the wedding and could only surmise her parents were searching for her.

"You shall be quite safe here, Lavinia." Oliver's deep voice broke into her thoughts. "Nothing and no one shall disturb you while you are under my protection. Not even a highlander."

She didn't realize she'd taken hold of his hand until

he squeezed her fingers. "They are quite fierce, I am told. How far are we from the border?"

Tingles spread from Oliver's warm hand up her arm and down her body, igniting a flurry of butterflies in her belly. She swallowed to ease the sudden dryness in her throat.

"A good day's ride." He paused, his tone gentle yet pragmatic. "I do not wish to dash your hopes, but many young ladies have come to stay and returned to their families unscathed despite our proximity to Scotland and her fierce warriors."

Turning to him, she discovered he had changed out of his riding clothes and into a pair of navy trousers with a silver waistcoat. They stood so close his navy velvet jacket brushed her sleeve and sent shivers of awareness down her spine.

Her breath caught in her throat at the sight of his dark, wavy hair tousled by the breeze and the intensity of his searching gaze. The enticing aroma of citrus, sandalwood, and leather clinging to his skin surrounded her, and her heart quickened. No warrior, Scottish or English, could compare to the intoxicating presence of the duke standing so close she could feel heatwaves rolling off his masculine body. Swallowing to ease her suddenly dry throat, she dropped her gaze to hide her attraction. Heat surged through her belly, weakening her knees as he shifted her to face him.

His hands settled on her shoulders and burned through the layers of clothing separating them, igniting a fierce longing within her.

"*I* do not wish to." Turning her face away, she stared at the line of trees in the distance and wondered what freedom would be like.

His gaze sharpened. "Remain unscathed or return home?" His gaze dropped to her lips for several heart-pounding minutes. Leaning closer, he ran the tip of his finger along her jaw, making her dizzy with desire. His warm breath blew against her cheek, smelling of forest, temptation, and sin. "Perhaps a lesson on perspective is in order." The words hung heavy in the air as she lifted her gaze to ask his meaning and met the intent in his.

Before she could blink, his hard, warm lips captured hers in a soft, exploring kiss that sent a flurry of wings fluttering inside her.

Her lips softened, and she sighed when he repeated the kiss.

Hudson's mouth had been hard and brutal. A branding of sorts, while the duke's lips made her tingle all over and yearn for more.

He murmured against her mouth and slid his hands around her waist, drawing her up against him.

She gasped with pleasure as her body melded with his from breast to hip to knee. Oliver's strong arms wrapped around her, creating a sensual heaven where nothing else existed but the two of them. Their breath intertwined, igniting a fire within her that left her weak and clinging to him for support.

"Open for me, Lavinia." His tongue teased the seam of her lips, and she gasped again. Before she could react, he slid his tongue into her mouth, caressing hers with languid strokes that sent waves of pleasure coursing through her. Never in her most intimate fantasies had she envisioned such an experience. Each deliberate stroke of his tongue made her heart pound harder, and her breath quicken.

"You taste so sweet, my dear. I think I will have

some more." And he did. His tongue explored the depths of her mouth until she shook in his arms, too dazed to do anything but cling to him and pray her trembling limbs kept her upright.

Tightening her grip around his neck, she gave kiss for a kiss as all the hurt, yearning, and disappointment of the last year poured out of her. Each frantic beat of her heart fueled her desire to drown in his embrace. Imitating his movements first with hesitation and then boldness, she pressed her body into his as he groaned against her mouth.

Her breath came fast as he turned her head and deepened his kiss. For long minutes, they clung together until the duke raised his head and gave her a sardonic smile.

"I believe you will discover English lords are more refined and are far more appealing than our fierce northern neighbors." Grasping her arms, he unwound them from around his neck and placed them by her sides. "Remember my kiss the next time you wish for a rough, uncivilized Highlander. We English have so much more to offer a delicate lady."

Lavinia stared at him as his words penetrated the sensual fog in her mind. She was no delicate flower despite the way she clung to him for support. English or Highlander, no man had kissed her so thoroughly before. Heat filled her cheeks as she gazed up at his impassive face.

His features could have been carved from stone for all the emotion they displayed. In that moment, it occurred to her their kiss meant nothing more to him than a lesson in comparison. Had he not said as much before he whisked her away to the stars?

Her head whirled with the pleasure of his kiss as she searched his countenance for any sign their embrace affected him too, but his hooded gaze revealed nothing of his thoughts.

Pride came to her rescue, and she stiffened her spine. If he could act as though nothing happened, so could she. Shaking the sensual cobwebs aside, she resumed their conversation as if she hadn't just received the most delicious kiss of her life.

"I do not wish to return home. Now or ever." Let him make of her comment what he would. She would never go back, unscathed or nay, for she knew what waited for her.

Or more whom.

Papa would punish her for running away and putting his precious hundred acres in jeopardy. His judgment would be harsh, but marriage to the viscount was out of the question. She had a better chance of survival alone. Or in Scotland where her father's considerable influence could not affect her.

Oliver remained silent for several seconds while he studied her face.

"What happened, Lavinia?" His soft voice hit her heart like a metal-tipped arrow, straight and true.

She flinched. He sounded as if he cared, and she might have fallen for his expression of concern if he didn't just kiss the bloody hell out of her and then step away with a comment about his superiority. He was a man and a wealthy, powerful duke. What could he know of having someone else dictate his life or the painful repercussions of nonconformity? Her heart hardened, and her blood cooled.

"Nothing." Shrugging, she stepped away from the

heat of his tall, muscular body. If he knew how she shamed her father and left her fiancé standing at the altar, he might not give her sanctuary.

Oliver tilted her chin up with his free hand. "Someone hurt you. Who?" His gaze searched her face while the heat of his finger sent thrills down her spine.

"Does it matter?" She swallowed, cursing her traitorous body for responding to his touch.

"It does to me." The concern in his voice and the gentleness of his finger caressing her chin made her quiver.

She almost believed him. Almost. But English Lords stuck together, and the laws of honor made it impossible for him to understand her plight. Whoever heard of a lady refusing to bow to the demands of society and protocol? No, he would expect her to behave like all the rest, and no doubt hand her back to her father tied up with a big red bow.

Removing her chin from his grasp, she squared her shoulders.

"Not to me. Thank you for your concern, but it is not needed." She cast him a small smile and took a determined step away from temptation. "My problems are my own."

Oliver's lids dropped over his eyes, shielding his expression. "I have two shoulders for you to weep on should you desire to do so. I do not know why you are here or what occurred to make you so bitter against my kind, but I am at your command, Lavinia. If you allow me, I will do all I can to help you."

He confused her. First with his heated kisses, then with his cold indifference, and last with his offer to help. She responded the only way she knew. Gazing up at him, she allowed the devil to take hold of her tongue. "As I see. Thank you for the kiss. It was most…instructional."

He wouldn't be so amiable if he knew what she had done. Turning on her heel, she fled. He couldn't know how his kind words wrapped around her heart and filled her with yearning for a unicorn she could never have.

Chapter Eight

Viscount Becker walked on the tips of his toes as he made his way across the rough wooden floors of the tavern, careful not to get any gutter muck on his pristine heels. He held his top hat in one hand and turned side to side to avoid contact with any of the patrons or the unclean furniture. He sniffed with disgust at the ill-clad crowd filling the seedy tavern on the dock. He should have insisted his contact meet him in a more genteel place such as Vauxhall Garden or the theater. Somewhere, he could stroll about and not worry about soiling his forest green jacket and fawn breeches.

But his man of business, Mr. Timberlay, assured him the Drunken Sailor would be a better choice. "No one will recognize you there, sir. You can sit at a table, have a sip of rum, and make your proposal without fear of being discovered."

His comment seemed reasonable until Hudson stepped through the rough-hewn door and took in the scene. A long bar ran the length of the room, with bottles of spirits on a shelf behind the beefy bartender. Four rumpled sailors sat on tall stools in front of the bar, engaged in a lively conversation, while the bald bartender hit flies with his rolled-up piece of linen and glowered.

Off to his right three tables held groups of unshaven, and if Hudson were to guess by the smell, unbathed men holding cards and drinking ale from tin tankards at their elbows.

To his left, four other tables were arranged to fill up the space. Men sat at three of them. The other held a thin man with a curling mustache and a steely glint in his gray eyes. He wore the clothes of a merchant and sipped from a tankard. He must be Mr. Marlboro, the finder.

According to Mr. Timberlay, Marlboro could find anyone and anything.

Hudson retrieved a lace-edged kerchief from his pocket and held it against his nose to mask the smell of the tavern. On tiptoes, he inched his way to the table in the corner where Mr. Marlboro sat.

A buxom woman in a low-cut dress gave him a wink as she refilled mugs of ale with a pitcher in her hand. "We don't get Toff's in 'ere much. Take a seat anywhere ye've a mind to, and I'll fetch ye a drink. What'll ye 'ave?"

He grimaced. No doubt they watered the ale down to the point it rivaled the Thames for taste. "Your best whisky, if you please."

She nodded as she finished her task. "I'll 'ave it right out for ye."

Arriving at the corner table, Hudson pulled out the closest chair and gagged. Brown with frequent use, the wood reeked of some God-awful scent. Urine? Vomit?

Hudson shuddered at the thought and opened his perfumed kerchief. Spreading the delicate lace-edged linen square over the putrid area, he sank down with careful attention to the location of his backside in relation to the square. He glanced around for a suitable spot to put his top hat and, finding nothing acceptable, placed it on his lap. He may have to have his valet burn his clothes after this unsavory adventure.

"Ye be Viscount Becker?" Marlboro studied him through half-closed eyes.

Hudson grimaced. "Do you see any other gentleman willing to risk a costly pair of fawn breeches to speak to you?" He studied the other man as he spoke and gave an involuntary shiver. There sat a man one wouldn't want to meet in a black alley. An aura of danger clung to him like cologne.

His companion sat back in his chair. "If ye don't confirm who ye are, I cannot do business with ye." His eyes narrowed to mere slits, and Hudson sighed with frustration.

"Fine. I'm Viscount Becker. My man, Mr. Timberlay, tells me you are the one to speak to about my missing fiancée." Did the man not realize his place?

"That's right. I'll need a description of the woman, a list of places and people she would run to, and your hundred pounds." Leaning back in his chair, he chewed on a small sliver of wood and twirled it around in his mouth.

Hudson withdrew a velvet bag and threw it out on the table with a thud. "Here." He didn't like the man, and as soon as he found Lavinia, he would pay someone else to kill him. "Half now and half when you find her." No man of worth wore a puce shirt without a collar. Hudson kept his gaze on the man's face, loathe to discover what he paired with the hideous garment.

Marlboro stared. "If ye think to cheat me, ye should know I bumped off the last Toff what tried it." He flicked the sliver of wood from his mouth. "They found the bloke in the Thames from a…suicide."

The popinjay thought to challenge him, did he?

Hudson narrowed his gaze on the man's face. "The last man I hired who didn't complete his job vanished into thin air. The police have been unable to find him or his body." He paused and fixed a piercing stare on the filthy man opposite him. "Only pieces."

The man under discussion tracked down Arthur Holbrook as he asked but failed to kill him. Hudson discovered the viscount at the docks, preparing to return to England in glory with the coveted title in his jacket pocket.

Pirate John had lied. Arthur Holbrook wasn't dead.

In retaliation, Hudson lodged his dagger in the viscount's back, retrieved the title from his jacket, and swaggered off to find a new assassin to kill his old one. Once the Earl of Holbrook caught a glimpse of the parchment, he would hand Lavinia over on a golden platter, and there would be no more talk about being unworthy of his daughter. *And* he would have her glorious dowry at his disposal. The arrogant chit and her family would learn not to offend him.

God, how the earl's insult stung. His face burned as he remembered asking for her hand during Lavinia's first season and the earl tossing him from his townhouse as if he were a pile of rubbish.

Hudson stewed in the highest quality gin available for a week, concocting plots to gain his revenge. Every scenario ended with the high and mighty Earl of Holbrook finding him in Lavinia's bed naked. Nothing would wound the man like having his daughter debauched and discarded.

For two seasons, he stood on the sidelines and lusted after Lavinia's voluptuous body. But every time he got close, her brother chased him off. Soon, Hudson burned with as much hatred for Arthur as he harbored for the earl.

And then, one glorious night, he learned of Arthur Holbrook's errand to France quite by accident. Hudson sat at a table in White's nursing a brandy when two of the dandies in his set mentioned the date and time of the meeting where Arthur planned to acquire the lost hundred acres of Holbrook Estates.

Viscount Arthur Holbrook made a fortune in investments and planned to use a good portion of his wealth to appease his father's obsession and return the acreage to the family holdings.

Smelling a mouthwatering opportunity to appease his wounded feelings and solve his currency problems, he rose to his feet and ordered his carriage. Everyone knew of the earl's passion for regaining the hundred acres, and with the sweet title tucked away in his strong box, Lady Lavinia would be his to do with as he pleased.

Revenge could be so sweet. Memories of the glazed look in Arthur Holbrook's eyes when he fell to the ground dying made him go hard.

Hudson returned to the present with a shrewd smile. He knew how to get what he wanted and damn anyone who got in his way. "I offer half now and half when the job is complete. Those are my terms."

The two men stared at each other for several long minutes, and then Marlboro nodded his agreement.

The buxom woman approached and set a glass of whisky by his elbow. "'ere ye go, love."

Hudson cast her a sour glance, anxious to get this meeting over so he could return home and wash the scent of the docks from his skin. He didn't think he could take the foul place anymore, and the thought of what his poor kerchief might be protecting him from made him ill. "I am not, nor will I ever be, your love." He tossed a coin at her. "Be gone. You cloud the air with your common stench."

She gasped, and Marlboro's chair legs hit the ground.

He smiled at the outraged woman. "Thank you, Rosie." Removing a gold coin from his vest, he tossed it in her direction. "I'd like another ale when ye have the time." His shrewd gaze shifted to Hudson. "If I were you, I wouldn't get on her bad side. She's been known to piss in a man's drink before serving it."

Hudson didn't doubt the truth of it and swallowed the bile rising in his throat. "Thank you, Rosie." He had a tough time getting the words past his stiff lips. "You are a delight, I am sure." He didn't think he could take a sip of the foul liquor now if he tried.

Rosie sniffed. "I'll be right back, Mr. Marlboro." Glaring at Hudson, she wiped her hands on the dirty white apron tied around her middle and huffed away, muttering about high and mighty Toffs no better than they should be.

Hudson leaned forward. "Can we get to business now? I have another appointment I must not be late to." Thinking about his brass tub filled with scented water made him giddy with longing. His skin positively itched from the common dust settling over him.

Marlboro nodded.

For the next twenty minutes, Hudson gave descriptions and answered questions about Lavinia and her family. By God, the lengths she forced him to go to made him froth at the mouth. The chit could learn her place and would soon understand where she stood in the grand scheme of life. Once he got the required heir out of her, he would make her life a hell on earth. Close enough, the earl would be forced to witness the show, and far enough away, he could do nothing to stop it.

Hudson rose to his feet. "If you have no further questions, I will take my leave. Send a note to my townhouse in St. James when you have information. Any other concerns take to my man of business, Mr. Timberlay. Good day."

When he stepped into the street, he discovered several men standing before his carriage arguing with his coachmen.

Bentley held a pistol in one hand and glowered at the group. "Get back, or I shall fire." He cocked the flint back and took aim.

The group scattered, and Hudson hurried to the carriage door.

Bentley glanced his way. "I am happy to see you, my lord. And I will be happier still to leave this wretched place."

"Agreed. Take me home."

"Aye, my lord." Bentley lifted the reins and clucked as Hudson closed the carriage door.

He tossed his best linen handkerchief out the carriage window and leaned back against the red velvet seats. He frowned at the passing buildings and wished for a second kerchief to place over his nose again. The scent of fish, putrid water, and the salty sea assaulted his senses. He thought of his absent fiancée and narrowed his gaze. When he met her, he thought her a timid miss, much like her mother, and considered her the perfect lady to fulfill the conditions of his father's demands. He would marry the chit, get her with child, and leave her in the country, out of sight and out of mind. Her dowry would ease his financial situation, and her body would ease his appetites…for a time.

But after recent events in the church on the day of their wedding, he discovered his mistake. Not only did her father and brother insult him, but she did as well.

The entire Ton thought her defection was a grand lark and nicknamed him Blown Off Becker.

He gritted his teeth. Of all the embarrassing labels to be dubbed, this one made him grind his teeth in rage. God, how he hated the smirks and laughter whenever he entered a ballroom or salon.

After Lavinia's desertion, it took him a good week to calm down enough to think of a sound plan. She had the biggest dowry on the market with Lady Abby Waterdown's coming in second.

Though but fifteen years of age, Lady Abby should be timid and shy, but she had the tongue of a shrew. And when Hudson approached the duke to ask for her hand, he tossed him from Waterdown Castle by the collar of his favorite velvet jacket, laughing all the while.

"Blow off, Becker." The duke's parting words were a shot below the waist. With a curt nod, he righted his top hat, patted his jacket back into place, and left Waterdown Castle in a rage.

His man, Timberlay, produced the idea to hire Marlboro the next day.

Hudson wiped his brow and shrieked in alarm when his lace cuff came away smudged with dirt. God, he hoped he made it home without being spotted in such a mortifying condition.

He made a fist and thought of the satisfaction he would feel when he struck Lavinia for her part in his humiliation. These last two weeks since her defection were a hell he didn't care to re-live. Ever. Rage raced through him as he toyed with other methods of punishment. No woman could treat him with so much disregard and get away with it. Once Marlboro found the wretch, he would marry her, collect her dowry, and mete out punishment to his satisfaction. To both her and her father.

Chapter Nine

Lavinia's days fell into a comfortable routine.

She had breakfast with her godmother and the duke. Afterward, she requested Grace or Belle and explored the vast grounds of the castle with a footman trailing behind for protection. During these rides, she rode north and scoured the perimeter of the property for another way through the forest other than the main road. If her parents found her, she would require a quick escape route to Scotland. A way few knew about, and she could traverse while they searched the main road in vain. But alas, every day, she turned back in disappointment, for the trees sprouted thick and dense from the rich black soil as far as the eye could see.

The first day, she dashed through the trees, hoping to shake off her chaperone and explore alone. But after riding around in circles for hours with no idea which direction to take to return to the castle, she admitted defeat and asked the dour-faced man for directions. They arrived at the castle in time for Lavinia to dress for dinner, having spent the entire day trudging through the dense forest in vain. Impressed with the man's ability to find their way back, Lavinia requested the same footman on her next ride and questioned him about northern routes.

But the man shook his head and pointed south. "Me horse knows the way home. He doesn't know the way north."

Disappointed, she left him to his duties and accepted other escorts. Somewhere, somehow, there had to be an answer.

The first week, she sent a letter to her mother's cousin Gwendolyn asking for refuge. She explained her situation and her determination to leave England as soon as possible. Lavinia hoped for a reply by Christmas and prayed the answer came before her parents found her.

At the end of the second week, the duchess invited three girls to a house party.

They arrived in time for tea, chattering and giggling as they curtsied to her godmother.

Lavinia accepted the cup of tea the duchess handed her and sipped the fragrant beverage as she studied the other women sitting around the salon.

Miss Myrtle Marshall was the daughter of a local baron. Three inches taller than Lavinia's five-foot-seven frame, she had dark brown curly hair and big chocolate eyes. Tall, reed-thin, and shy as a goose the day before Christmas, she flushed a deep crimson whenever the duke strolled into the room.

Lady Priscilla Covington was the exact opposite. She was the daughter of the Earl of Covington, and though she stood equal height to Lavinia, she had honey-brown hair, hazel eyes, and a dimple in her left cheek. Outspoken, bold, and prone to bluntness, she kept the conversation going. One never had to guess her exact location because her lilting voice carried through the corridors and grew louder the closer one became. Curvaceous and adventurous, she transformed whenever the duke entered the room. Her unnatural silence was as hard to bear as Miss Marshall's painful shyness.

Lady Elspeth Perth from Bath proved to be the most resourceful. Red-haired, of regular height, and as thin as Miss Marshall, she refused to join the conversations unless the duke was present. And then her musical laugh rang out while she gushed with authority on every topic. Her hand movements grew more exaggerated the longer he remained, and her voice became quite breathless. She flushed with color, and her gaze stalked him like a tigress eyeing a potential mate.

The first time she witnessed the transformation, Lavinia raised an eyebrow at Lady Elspeth and peeked at the duke beneath her lashes to gauge his response. Within three minutes, he remembered some urgent matter requiring his attention and fled.

Lady Elspeth came from a prestigious line of Perth's and her self-importance manifested in waspish comments to the servants or a disdainful tilt of her nose when someone she deemed inferior crossed her path. She never, however, displayed this attitude in front of the duke.

Although Lavinia enjoyed the girls' company, Arabella did little more than take tea with them before disappearing until dinner time. After their second day at the castle, Lavinia wondered why her godmother invited them at all.

Until she overheard her maid, Annie, having a conversation with Cecil and learned about Arabella's wager.

Today, as she sipped her tea, she took note of her godmother's attempts to direct her guests to Oliver's notice and noted with interest how he deflected every maneuver with a wry glance or a dry comment.

On the third night of the house party, the duchess

announced a rousing game of hide and seek would add a dash of fun to the evening.

Lavinia caught the quick grin on Cecil's face and the glance he shot the duke before Oliver made his excuse and escaped to his study.

She didn't understand the importance of the interaction until her turn came to find the other girls. As she patrolled the corridors, searching for her quarry, cursing came from within the duke's chamber- female cursing followed by a muffled cry of alarm.

Moments earlier, Lavinia passed the duke's study with his door ajar and knew him to be in a conversation with his valet, Batty.

Pausing outside his closed chamber door, she frowned, and then she recognized the voice.

Lady Elspeth.

She wouldn't be in there for any good reason, and a surge of righteous indignation shot through her. The duchess was her godmother, and by rights the duke could be considered family, too, couldn't he?

The girl turned with a surprised expression, which exploded into rage when she discovered Lavinia standing at the door. "Get out. You'll ruin everything!" Clad in her corset, chemise, and pantalets, she planted her hands on her hips and narrowed her gaze. "I said, get out!" Her gown lay in a heap on the floor beside her satin slippers and stockings.

Realization dawned as Lavinia took in the scene. The bedclothes were rumpled, and the girl's hair stood on end. Shock and horror rooted her to the spot.

Lady Elspeth orchestrated this compromising situation with the intention of forcing the duke to ask for her hand. And the worst part? She cared not one whit if she ruined her reputation in the process.

Oliver's dry comments when she entered his chamber by accident on her first night in the castle flashed through her mind, and she flushed. *She* would never stoop to such an underhanded plot.

Frowning, she called for a footman and stepped into the room. "What *are* you doing?"

Lady Elspeth shrugged and tugged on the strings of her corset behind her back. "This is not your concern. Now, go away."

"I beg your pardon, my lady. *Why are you in His Grace's chamber?*" Cecil appeared at her elbow and glanced at the footman who hurried in behind him. "Willoughby, cover your eyes and go get Her Grace."

Lady Elspeth cast Lavinia a hate-filled glare before placing the back of her hand against her forehead. "I am so dizzy. I fear I will swoon." She stumbled around as if in a daze. "Where am I?" Reaching the hearth, she sank down, making sure she collapsed onto the tufted satin armchair standing there. Once settled, she blinked up at Cecil. "I...uh...believe I lost my way and..." Her voice trailed off as she slumped back and closed her eyes.

Lavinia rolled her eyes. Could she be any more obvious?

Cecil grunted his disapproval and covered the undergarment-clad lady with the coverlet from the bed. Folding his arms over his chest, he glared down at her and waited.

Cecil would defend his master to the death, and his expression said he dared the devious miss to stir. No wonder Oliver flinched whenever an unmarried female crossed his threshold. Did he have to deal with this sort of subterfuge on a regular basis?

The object of her thoughts strode down the corridor a moment later with the duchess two steps behind.

Four footmen and two housemaids brought up the rear.

The duke's frosty voice came from the corridor. "You will leave at once, Lady Elspeth, and never return. I sent a footman for my carriage. He has instructions to return you to your parents with a full account of your activities tonight. Including how Lady Lavinia caught you in my rooms."

"Oh dear." Standing at the door of the master chamber, the duchess frowned at the scene. "Lady Elspeth! I cannot fathom what you are about."

Oliver gave her a mocking smile. "Can't you, mother? I wouldn't be surprised to discover you put her up to this." He waved his hand in the unfortunate lady's direction. "I will not be manipulated into wedlock in such a fashion."

For once, Lady Elspeth did not burst into animated speech. Her chin lifted, and she glared at her audience. "A lady can hope and plan."

"Not with me." Oliver tilted his head at Cecil. "My butler will see you out."

Turning on his heel, the duke strode away, and Lavinia caught a small smile on her godmother's face.

Did she plan to entrap the duke? Her eyebrows rose in surprise. She thought only women had a tough time of it and stared after Oliver. Sympathy or empathy, she had no idea which, filled her chest. Stupefied, she kissed her godmother's soft cheek and wandered off to her chamber, deep in thought.

The next morning, Oliver did not appear for breakfast, and she learned he had gone riding before dawn and hadn't returned.

Lavinia shook her head. She didn't blame him the least little bit. No doubt, he hoped for a little solitude. And who wouldn't after last night?

The girls burst into laughter over some trivial conversation, and she glanced out the window toward the forest. The noise of the guest's chatter made her head throb, and she wished for silence to ease the dull ache.

Envious of the duke's solitary ride, following breakfast she sent a footman to the stables to saddle Grace and changed into her navy riding habit with the white braiding. The form-fitting jacket hugged her waist and arms and drew attention to the curve of her full breasts. Her full skirt billowed around her as she swung her fur-lined cloak over her shoulders and tied the ribbons beneath her chin.

Steel gray eyes smiled into hers as she accepted Tom's help into the saddle and looped her right knee over the pommel. Her normal escort had been sent to the village on an errand, and a new stable hand stepped forward to volunteer for the duty.

"My name is Maurice." He replied when she inquired about his name.

Lavinia tilted her head as she studied him.

Tall and thin with a curly mustache and a gallant manner, he moved slower than most of the footmen and took several minutes to climb into the saddle.

"You shall do just fine." This man wouldn't be able to keep up, much less stop her from exploring.

Smiling with relish, she picked up her reins, nudged the beautiful mare into a trot, and guided her north.

Cool, crisp air bit her nose and cheeks as she galloped across the grassy area toward the dense forest.

A shiver raced down her spine, and her teeth chattered. Gray clouds, forbidding and angry, hovered overhead, but she didn't care.

Racing forward, she smiled as they flew over the stark ground, enjoying the bite of the wind and rolling motion of the mare beneath her.

God, she felt so…*free.*

Glancing behind her, she smiled when she noted the stable hand three hundred feet behind, struggling to keep up. Good. If he kept his distance and didn't try to stop her, they would get along fine.

Savoring the liberty of the moment, she guided Grace north through the trees, dodging limbs and bushes. Lost in thought, she rode on, paying no attention to the passing time or the bite of the wind.

What if Cousin Gwendolyn didn't answer? Or worse, if she did respond but refused to offer Lavinia asylum?

Her hope of disappearing into the highlands would die a premature death. She worried her bottom lip with her teeth as she rounded a large pine tree and came to a stop.

Having left her slow escort far behind, nothing but the silence of the forest surrounded her. Far removed from the castle and other people, she allowed the stillness to envelop her. Peace and serenity flowed into her soul, calming her frayed nerves.

If she could stay here forever, she would. Closing her eyes with a satisfied smile, she sighed as blessed solitude settled around her. She cherished this place, so far away from London, her parents, and Hudson. Away from the gossip, scandals, and the pressure of the peerage.

Staring at the quiet beauty of the oak, alder and pine trees surrounding her, she clasped a bough and ran her gloved hand down the branch. Her leather covered palm came away with a fistful of dark needles. She stared at them as they slipped through her fingers to the forest floor.

Like sand in an hourglass.

A bird called from a nearby tree, and she jumped.

Frowning, she stared up at the canopy above her as if the answer to her problems would fall from the sky. She had little time to come up with a sound solution to her dilemma. By now, everyone knew she broke off her engagement and left Hudson waiting at the altar.

Nudging Grace into motion, she continued north.

Her parents could arrive ahead of schedule, and then what? She would have little choice but to accept whatever fate they planned.

A branch snapped to her right, and she jumped. Apprehension rippled down her spine, followed by a shiver.

"Who is there? I have an armed escort who will not hesitate to come to my defense." *If he finds me in time.* Her voice drifted away, followed by silence. After five minutes of stillness, she shrugged and resumed her musing.

Papa's punishments were never pleasant.

Mama would hide in her chamber until any unpleasantness passed. And then she would emerge with a careful smile and unseeing gaze, pretending everything was normal.

After a scandal like hers, there were only bleak options for her future.

Lavinia needed a miracle.

She thought of London, her friends, the theater, balls, soirees, and all the parties.

They dazzled her during her first season, making her shiver with excitement and anticipation. During her second season, they kept her entertained, and during her third, they no longer held any appeal.

Her friends enjoyed promenading on Rotten Row and planning trysts in Vauxhall Garden. They loved riding in Hyde Park in the afternoon, noting who rode with whom, and sharing stories about the newest scandals. Most of them related tales of stolen kisses and would-be lovers to enthrall each other with at tea.

While she did not.

Although not lacking for partners nor opportunity, she had yet to meet a man who made her heart race and her palms damp.

A fleeting memory of the duke's hot kisses flitted across her mind, and she frowned. If he knew such thoughts occurred to her, he'd toss her out like Lady Elspeth.

Forcing her mind back to the present, she urged Grace into a trot.

To see and be seen were the only two things most of the Ton were faithful to. Not so with her. In her heart, she yearned for love and a family—a man who would defend her with the ferocity of a panther yet also made her weak in the knees with his kisses. Did such a man even exist? Running her hands down her mare's side, she patted Grace.

A new gust of wind tugged at her cloak laden with the scent of…*snow?*

Glancing up at the darkening sky, she held her hand out as the first few white flakes drifted down through the canopy overhead.

Holding her tongue out, she laughed as the frozen droplets landed and melted. The wind howled through the branches, and her first stirring of unease settled in her stomach.

Turning Grace, she retraced their steps with reluctance. Her afternoon of solitude had been cut short. But then, if this storm turned into a blizzard, the roads would be impassable.

A smile lifted the corners of her mouth as her miracle started to fall thick and fast. Stopping to cast her glance heavenward in gratitude, she laughed aloud.

And then she spotted him sitting beneath the trees astride a massive horse watching her.

His plaid, bare legs and knee-high woolen stockings gave him away.

A Scot!

Lavinia gaped in astonishment. Turning to look at him, she didn't see the branch in front of her until it was too late.

The hard ground knocked the breath from her, and she lay startled as the edges of her vision darkened. She caught a glimpse of dark brown, curly hair, a rugged chin, and deep blue eyes before blackness claimed her.

Chapter Ten

Lavinia awoke with a start. She lay beside a fire on a thick woven green and brown plaid. The other end of which covered the length of her body. Warm, and disoriented, she frowned at the flames wondering how they burned so brightly when she remembered snow. And a man. The plaid…

"Wait!" Struggling, she sat up and took stock of her surroundings. Her heart slammed against her ribs when she spotted her companion. The world twirled before her eyes, and she dropped her chin to her chest to make it stop.

The Scot, wearing a skirt made of the same fabric as her blanket, sat on the other side of the fire, bandaging a wound on his thigh.

A day for miracles, indeed! She found a Highlander! But why was he in England? And all alone? The stories always started with a group of warriors, raiding parties, and the like. Staring, she studied him through her lashes.

Dark brown curly hair, a trimmed beard, and piercing blue eyes held her attention. A dark, thick woolen jacket stretched over broad shoulders as the reflection of the flames danced across his high cheekbones and broad forehead. He wore knee-high woolen stockings with a dirk slid inside the right one.

Taking in every inch of his impressive form, from the top of his curly brown hair tied behind his neck with a strip of leather across the broad planes of his shoulders to the muscular calves visible beneath his kilt, Lavinia sighed with appreciation. The tales did not do the man justice. Although he looked every bit as fierce and shocking as the stories suggested, he made no effort to touch her. Shouldn't he be throwing her across his saddle and racing for the border? Or something? Every tale she knew of the fierce highlanders contained some form of violence.

Bronzed, muscular, and intimidating, he shot her a glance.

"Yer awake at last, lass." His mild tone suggested she wasn't worthy of his notice, and he kept his gaze on his task.

Not sure if she should be offended or relieved by his lack of attention, she answered. "Yes. The last thing I remember is riding through the woods and your face." She glanced around, remembering her escort, and wondered if ditching him had been her smartest idea. She should have been frightened, but curiosity took over. She jested with Victoria about marauding highlanders, and with a Scot less than ten feet away, she had questions. "Why am I here, and where is my horse? You are on Chauncy land. When the duke learns of your presence, he will detain you."

"He willna get the chance." The man's muscular leg, bare and covered with dark hair, had a three-inch laceration right above the knee. His expression didn't change as he sewed the jagged edges together with a bent needle. "By the time His Grace hears of me, I'll be long gone. I'll thank ye to keep still until I finish with my wound. I canna have the English chasing me off again until I get what I came for."

The wind whipped around her and nipped at her face while thick, fat snowflakes fell around them with quiet determination. The frigid air made her tremble, and she drew her cloak tight against her chest.

"What did you come for?" Lavinia frowned when her voice came out breathless and hesitant, as if she were a first-season debutante.

The man glanced up with a frown. "A woman."

Then, he *did* plan to carry her off to the highlands. Lavinia couldn't breathe. "What are you going to do to me?"

He glanced up in surprise. "With ye?" Astonished eyebrows rose to his hairline. "Nothing," he scoffed. "I'm here to find my sister and return to Scotland before anyone knows different."

She frowned. *Nothing?* "Then…you have no plans to ravish me and carry me away on your steed?"

The man's jaw dropped open. "Good God, no! I'm no heathen, and I wouldn'a take advantage of a lady, especially an English one." The way he pronounced *English* as if the word were a bad taste in his mouth made her gape. Did he think her unworthy, too?

She must have a bloody note on her face that read, *I have no value.*

"Do I have no appeal to you at all?" She sounded piqued to her own ears and flushed.

Her companion stared at her. "I am sure ye have *some*, lass. But I canna be knowing what an Englishman finds attractive."

Her mouth dropped open, and she grappled with how to answer such a comment.

He glanced her way when she remained silent, and his face softened. "I dinna mean to upset ye, and for that,

I'm sorry. I came to find my sister. I canna understand why she ran away and what she hopes to find by coming to this Godforsaken place." Grunting as if the conundrum irritated him, he kept at his task.

Lavinia sighed and tilted her head. "Why did she run away?" She had to know why any woman would leave the place she came to think of as a haven.

A long, deep sigh escaped his well-shaped mouth. "She dinna wanna marry Angus Foust and has some notion she's in love with an English lad who visited our clan over the summer." He grimaced. "She fancies running away will solve all her problems." He shook his head. "But I dinna think she knows what trouble she invites by taking off alone. Clarice is a pretty lass, and any man who dares to touch her will feel the sting of my blade."

Lavinia digested his comments for a long minute with more than a little discomfort. She had a brother, too.

Once.

He would be livid if he knew of her plight. The feeling of being loved swept over her like a mist, a vague memory of a long-ago time, and then disappeared in the blaring light of reality. Her brother was dead and would never champion her cause again.

The hope she experienced five minutes prior fell flat and drained away, leaving despair behind. But another thought raced in. "What were you doing in the middle of the forest and not on the main road? You must have followed some kind of trail, and I must know where it is. Will you show me?"

The man knotted and snapped the thread. "Why?" Picking up a jar from the ground beside him, he dipped his fingers inside. Thick, gray paste emerged which he rubbed across his wound without looking up.

He didn't deny such a trail existed, she noted with satisfaction. Lavinia licked her lips. "Because I may have to leave England in haste without being detected, and a trail would be very fortuitous." The smell of his paste hit her with a foul eye-watering sting. "What in God's name are you putting on your wound? The stench could wake the dead."

The man chuckled. "My mother claims it will cure everything that ails ye. The recipe has been in her family for generations." He wrapped a long piece of plaid around the wound and tied the ends. When he glanced at her, all traces of humor were gone. "I apologize, my lady, but I dinna have time to play lady's maid. I must be on my way."

Lavinia swallowed and lowered her gaze, changing the subject. "How did you hurt your leg?" She hadn't meant to ask, but the question popped out before she could catch it. "And how did you make a fire?"

Her companion tilted his head. "Your English friends in the village dinna like me knocking on doors and asking if they had any pretty brown-haired, blue-eyed lasses. They chased me off, and I shouldn'a ride through the forest so fast." He glanced up at her and waved a hand at the fire. "I always carry a bundle of dry kindling on my horse when I travel." He gave her a wistful shake of his head as though he found it curious she inquired about such a commonplace practice.

Clearing her throat, she asked, "This man she is in love with, he lives in the village?"

"Aye. That's what she claims." He sighed. "I dinna mean to frighten ye earlier. I am Wallace Armstrong. My da is laird of our clan." His blue eyes held her captive.

"We live in the lowlands on the other side of the border."

Lavinia swallowed her disappointment. Not a Highlander after all."I am Lady Lavinia Holbrook, and I am delighted to make your acquaintance."

The Scot snorted and shook his head. "Ye shouldna be alone in the forest. Most English ladies have servants trailing along behind them. Why don't ye?" He cast her a suspicious glance.

"I, uh, sent mine back to the castle." A sinking feeling settled in the pit of her stomach. She had to find a solution and fast. "If I help you find your sister, will you show me the way to Scotland through the forest?"

Wallace rose to his feet. "Whatever ye are running from, Scotland is not the answer."

Exasperated, she leaned back and fixed him with a determined stare. "You know nothing of my plight."

When he bent to gather up his things, she tried a different approach. "Returning to the village in search of your sister is not advisable. The village men will not welcome your presence. I, on the other hand, can make discreet inquiries without drawing attention."

The angle of her head made the world twirl again, and once more, she dropped her chin. A sudden fit of chills racked her body, sending her burrowing beneath the heavy plaid.

"What ails ye, lass? Are ye feeling ill?" He strode over and knelt beside her, running his hands over the top of her head. "When ye hit yer head on the branch and swooned, I worried ye wouldn'a wake for a bit." His fingers grazed her cheek before coming to rest on her forehead. "Yer face is hot as coal. Ye have been out in the weather too long." Rising to his feet, he planted his hands on his lean hips, giving her an eye-level view of his muscular thighs. "We need to get ye back to yer castle before ye catch yer death of cold."

She should be quivering with feminine appreciation instead of cold. His heat, the strength of his fingers, and his gentle touch did nothing to ignite her feelings. Unlike the duke…God, what she would give to be back at the castle right now playing chess in the duchess's salon.

Wallace kicked snow and wet leaves onto the fire. Pointing, he said, "Yer castle is that way. I will ride with ye until I am sure ye will make it, but no further."

"If you have no intention to carry me away to Scotland, why did you stop to help me in the first place?" Irritated with her naive belief in the romanticized tales of Scottish Warriors her school friends told and her failure to attract this one's interest, her voice sharpened. Somebody out there somewhere wanted her for who she was, and she would find him even if it took a lifetime. "Scratch Scots from the list."

Wallace arched a brow at her acidic tone and turned away to untie their horses. 'I dinna dare ask what list ye are meaning."

"You wouldn't understand if I told you." Lavinia sighed. If he hadn't stopped to help her, she would be at the mercy of the storm and no doubt catching her death of cold, as he suggested. This predicament wasn't his fault. Softening her tone, she sighed. "You sacrificed a good deal of time making a fire and such. Thank you."

"Ye are welcome, lass." His frown eased as he studied her face. "Ye are somebody's sister, and ye fell from yer horse at my feet. When I touched the side of yer neck, ye were cold as ice. I know I lost time looking after ye, but ye are a lady and I couldn'a leave ye face down in the forest alone with the snow coming down so fast.

My mother would take an inch off my hide if she knew."

Lavinia shook her head as she reflected on the situation. Victoria would have plenty to say about her lack of attention if she were here. "If you decide you want my help with your sister, leave a message with the village merchant. If you go to the door in the back and don't ask questions, he won't bother you. My lady's maid is the merchant's sister, and she will get your note to me. The price for my help is the path to Scotland."

He stared at her for a long minute. "Agreed." Wallace held his hand out. "Now, up with ye. Let's get ye on yer horse and on yer way."

She didn't make it, and he ended up riding behind her most of the way, one arm around her waist and the other leading his horse until he heard the hounds' bay.

"I wish ye luck, me lady." Sliding to the ground beneath a giant oak, he mounted his own horse in one swift movement.

Lavinia lifted her head from her stupor. "I must find the way to Scotland." She had no idea if he answered, and the next moment, she was alone beneath the frosty canopy as thick snowflakes fell around her. Dizzy and feverish, she stared into the storm, hoping to remember which way Wallace said to go.

The howling wind carried the hounds' baying voices first from one way, then another.

Lavinia gripped her reins and swayed in the saddle.

Whiteness swirled around her face until she could not see a thing. Chills raced up her spine and set her teeth chattering. Hanging suspended in a bleak, freezing world, she gripped Grace's reins tighter, urging her toward the hounds as their voices grew louder. The next thing she knew, the duke lifted her from her saddle into his arms and tucked his fur-lined cloak around her. "I have you, Lavinia. You are safe now."

She smiled against his broad chest and snuggled into his embrace. If only it were true.

Chapter Eleven

Earlier, as the weather took a turn for the worst and the first flakes fell, the duchess cut her house party short. "You must return home before the snow becomes so deep traveling is impossible."

The remaining girls protested and cast covert glances toward the door as if hoping the duke would appear.

But alas, their carriage arrived before he returned, and they departed with frowns of unhappiness as their black carriage, drawn by four black horses, made its way down the long tree-lined drive toward the village.

Oliver did not appear until tea and stepped into Arabella's salon with a stern expression. "I wish to speak to you, Mother. Enough is enough. Did you truly believe such a trick would work on me after all this time?" Running a hand through his thick black hair, he grimaced. "Since the moment you invited the ladies to stay, I have slept everywhere but in my own bed. *If* I marry, Mother, it will be because I desire to and for no other reason."

Arabella turned to him with a tilt of her head. "You may not believe me, but what Lady Elspeth did, she did of her own accord. I had no hand in it."

He snorted. "You expect me to believe you after you offered me a wager to the contrary not twenty-four hours ago?"

She smiled and set her dainty porcelain teacup down on the marble table at her knees. "I do. What I wish is for you to find the same happiness I did with your father, not just a wife. When the heart is involved, life is so much more fulfilling in every way. The simple things become priceless, and everything takes on a rosy hue. Nothing is impossible, my dear."

Oliver grunted and glanced back at the door. "Are we about to be invaded with your prattling, giggling company?"

Noting his readiness to flee, she smiled with amusement. "Nay. I sent them home when Cecil informed me of the weather."

"Thank God."

Unsure if he knew he said the words out loud or not, she shot him a glance as she poured him a cup of tea.

He murmured his thanks and leaned forward to take a slice of cake. "The temperature has dropped at an alarming rate. I'm happy you made the prudent decision to send your company away. Did Lavinia grow tired of our company and leave as well?"

Arabella cast him a questioning look. "She went riding after breakfast. I assumed she found you."

He froze with his fork halfway to his mouth. "She hasn't returned?"

Arabella shook her head. "I would say not if you are unaware."

He cursed under his breath and rang for Cecil.

"Yes, Your Grace?" The man stepped into the room, standing at attention.

"Has Lady Lavinia returned from her ride?" Oliver rose to his feet and strode to the window to gaze out at the whiteness. The snow fell thick and fast. A blizzard.

"Nay, Your Grace. Tom stepped inside a moment ago to inform me of her continued absence. I was on my way to inform Your Grace when you rang the bell."

"Did Smithy accompany her?" Her usual escort would ensure her safe return like he did every time she went riding.

"Nay, Your Grace. One of the new stable hands offered to go. Maurice is his name. We had no other footman ready, so Tom agreed to the change in escort." Cecil frowned. "Do ye think her ladyship is in trouble?"

Oliver turned around. "I do. She has been out in the cold too long. Send a footman for my thick boots and overcoat. Prepare tea and blankets. Ask the master of the hounds to ready the dogs." He issued orders like a seasoned general, and Arabella nodded in agreement.

"I will be here waiting with hot bricks for her feet and a hearty fire in her chamber. She's very dear to me, Oliver. The daughter I never had."

He nodded, already striding from the room with determination ringing in every step.

****

Oliver mounted his stallion in one fluid motion and waited for the master of the hounds to ready his dogs. "Her mare's tracks lead north, toward the forest. We unleash the hounds once we are under the trees."

Five of his men rode beside him as they entered the tree line. Had he not taken note of Grace's tracks on his return ride, he wouldn't know which way to search, and he thanked the gods for this stroke of luck.

Oliver drew his mount to a stop and waited while the master of the hounds held one of Lavinia's shawls for the dogs to sniff.

The dogs pressed their noses into the garment and

then circled the ground. One lifted his head and gave a short bark. The pack trotted north, stopping to sniff the ground and the air as they circled. Once they caught her scent, they raced off to the northeast, baying with their discovery.

Two long, weary hours later, the dogs' barking changed, indicating they had found their target, and Oliver nudged his mount forward, his heart pounding with hope and urgency.

They found Lavinia clinging to the saddle, confused and disoriented, mumbling something about a sister. She waited beneath a giant oak where the ground bore evidence of more than one horse. Grace lifted her head and whinnied when Willoughby took hold of her halter as if she understood he came to rescue her and bring her back to her warm stable.

Lavinia swayed, holding the reins in a death grip with her head bowed. Her face, chest, and arms were pallid and shaking. She didn't look up or respond when Oliver called her name.

"Are you all right, Lavinia?" Urgency spurred him forward.

The dogs sniffed every inch of the ground beneath the oak and growled.

Oliver dismounted and checked the area. He found two sets of horse tracks in the snow. One belonged to Grace, but the other tracks bore a strong resemblance to the heavy draft horses ridden by the Scots. Those tracks led north.

His chest tightened, and a heavy feeling settled in the pit of his stomach. "Bloody buggering hell." The northern men hadn't crossed his land for months. Why now when he had Lavinia to think of? And her foolish notion a Scot would solve all her problems?

Oliver ground his teeth together and remounted, riding his horse alongside Grace so he could scoop Lavinia into his lap. Where the hell had she been all this time, and to whom did the other tracks belong? He wanted answers.

But first, he had to get Lavinia back to the castle.

She offered no protest, collapsing into his arms as if too exhausted to do anything else.

Oliver wondered if she knew who rescued her, for she wrapped her arms around his waist, tucked her head beneath his chin, and cuddled against his body as if he were a roaring fire.

Two minutes later, her tremors intensified.

Oliver drew to a stop and wrapped one of the blankets from the saddle bags around her. Motioning for a cup of the warm tea one of his men carried, he held the cup against her pallid lips and urged her to drink.

She managed two swallows and then turned away, tucking her head beneath the blanket and plastering her shivering body against him. "Oliver."

She burned with fever.

"I have you, Lavinia. You are safe now." He glanced at his men. "Willoughby, Stratton, ride back to the castle and fetch the doctor. Tell Mrs. Whittle to prepare Lady Lavinia's room. We will join you there." He frowned at the tracks beneath the tree. "Dougan, mark this spot, and tomorrow, assemble a squad to search the forest. I want to know who those other tracks belong to and where they lead."

It seemed an eternity before the castle lights came into view. And all the way, questions about Lavinia's afternoon ride burned in his mind. Thoughts of a Scot on his land deepened his frown.

In the morning, his men would scour the forest for clues. And when he found the intruder, he would make sure he stayed where he belonged. And away from Lavinia,

Holding her close, he slipped to the ground inside the courtyard and tucked the blanket tighter.

Willoughby took his horse as soon as he dismounted.

"Rub him dry and see he is taken care of," Oliver commanded as he took the front steps two at a time.

"Aye, Your Grace. The doctor will be here soon, and Mrs. Whittle has everything prepared." He cleared his throat. "Lady Lavinia's escort rode into the castle grounds an hour after you left. Maurice reported Lady Lavinia galloped away into the forest, and he spent the entire afternoon searching for her. He returned when the snow got too deep to track her."

"He did not make a sufficient effort. Send him to me in an hour. I wish to question him."

"Aye, Your Grace." The groom nodded and led the duke's stallion away.

Oliver strode through the entry hall, down the corridor, and ascended the curved steps to the family apartments. When he entered Lavinia's chambers, Annie rose to her feet and stood ready as he set Lavinia on the bed.

"I'll attend to her, Your Grace." She gave a bob and set about removing Lavinia's cloak and shoes.

He remained rooted in place, his gaze fixed on Lavinia's pallid face, a peculiar knot forming in his stomach. He hadn't felt like this since the morning his father passed, and he found the unpleasant memory unsettling.

Annie glanced at him. "I cannot remove her ladyship's clothes and prepare her for bed unless ye leave, Your Grace."

He nodded and strode from the room. Retracing his steps, he entered his study and stopped beside the hearth. Leaning his forearm against the warm marble, he gazed into the flickering flames and tried not to think about how feverish Lavinia had felt to the touch. Why the hell would she remain outside for so long in the biting cold? And who had she been with? Did her unknown companion have something to do with her delay? Oliver ground his teeth together. If the unknown man touched her or caused her any distress, he would seek swift and severe judgment. And God have mercy on him then because Oliver would not.

Turning, he crossed to the drink trolley and poured a splash of whisky into a glass. The amber liquid burned all the way down his throat, and he welcomed the heat.

What if she died? The thought unsettled him, and he rolled his shoulders to shrug it off. His chest tightened, and he took another long swallow from his glass. God, she'd been exposed to the elements for hours. Rubbing his hands together, he held them close to the fire on the hearth. The familiar ache of loss settled in his gut, and he winced. He experienced the same dark feeling the night his grandfather passed, too. As if his entire world condensed and dissipated into a shadowy mist, vanishing into the night.

A knock sounded at the door.

"Come in." He took another sip and turned to meet his mother's concerned blue eyes.

"You found her." She sighed and stepped into his

study, taking a seat beside the hearth.

"Yes, but she is not well. No doubt Cecil informed you I sent for the doctor. She's been out there for hours…" His voice trailed off. The weight of his words hung heavy in the air. "But there's more. She wasn't alone. We found another set of tracks leading north. They bear a striking resemblance to the draft horses ridden by the Scots."

Arabella gasped. "Bloody hell. Do you think she's been alone with a highlander all afternoon?"

Oliver suppressed the fury her question ignited in his chest and set his glass back on the trolley with a careful, deliberate gesture. He refused to dwell on the potential implications. If he did, his rage would know no bounds. Taking a seat beside his mother, he gripped the arms of his chair and gave her a pointed look. "I believe it's time you told me why she's here, Mother, and don't leave anything out. I want to know everything."

For once, his mother didn't argue, nor did she quirk an eyebrow over his interest; she simply folded her hands in her lap and spoke in a quiet voice. "She ran away from Viscount Becker on her wedding day and refuses to go back."

The duke sat in silence for long minutes. "Did he mistreat her?"

The duchess shook her head. "Not in a physical sense. He humiliated her by bringing his new mistress to the wedding. Her aversion to churches and weddings stems from other situations she's witnessed." Princess jumped onto her lap, and his mother stroked her pet as she gazed into the fire.

Long minutes passed, a myriad of emotions flickering across her face before the duchess lifted her head and spoke again. "And from being a woman. She has a quick mind and dislikes being treated like a child."

Oliver frowned as images of her soft, round body clad in her undergarments danced like sugar plums in his head. "She is no child."

A faint smile tugged at the corner of his mother's mouth. "No." She shot him a meaningful glance and told him the rest of the story. "I cannot say I blame the girl. I would have run away, too."

"Your Grace." Cecil stepped into the study. "Dr. Smythe has finished his examination and is waiting for you in the blue salon."

Oliver nodded, extending his arm to his mother. "Shall we?"

Together, they descended the stairs and entered the blue salon to hear the doctor's assessment.

Tall and thin with sparse gray hair, the elderly man pushed his spectacles on the bridge of his thin nose up and greeted them. Clearing his throat, he gave his diagnosis.

"The lady is quite ill, though not afflicted with lung fever as you feared, Your Grace. Her condition is the result of prolonged exposure. The lump on her head and the bruising on her right side suggest she fell from her horse. She must remain in bed and take the prescribed medicine I left with her maid. Under no circumstances is she to be burdened with undo anxiety. She must rest and not think too much. Tea and broth should sustain her for the next few days until her fever subsides. The cold is responsible for her aching throat. With proper adherence to my instructions, I anticipate a full recovery. I will return tomorrow to check on her." With a tip of his hat, he left the room.

Oliver stared after the doctor and then turned to his mother. "I sent word to my man in London to investigate Lavinia after overhearing Lady Victoria and her discussing a scandal. If the situation is as dire as you suggest, the viscount may have hired someone to find her. There is also the mystery of her companion and the doctor's suggestion she fell from her horse." He steepled his fingers and stared into the fire. "Lavinia is too skilled a rider to fall from her horse unless there existed compelling circumstances. Then, there is the unsettling matter in France involving Arthur Holbrook and Viscount Becker. I haven't been able to figure out what bothers me about the whole affair. Arthur wrote me last year, claiming he found the title to the lost acreage and would return to England within a fortnight. The next communication I received, we were informed of his death.

"I do not like Viscount Becker and never have. What's more, I do not trust him." Oliver ran a hand through his hair and gave a deep sigh. "Thank God Lavinia came to you. I will not tolerate anyone pressuring her into getting out of bed before the doctor declares her well enough. Not even the earl, should he and the countess discover her whereabouts."

Having made his resolve clear, he bent and kissed his mother's cheek. "Get some rest. I intend to. See you in the morning."

The duchess rose to her feet. "And if the viscount arrives and demands you hand over his bride? What will you do then?" Her eyes roamed his face with an assessing look.

Oliver shook his head. "Quit smiling. I am not in love with her, nor do I intend to marry her, but I will keep her safe. Of that, you can be sure."

She nodded. "That's all I ask." And only as he closed the door did he hear the rest of her sentence. "For now."

Chapter Twelve

Alone in his study the following evening, Oliver stared into the flames dancing in the marble hearth, his mind swirling with frustration and concern. He muttered every foul word he knew in all five languages.

His men tracked Lavinia and her mysterious companion from the oak tree to a protected area in the forest near his northern border, aided by the hounds. There, they discovered the remnants of a fire and a flattened area where one or possibly two people rested.

"A spinster I shall be unless some handsome Scot carries me off to his highland home to ravish me, far away from English lords, the Ton, and polite society. I have no use for the lot."

He slammed the rest of his whiskey down his throat and glared at the flickering flames. When he found Lavinia the previous evening, her clothes were as they should be, and she bore no signs of violence. She cuddled into his chest like a homing pigeon coming to roost, leading him to wonder if she knew who held her. A ravished woman would be defensive and mistrustful.

Whatever transpired between Lavinia and her companion did not include the loss of her innocence.

Nay. He wouldn't allow his fears to garner any of his attention.

Oliver's gut tightened, and he took a deep breath to steady his rising anger. Until he found evidence to the contrary, he would continue to believe in Lavinia's innocence. And he vowed to track down the bastard who shared her afternoon.

His gaze hardened.

Unless he misread the entire situation and whoever Lavinia spent the afternoon with had a more lethal objective, such as abducting her for her bastard ex-fiancé.

But why not take her if such were the case? They were alone, and he had hours to perform the evil task. Alone.

Maurice, her escort the previous day, abandoned her in the forest, leaving her vulnerable to both the weather and her unknown companion.

Oliver demoted the man to stable duty and assigned him to shovel dung for the next week as punishment.

After their discussion, the older man apologized and vowed to be her protector for the remainder of her stay at the castle.

Oliver accepted his apology and allowed him to leave. He spent the night monitoring the corridor for activity, unable to shake Lavinia's pale face and shaking body from his mind. Turning, he stared at the closed door of the master chamber.

With all his mother's guests gone, he could sleep in his own bed without fear of being discovered and accosted. The soft mattress and familiar surroundings should have lulled him into a deep sleep, but the coveted state of bliss remained elusive as concern for his mother's goddaughter plagued him.

At two in the morning, Oliver abandoned any hope of rest and rose, dressing with haste. Strolling down the corridor to Lavinia's chamber, he tapped and informed

Annie he would be in his study if anything changed.

With a last glance at Lavinia's white face swallowed in the depths of her feather pillow, he closed the door and turned his attention to the pile of correspondence on the desk in his study.

A busy mind has no time to dwell on impossible situations one can do nothing about but wait.

As he opened the first missive, his father's words flashed across his mind, and he prayed the words were true.

Dipping his quill in the inkpot on his desk, he formed a reply to his man of business' request.

The servants would alert him if Lavinia's condition deteriorated.

Now, a day later, weary from worry and lack of sleep, Oliver placed his glass on the drink trolley and strolled toward the door to check on Lavinia before he retired.

****

Lavinia woke to a terrible pain in her head and an aching throat, unable to quench her parched mouth.

Several times, an unseen hand dabbed a cool cloth against her fevered brow, and she sighed with delight.

"That feels so good," Lavinia murmured and groaned when the hand stilled and then withdrew. "Please don't stop. Do it again." Her breathless plea lingered in the silence until the hand dabbed at her brow once more. Hot, feverish, and sticky, she stripped her clothing off and lay back. "Please cool all of me. I burn."

Lavinia moaned with pleasure as the cloth moved over her neck and dropped down to press against the heat of her chest. "Again," she demanded when the hand withdrew. "More. I need more." She arced up from the bed, panting for air as the stuffy, overheated chamber pressed down on her like molten lava.

No answer came, but the figure beside her shifted, bumping into the side of her bed. She could hear quick, shallow breathing from her left. She sensed the figure rising and stepping back. Struggling to open her eyes, she lifted a hand to sweep her hair back from her neck. "Please don't go. I am so hot, so thirsty. Do not deny me."

After what seemed like an eternity, the cool cloth slid over her bare chest and down to the flat plane of her belly. She gasped and arched against the hand. "Yes, please. I burn."

The rapid, shallow breathing continued as the cool linen cloth drifted over every inch of her front.

The figure smelled of pine trees, fresh air, and…citrus.

Lavinia found the scent intoxicating. She caught the hand holding the cloth and lifted it to her nose. "You smell good. I suppose there are trees and forests in heaven. There would have to be. They're so beautiful." She sighed. "Thank you for soothing my burning flesh. If I turn over, will you run the cloth over my back, too?"

Without waiting for a response, she rolled onto her belly and moaned with delight as the cloth slid with slow, methodical movements over the back of her heated body. Dying wouldn't be so bad if angels like this were there. Did Arthur have one, too? She asked and waited for an answer while the angel soothed her with his touch.

His?

Lavinia jerked awake and sat up, taking in her surroundings. She lay in her chamber beneath her fine bedclothes in her silk night rail. Alone.

Her gaze darted to every corner of the room and landed on the two chairs before the hearth. No one occupied the chamber but her.

The fire crackled, sending a tiny explosion of sparks into the air as a log settled.

Turning her head, she noted a ceramic bowl on a small table beside the bed. A cloth floated in the clear water, and two dark bottles with stoppers stood beside it.

She blinked, realizing she hadn't imagined the cool linen against her skin.

In her feverish state, she imagined an angel, but it must have been Annie tending to her. Heat rushed to her cheeks as she recalled removing her night rail and undergarments. The dear woman helped her bathe, so seeing her nude body wouldn't be much of a shock. Her brow furrowed in confusion. Then, where did the male voice come from?

The ceiling held no answers no matter how hard she stared at it, and with a sigh, she put the matter out of her mind. If her fever produced and angel, why not a man, too?

The door opened a crack, and Annie peeked inside. "Oh, thank goodness, yer awake. The doctor said the danger is past now yer fever is gone. He said ye can go downstairs for an hour at a time until ye feel better. Her Grace sent me up to check on ye."

Lavinia nodded. Her head felt better than it had since—"How long have I been here? I remember going for a ride…" Her gaze shot up to Annie's. "Grace! I rode north, and then it snowed. I couldn't tell which way to go, and Grace kept turning around. Where is she?"

Annie clucked her tongue as she came forward to straighten the bedclothes. "His Grace found ye and brought ye home. Grace is in her stall, safe and warm. Ye were burning with fever, and the doctor came. Ye've been asleep for four days. We wondered if ye would catch lung fever. Ye burned so hot. But here ye are, fine as an apple tart."

Her gaze widened. Four days? "Is there—" She paused. "Have there been any messages or visitors?" She didn't have time to lay abed for four whole days. What if her parents figured out where she had gone? And what of Wallace? Did he find his sister? Lavinia gave a brief overview of her encounter with the Scot, omitting how long they were together and the fact they were alone. "I am hoping for a note from him. Have you seen one?"

"Nay. There's too much snow. No one has been to the village since ye fell ill." Annie poked the fire and returned to her side. "I am to ask ye if ye'd like to come to the blue salon. Her Grace would like yer company if yer feeling well enough."

Lavinia nodded. Her body ached from lying in one place for so long. "Yes, please."

Annie helped her into a clean night rail and brushed out her tangled hair. She plaited the blonde length with nimble fingers and tied a blue ribbon on the end. "Let's get ye into yer dressing gown, and I'll fetch a footman to carry ye down the stairs."

Lavinia frowned. "I can walk." She held her arms open as Annie helped her into a lavender velvet dressing gown and matching satin slippers.

Annie shook her head. "Nay. His Grace ordered me to call a footman for ye."

As the maid opened the door, Lavinia slid to her feet. She could do this on her own without a man's interference.

Her knees buckled, and the room swirled around her head. She caught the bedclothes in a frantic grip and would have fallen, but the duke appeared at her side.

Catching her up in his strong arms, he frowned down at her. "You've been ill, Lavinia. Give your body a chance to get well. There is no shame in asking for help."

The heat of his body surrounded her, and his gaze softened as he stared down at her. "I am happy you did not succumb to the fever. The duchess and I were quite concerned when you did not respond to the doctor's remedies."

Her breath caught in her throat when he leaned close, his lips hovering just above hers. "Thank God, my mother remembered what her nurse taught her and ordered your maid to bathe you with a cool cloth."

She stopped breathing and stared. In a squeaky, high-pitched voice, she asked the burning question, nagging her. "Did anyone besides Annie tend to me?"

A wicked glint entered his eye as he took the stairs to the lower level. "We all took a turn. Someone sat beside you day and night. You mean a great deal to my mother. The daughter she never had, as it were. How could we do less?"

Lavinia had no idea what to say. She shrugged and studied the passing walls with great attention, ignoring the heat rushing through her body. She wished she were back in her chamber where she could tug the bedclothes over her head. God, what if *he* were the one with the cloth when she tugged her night rail and undergarments off?

Her cheeks flushed with embarrassment, and she fought to keep her composure. "I owe you my gratitude, then." She managed to get the words past the lump in her throat as she resisted the urge to bound from his arms and flee.

Oliver smiled. "No thanks are necessary. Just focus on getting well."

As they reached the lower floor, Lavinia glanced at him out of the corner of her eye, wondering how much he had seen and how much he knew. Uncertainty gnawed at her, but she resolved to put it out of her mind for now. She had more pressing matters to attend to, like finding an escape route to Scotland before her parents found her. With or without Wallace's help.

****

Oliver would never be the same again. Not since the night he ordered Annie to get some rest and sat beside Lavinia, mopping her heated body with a damp cloth.

Her moans of pleasure pulsed through him like molten lava, firing his blood. Every whimper and moan from her soft pink lips had him shifting in his seat, his mind conjuring a very different scenario. She arched into his hands, her voice husky as she begged him to continue touching her. He'd been forced to turn aside and draw on his reserves for strength.

But then, she tugged her night rail over her head and tossed her undergarments to the floor a moment later. God, he could still see the firelight glinting on her pale skin and the taut pink buds of her nipples hardening in the cool air. Her full breasts, narrow waist, and the gentle flare of her hips haunted his dreams. Her long, shapely legs added to his torment. Pure willpower and ferocious self-control kept his hands busy with the cool linen cloth instead of exploring her beautiful satin skin as he longed to.

Swallowing the sudden dryness in his throat, he bathed every inch of her silken body until she turned to her belly and presented her backside.

Even now, the memory made his hands shake. He prayed for mercy the entire time and sank to the chair before the hearth with relief when her rhythmic breathing announced Lavinia had fallen asleep.

When he regained control of his breathing, Oliver helped the siren back into her clothing with gentle hands, careful not to wake her. Tugging her bedclothes to her chin, he tucked them around her and tugged the bell to summon Annie.

Once he returned to hs chamber, he took an icy cold bath and soaked until his ardor cooled to a comfortable level.

How could one slip of a girl make him lose control the way he had? Shaking his head, he offered silent thanks that his mother hadn't been awake and prowling the castle. Such a situation would no doubt have her sending a footman to the village to order a wedding gown and a baby cradle.

Speaking of a baby cradle, he received word from Tom that the men resumed their search and followed the intruder's tracks from the oak back to the border, confirming his suspicions about her companion.

Lavinia found her damn highlander!

Oliver wanted to know why the Scot crossed into England in the first place.

On his first trip to the village following the storm, he found his answer.

"A Scot walked in the other night, banging on every door and asking to see our women. We aren't too partial to strangers or Scots, so we…encouraged the man to go back where he belongs." Tim Gallagher and his wife owned the inn and were privy to everyone's business.

"Thank you." Oliver tossed a gold coin on the counter and visited a few more shops. Every shopkeeper told the same tale, and he rode home deep in thought.

The Scot came to find a woman. The stone in his belly grew.

Lavinia evaded any questions about her night in the woods and gave him a blank stare when he demanded an answer. Although he no longer believed the Scot touched her, he couldn't shake the feeling she had a secret. And he didn't like how much time she spent alone with the man.

If anyone discovered the truth, her reputation would be destroyed. More than now. Leaving your groom at the altar and spending the afternoon alone, unchaperoned, were two separate issues. The former was reprehensible, the latter unforgivable.

But what could he do except keep an eye on her?

Oliver frowned and released a deep sigh. He kept his distance, believing he had his body under control, until he strolled past her chamber and caught sight of her slipping from her bed. One touch and he lost the war.

Glancing down at her now, safe in his arms, he entertained the desire to carry her to his chamber and keep her there until the feverish need to possess her dissipated. How long would it take for his craving to fade? A week? Two? A month?

Oliver didn't know, nor did he intend to find out. His mother waited for the girl, thank God, providing him with the necessary willpower to carry her downstairs rather than down the hall to forbidden pleasure.

"Lavinia, my dearest child. I am delighted to see

you." The duchess straightened in her chair and raised an eyebrow at him when he came into view with her goddaughter in his arms.

"Oliver." She nodded in his direction. "Thank you for fetching her. You may place her here." She waved a hand at the empty seat beside her and rang for the butler.

"A tray of refreshments, Cecil. I hope to tempt Lavinia into eating. Annie informs me she's had little else but a bit of broth."

"Aye, Your Grace." The older man bowed and left the room with a soft click of the door.

The duchess's frown betrayed her concern over her goddaughter's appetite, and Oliver smiled.

According to his mother, every ailment, injury, or emotional state could be remedied with a cup of tea and a well-made biscuit.

Placing his soft burden on the settee beside his mother, he turned to depart, but Lavinia halted him by placing a hand on his arm.

"Will you join us?" Her large lavender eyes met his, and before he knew what happened, he sat across from the two women holding a cup of tea and a small sandwich.

To his astonishment, he discovered he enjoyed the small talk between his mother and Lavinia as they discussed her childhood visits.

He'd been away at Eton, and then serving a commission in the army and had not been present for any of the visits.

"Remember the day you wanted to make tarts and caught the kitchen on fire?" The duchess laughed until tears glistened in her eyes.

Lavinia flushed. "I befriended one of the goats and

thought he might like to see how tarts were made. I hid him in the larder until Cook put the tray of tarts into the oven."

Oliver's eyebrow rose." And Cook didn't know?"

She flushed anew and twisted her hands in her lap. "She found out. I planned to return the goat to his pen, but one of the scullery maids discovered him first and shrieked as if she found a rat. Cook came running, and when she caught sight of the mess he'd made in her larder, the very foundation of the castle shook from her cries of outrage." Lavinia shook her head. "I still don't know why you allowed me to come back. Cook caught me and made me help clean up the spilled food and broken dishes while one of the footmen escorted my goat back to his pen. We were so busy wiping and cleaning we forgot all about the tarts. When Cook took them from the oven, they smoked something fierce. I thought I'd clear the air by waving a cloth over the burning mess. But instead, my tarts burst into flame. I tried to smother the flames with the cloth before Cook noticed and only succeeded in setting the cloth ablaze. I screamed and waved the cloth around to put out the flame…" She trailed off as if she couldn't finish telling the story.

Arabella chuckled. "And managed to set half the kitchen aflame. Cook never let you near her ovens again." She smiled. "Or her larder."

Lavinia glanced up. "I am sorry. I don't know to this minute if Cook has forgiven me for that day."

The duchess patted her knee. "She has. If your visits lengthened longer than six months apart, she would contrive some reason or another for me to send a personal invitation for you to come and stay. You brightened this old castle with your antics."

Just as she does now, Oliver couldn't tear his gaze from the delicate blush of embarrassment dancing along Lavinia's cheekbones and the shine of memories in her bright purple eyes.

A warm, contented feeling settled in his chest, and a sense of peace enveloped his soul as he sat with the two women opposite him. Everything about this moment felt harmonious and right. Just the three of them, enjoying each other's company.

It felt perfect.

The unsettling thought crept into his mind, and Oliver sat up, horrified by its implication. He didn't like the path his mind chose to explore. Perfection with his mother *and Lavinia*?

Not if he could help it.

Spurred to action by the thought, he rose to his feet, mumbled a hasty excuse, and raced up the stairs to bolt his study door behind him. The locked door served as a barrier against the temptation of Lavinia's luscious lips. If he didn't watch his step, the duchess would win their wager. And the worst part? He'd help her of his own volition.

Love, marriage, and all the nauseating complexities they entailed had dropped greater men than he to their knees and made them as weak as kittens.

Grimacing, he took a seat at his desk and glanced out the window.

Icy, sparkling whiteness drew his eye. Snow evoked thoughts of Christmas, holiday cheer, and wishes. Which, in turn, made him think of miracles, family, and…Lavinia.

Oliver froze.

Time to think of something else, old man.

Running a hand through his hair, he straightened the pile of correspondence on his desk and flipped his letter opener over in his hand. The fire's flames danced along its metal surface, and he cast a glance at the hearth.

At breakfast, a maid spilled some ash as she cleaned the grate and produced a small broom to sweep up the mess. The bristles were made of caramel-colored straw, which made him think of hay, sunshine, grass, and lilacs bordering his mother's gardens. Lavender blossoms adorned with dew, the exact color of Lavinia's black fringed eyes.

Bloody buggering hell!

Oliver groaned and turned to stare at the offending flower garden. He forced his mind to think of thorny bushes dormant for the winter. Nothing about their sharp sting could be linked to…what's her name? Cold, spiny, and dark, they would hibernate through the winter until the sun's rays warmed them, coaxing forth dewy, fresh, pale pink blooms—the exact shade of pink sprinkled along Lavinia's delicate cheekbones.

Dropping his head in his hands, he groaned, and he wondered if he should check his tongue for spots. God, he had the willpower of a gnat.

A vision of his mother and grandmother's grief-stricken faces on the day they lost their husbands flashed across his mind, and Oliver's resolve hardened. They damn near succumbed to the pain of loss, and he would never be that weak, no matter how tempting the woman.

With a determined set of his jaw, he straightened and opened the top missive, scanning its contents. His mother's younger brother requested to spend the Christmas holiday at the castle.

Oliver retrieved a fresh parchment from his

secretary and penned an invitation. Another male in the vicinity would be beneficial if the duchess intended to host any more house parties. With any luck, the Earl of Corbet would depart with a prospective wife while he remained unattached.

But not with Lavinia. Never her.

Let Corbet pursue any other over-eager, young lady determined to catch a duke, and he'd be welcome to them. God knew his mother invited them often enough.

With Christmas coming and relatives making social calls, he had a full schedule. He would make a point of visiting each one of his tenants before the blessed holiday to make sure they were healthy and happy. Well-cared-for tenants created a well-run estate, and everyone prospered. As an added bonus, his time away from the castle kept him away from Lavinia and her intoxicating allure.

His resolve lasted until he strolled past the blue salon the following day and his mother invited him to join them for tea.

Chapter Thirteen

Lavinia spent more time in the salon with the duchess as she grew stronger.

On Monday of the first week, Annie delivered news from the village. Wallace had not yet found his sister and agreed to let Lavinia assist in the search, as per their agreement. Lavinia resisted the urge to jump to her feet in a victory dance when she caught sight of Annie's frown.

"His Grace won't like ye making a deal with a Scot. They cannot be trusted." She shook her head before adding, "He won't like ye speaking to another man, either."

Lavinia's brows knit together. "I doubt he will care. In any event, he will not find out unless you tell someone, and I am asking you to keep my secret."

Annie's rebellious expression made her sigh.

Using a soft voice, she explained the situation in more detail.

"And getting away from the wicked viscount is the reason yer helping the Scot find Clarice?" The maid's gaze grew thoughtful as she waited for Lavinia to answer.

"Yes and no. Escaping Viscount Becker is why I proposed the deal to Wallace. But I would help his sister, regardless. No woman should have to marry someone they do not love because society demands her compliance."

Convinced of the importance of Lavinia's cause, Annie agreed to assist and left the chamber with a note tucked inside her pocket for Wallace.

With renewed hope blooming in her heart, Lavinia wandered down to join the duchess in her salon.

Oliver surprised her by joining them for tea, and afterward, he challenged her to a game of chess.

For the next two weeks, while Annie scoured the countryside for Clarice and exchanged notes between her mistress and Wallace, Lavinia focused on getting well.

Sometimes, Arabella stayed to watch Oliver and Lavinia play chess in her salon after tea. Other times, she left the door ajar and made her excuses to depart.

Mrs. Whittle would arrive with her knitting basket as soon as the duchess disappeared and sit beside the hearth to maintain propriety.

Oliver and Lavinia spent the last week of November and the first week of December discussing their childhood, holidays, and families before their talks turned to debates about politics.

Lavinia read the newspaper every day at home and knew a great deal about the bills being presented to Parliament.

Surprised by her depth of knowledge, Oliver listened attentively to her opinions and challenged them as if she were his intellectual equal.

His attention and respect made her burn with happiness.

She studied him through her lashes and shook her head in disbelief when he accepted her intelligence without reservation. He never belittled her, threatened her, or seemed the least put out when she voiced her thoughts with authority. Instead, he seemed to enjoy their heated debates. For several days, he came to breakfast with a knowing gleam in his eyes, threw out a comment, and waited for her reaction.

And when she argued the point, he would lean back in his chair with amusement until she said something he objected to, and then he would challenge her again.

They held heated discussions and argued for days until they exhausted every other topic but the holidays.

And marriage.

"What about an heir? You must have one. I believe it's a requirement," Lavinia remarked, studying his reaction over the rim of her teacup.

"My younger brother Algernon is my heir. He shall inherit the dukedom when I pass on." They were finishing tea in the blue salon, and Oliver stood with his back to her, staring into the snow-covered rose garden.

"I have never desired a wife, and I doubt I ever shall. Matrimony weakens a man. You would think my mother would be satisfied with Algernon's blissful marital state, but for reasons I cannot fathom, she is determined to drop me to my knees as well."

Lavinia stared at the back of his black head and shook hers. "Did your parent's marriage sour you on the idea as mine has, or is there another reason?" She couldn't help asking, sensing they were more alike in their convictions than she thought.

Turning to face her, Oliver's gaze softened as memories flickered in his eyes."My parents shared a love very few couples do. The castle brimmed with it. And when my father died, part of my mother did, too. She is not the same woman she was." He turned back to the window. "I could not bear to see her suffering. She refused to eat or drink and shriveled away to nothing the first year after he died. My grandmother suffered the same pain and never recovered. Gran died of a broken heart six months after my grandfather passed." He paused to clear his throat. "I have never been inclined to seek the blissful state because I do not wish to rely on someone else for my happiness. 'Tis a weakness I cannot afford."

Lavinia sighed. "My experience is quite the opposite. I have no wish to marry because of the misery my mother endures. I do not believe my father is happy either and uses other women to fill a void within him." She dropped her gaze. "I could never endure what my mother has, turning a blind eye as woman after woman shares my husband's bed. I have yet to witness a happy union."

Silence filled the salon until the duke turned. "I believe on this subject we are at an impasse. To love or not to love seems to be the question. My parents loved each other too much, and yours too little. Shall we raise a toast to our mutual decision to remain unwed and unattached?"

She nodded and smiled. No lectures on duty or honor and no arguments. Accepting the glass of sherry he handed her, she raised her gaze to his.

"To freedom."

His deep voice filled the room as she tapped the rim of her glass to his.

"To freedom."

Tossing back the liquid, a surge of warmth spread through her chest and surrounded her heart. Fire coursed through her veins, and butterflies took flight in her belly.

Their gazes locked, and for a moment, the world

around them faded away, leaving nothing but the two of them. And the thunderous beat of her own heart.

Lavinia's breath caught in her throat.

The long paned windows behind Oliver bathed him in golden light as if he were a god descended from the heavens, and she couldn't breathe.

Neither one broke eye contact.

His handsome face softened, and a warm smile curved his lips. "Lavinia."

The husky timbre of his voice made her limbs turn to jelly. A strange excitement raced through her blood as she stared into his vivid blue eyes.

A kinder, more understanding man never existed, she mused. As a young girl, she pondered the existence of Christmas miracles, wondering if they were real or merely tales spun by imaginative authors. But as she stood there, staring into Oliver's entrancing blue eyes, she prayed they were true. For if Christmas were a time of magic and wishes fulfilled, she knew in her heart what hers would be.

"Yes, Oliver?" She wanted to go to him and throw her arms around his lean waist, to run her fingers through his dark hair, and kiss his warm lips. Her mouth dried at the thought, and she ran her damp palms down the side of her pink muslin day gown to rid them of the itch.

Trembling from head to foot, she swallowed and waited for his answer.

His smile deepened, drawing her gaze to the curve of his mouth, the line of his chiseled jaw, and back to his magnificent blue eyes. As she did so, her heart shot out of her chest, filling her with glorious golden rapture.

His smile enticed an answering one to her lips.

She would never grow tired of being with him, of

listening to the rumble of his deep voice or drowning in his incredible blue eyes.

The thought tripped her racing heart, and she gasped as the full weight of her emotional state settled over her like a damp blanket. Her mouth made a perfect O as she stared at him in disbelief.

She'd fallen in love with the duke at the very moment he toasted his decision never to marry.

Unwed and unattached.

Panic flared in her chest, followed by the awkward thump of her heart.

Lavinia closed her mouth, casting her gaze downward as a rush of heat flooded her face, coloring her cheeks with deep embarrassment.

If Oliver guessed how she felt, she feared he'd toss her out into the snow and never let her return. Panic made her dizzy, and black spots danced before her eyes.

Gazing down at her empty glass to shield the truth from his intense stare, she swallowed. "I think I will retire to my chamber and lay down. I'm feeling rather weary."

Before he could take a step in her direction, she placed her glass on the marble table at her knees and fled.

****

Oliver stared after her, confused. He swirled the remaining sherry in his glass and frowned. Why had she run away? He thought she enjoyed their debates as much as he did. Did he miss something?

For one moment there, he thought they were in complete harmony. As if they were one mind in two separate bodies, and the free flow of understanding between them held him spellbound. He thought all women wanted to marry and plotted to capture the wealthiest, most titled nobleman available. Social standing, baubles, fashion, and gossip were the sole aim of every noblewoman's aspiration. Or so he believed until he met Lavinia.

Rehearsing their conversation in his head, he frowned. Perhaps the mention of her parents' unhappiness made her feel trapped. And like all caged creatures, she ran.

"Your Grace." Cecil appeared in the open doorway and bowed. "There's a messenger here from your solicitor." He held out a silver salvor containing a roll of parchment tied with a red ribbon.

"Thank you, Cecil. I will read it in my study." Setting his glass on the drink trolley, he caught the scroll in one hand as he strode toward the door. His man would have information on Lady Lavinia and Viscount Becker. Though his mother related all she knew, his man would be thorough.

Ten minutes later, he set the scroll down on his desk and stared into the flames. He had no liking for Viscount Becker and after reading the information his solicitor gathered, he wanted to shoot the snake.

The man belonged to a shadowy group of men whose tastes ran to children, young girls, and sadism. When Becker's father discovered his revolting secret, he issued an ultimatum. To stop his revolting behavior, get married, and produce an heir or be cut off. He gave his son two months to find a fiancée and a year to produce a child following the wedding.

Viscount Becker visited Lavinia's father two days later to ask for her hand, and according to the account his solicitor compiled, the Earl of Holbrook refused his suit. Becker spent the next two weeks drowning his sorrow at his club and vowing revenge.

Oliver retrieved his letter from Lavinia's brother, Arthur, who left for France the same week. In the letter, Arthur explained he would return with the title to the lands his father coveted and informed the duke he planned to wed Lady Victoria Beaumont on his return.

But he never came back. A French Inspector found his body in a back alley in Paris, with a knife in his back.

Oliver glanced back at his report. Viscount Becker sailed for France two days after Arthur and returned the same week with the title in his possession. When questioned, Becker informed his man of business that he had won the title in a game of cards.

But Arthur didn't gamble. This reason alone made Oliver suspicious of the circumstances surrounding Arthur's death. Now armed with the unsettling knowledge of Becker's true nature, his apprehension increased.

Upon Becker's return from France, he once again paid the Earl of Holbrook a visit, resulting in the signing of a marriage contract. The Banns were read, and a date for the marriage was set. However, the viscount's grandfather passed a week later, delaying the wedding for six months until the time of mourning passed.

Lavinia was right to leave the bastard at the altar. Thoughts of her in Becker's bed fueled a blaze of fury within him, tightening a vice around his chest. His hands fisted, and the muscles in his jaw tightened.

The last paragraph of his solicitor's letter caught his attention.

I have discovered Viscount Becker hired an investigator named Marlboro to find Lady Lavinia. Marlboro is known for his ruthless demeanor and disregard for life. If you know the lady's location, be advised this man poses a serious threat and will not hesitate to use foul methods to achieve his objective. I am informed the marriage between Viscount Becker and Lady Lavinia Holbrook is scheduled for the week preceding Christmas.

Oliver placed the letter on his desk and uncurled his fingers.

Marlboro.

He recognized the notorious name and leaned back in his chair. Lavinia was lucky to be alive, as many before her were not. The bastard wouldn't get the chance to hurt her. And if the earl rescheduled the wedding, he also knew of his daughter's location. Glancing out the window, he frowned as he recalled the fear in Lavinia's face when she mentioned Becker. Did she know of his vile inclinations?

Even before the question finished forming, Oliver dismissed it with a shake of his head. Nay. How could she when she didn't know the first thing about kissing? No innocent would understand Becker and his cohorts' depravity. He didn't, and his own desires were those of a healthy, normal man—nothing akin to Becker and his degenerate associates.

No harm would befall Lavinia, not while under his protection.

If Becker or the Earl of Holbrook dared to trespass on Chauncy land, they would face swift and lethal consequences. As for Marlboro, he dug his grave the moment he targeted his mother's goddaughter. His men would shoot to kill.

Not bothering to delve too deep into his violent need to protect Lavinia, Oliver retrieved his pistol from the mantle and checked the mechanism. Cleaned, oiled, and in perfect working order, he kept his weapons ready. And a battle loomed on the horizon.

Oliver doubled the guards and increased their rounds by twice.

"Every able-bodied man will take a watch, including the new recruits. Lady Lavinia's safety is our utmost priority." Cecil and Tom nodded in solemn agreement.

Every fifteen minutes, a set of guards circled the castle. Two footmen were posted at every door, and pairs were stationed at the end of every corridor.

Arabella commented on the extra footmen the next morning at breakfast. Lavinia had not appeared and the two of them were alone.

When he disclosed the contents of his solicitor's letter, Arabella's expression turned grave.

"Do you anticipate this assassin will come here?" A heavy silence hung between them before she sighed. "You must, or you would not have stationed extra guards."

Oliver set his fork down and gazed at her. "Lavinia's safety is my responsibility. I failed once when she spent all afternoon in the woods, and I will not do so again."

Arabella tilted her head and nodded. Taking a bite of her toast, she changed the subject. "Christmas is in three weeks, dear. I suggest we keep Lavinia busy with holiday preparations, and her mind off her worries. The poor girl hasn't eaten a thing in days." Picking up her teacup, she added. "If this assassin finds her, it won't be long before Madalaine appears."

He frowned. "And will you force Lavinia to go back? You know what the bastard will do with her."

His mother let out a deep sigh. "What is the

alternative? You know I have no authority in this matter."

He never thought the words would come out of his mouth, but they did. "What about Scotland?" The thought made him cringe, but in comparison to Becker, the former would be welcome. His stomach rebelled at the thought of another man touching her, of fathering a child with her…Schooling his features, he shoved his feelings aside and focused on his mother.

Arabella shook her head. "There's been no word from her cousin Gwen. I fear Lavinia will have no choice but to return home with her parents and marry Viscount Becker." She paused and stared into the hearth. "Unless a Christmas miracle arrives in the form of a different husband. We should resume our search for this mysterious Scotsman. Or invite all the eligible men in the area to a Christmas Ball. What can the viscount or her parents do if Lavinia is married?"

Oliver finished his tea and set his cup down. Her words cut through him like a carving knife. "Excellent plan, Mother. I will have the men make inquiries about the Scotsman. If we find Lavinia's woodland acquaintance, we shall put your excellent matchmaking talents to effective use. The two were alone together for an unspecified amount of time. If all else fails, we could force them to wed." His gut twisted as he said the words. God, what a conversation to have. Taking a hasty sip of tea to soothe his raw throat, he continued. "I received a note from the Earl of Corbet a few days ago expressing his intent to join us for the holiday. Your suggestion we host a ball and a week-long house party is wise. We will invite every other eligible man within traveling distance. With any luck, Lavinia will be swept off her feet, and the problem will be solved." His throat tightened, and he paused, giving the unsettling discomfort in his chest time to dissipate. But it twisted into a knot instead.

"What problem?" The object of their discussion strolled in the open door dressed in a pale blue day gown. Her golden blonde hair hung in curls down her back and framed her heart-shaped face. Large lavender eyes gazed into his as she strolled toward them.

Oliver couldn't tear his gaze away from her slender figure and frowned when his hands shook. Rising to his feet, he waited to resume his chair until she took the seat the footman held out for her. The less she knew about their Christmas surprise, the better, especially if she shared his sentiments about the whole affair. "A Christmas tree. We are lacking one, and thus it's a problem. The holiday is a mere three weeks away, and a tree expedition is of utmost importance. I plan to remedy the situation following breakfast and would be delighted if you joined me." Along with a contingent of his men.

A flush stained her cheeks when she glanced up and met his steady regard. She hesitated for a bare second. "I would love to go. Thank you."

He never considered a woman's voice intoxicating until he met her. And now the melodious husky timbre of her voice raced over his skin like angel dust, compelling him to draw nearer. If she perished at the hands of some lawless bastard sent by her loving fiancé, he wouldn't be held responsible for his actions. "Then it's settled." Motioning for more tea, he leaned back in his chair. "Mother is hosting a Christmas Ball three days before the holiday, and several guests will be staying here the entire week. If you know where your Scottish friend is, invite him along. The more guests, the livelier the holiday. The duchess will require assistance with invitations and decorating the tree. Are you up to the task?"

He quit breathing when she flashed him a wide, joyful smile.

Her beautiful eyes sparkled with pleasure, and the flush on her cheeks turned a deep pink. God, she was beautiful.

He couldn't swallow, and his heart thumped so hard in his chest that he wondered why it didn't break free. Narrowing his gaze, he schooled his features into an impassive mask, concealing how much he yearned to touch her, to embrace her, and to kiss her as he did in his feverish dreams.

Morning light streamed through the window behind him, casting a halo around her golden hair, illuminating her long, elegant throat, and highlighting her slender figure. His gaze trailed down to the rapid rise and fall of her soft breasts swathed in pale blue muslin. God, she enticed him to caress her, to taste her, and to hold her in his arms.

Oliver shifted in his seat and placed his napkin over his lap to disguise his ardor.

His gaze swung to his mother, who smiled with smug satisfaction. He shook his head in response.

Get control, man!

Lavinia was not meant for him. Self-preservation and common sense demanded he maintain his distance and give the house party a chance.

His thoughts drifted to the Scot, and his mood darkened like a thundercloud blocking the light of the sun.

He swore he would never wed, never commit.

But if by some impossible twist of fate hell become a frozen wasteland, the woman he would choose would be Lavinia. Everything about her drew him like hot cocoa on a cold Christmas Eve, sweet, intoxicating, and bliss to his soul.

And yet, the prospect scared the hell out of him.

"Of course. Christmas is my favorite time of year. I love everything about it." The joy in her expression made the restrictive band around his heart tighten.

"As do I, my dear." His mother shot him an amused glance as if she sensed his accelerated heartbeat and rapid breathing. "When you return from your tree expedition, join me in my salon. I will compile a list of guests, and we can get started on the invitations."

"I'll see to the sleigh. Dress warm, Lavinia. I'll meet you out front in half an hour." Oliver rose to his feet. "Good day, Mother. I'll see you at dinner."

He strode away before the duchess could make any further observations. Just because he allowed her to host a husband-finding house party didn't mean he planned to be one of the candidates. He would ensure Lavinia's safety and leave the wooing to his guests. Satisfied with his decision, he made his way to the stables, determined to enjoy the day. Why, then, did he feel as though the future held no happiness?

Chapter Fourteen

Lavinia gazed at the twenty-foot tree in amazement.

Workers carried the tree into the ballroom and crafted a sturdy wooden stand around the base while she sat beside the duchess overseeing the project. True to his promise, Maurice stood by her side, anticipating her every desire. If she required more cranberries, he brought them. If she asked for water, he ran to fetch some. Though slow, he took his duty as her protector to heart.

Oliver disappeared the second they returned from their tree-finding expedition, mumbling something about having work to do in his study, and hadn't reappeared since

With a sigh, Lavinia picked up her needle and resumed her task of stringing cranberries for the tree.

A week passed with little communication between them.

Determined to keep her bargain with Wallace, she focused her efforts on finding his missing sister. His knowledge of the forest north of the duke's property may be her saving grace.

During the second week in December, Annie discovered the girl scrubbing floors for one of Oliver's underlords, Lord Knightly. Clarice's lover, now her new husband, worked as a stable hand for the same lord. And they both professed contentment with their new life.

When Annie related the news, Lavinia's hope sank

like a stone in a pond. Would Wallace assist her if his sister remained in England?

Nibbling on the end of her quill, she debated what to say. Several minutes passed before she penned a quick note to Wallace, updating him on his sister and proposing a meeting the following Friday night at the edge of the forest bordering the castle. She expressed her earnest desire for him to attend so they could discuss Clarice and his part of their agreement.

If she were clever, she could get away long enough to come to a resolution. Ever since the eventful afternoon in the forest, the duke and his men kept her in sight at every hour of the day and, she suspected, every hour of the night.

Even Maurice, though a dedicated companion, proved to be an effective guard.

Handing the missive to Annie to take to the village, Lavinia returned to her cranberry strings with a heavy heart. What in God's name would she do if her parents found her before Wallace showed her the way north? She knew they would find her at some point, but then what? Bending to her task, she shoved the thought aside and whispered, "'Tis the season of miracles if you believe."

Her old nurse used to repeat the words as if reciting a prayer, and her wishes always came true. Without fail.

As a child, Lavinia believed Nurse might be a fairy godmother or a giant elf, able to summon wonderous events into existence.

But now she knew better. Unsure if the words, the fervency, or Nurse's blind belief in the spirit of Christmas created miracles, she could use a few right now. She whispered the words and then repeated them until her mouth grew dry.

After a bit, her mood lightened, and her smile returned.

While she strung cranberries, popcorn, dried fruit, and candy to hang on the massive branches, footmen set up scaffolding and draped the treats while the duchess and Lavinia directed from their seats below. Strings of metal foil and bright-colored paper came next, followed by candles.

When the delicate porcelain and satin angel sat atop the glorious tree, Lavinia sighed with delight and stepped back to admire the scene. Her problems drifted to the back of her mind as she stared in delight.

Candlelight from the tree glinted on the gleaming wooden parquet floor, making it appear golden brown. Three crystal-cut chandeliers hung above the ivy-silken walls of the ballroom, throwing slivers of light over the magical scene and creating an ethereal wonderland. The sweet scent of cranberries mixed with the warm aroma of cinnamon and burning candles filled the air, making her nose twitch with delight. Earthy pine wafted past, laced with the sweet, buttery smell of roasted chestnuts, and her stomach growled in response.

Turning, she smiled at the duchess. "It's so enchanting and beautiful. In my mind, I can hear the orchestra swelling and see the dancers' swirling skirts accompanied by the gentlemen's stiff, dark attire. Wreaths of ivy, mistletoe, and pine are draped along the walls and across the doors, tied with red velvet bows. The murmur of voices and the smell of hot apple tarts, hot chocolate, mincemeat, and ginger molasses cookies makes me faint with yearning."

"Who makes you faint with yearning?" The duke's deep voice rumbled behind her, causing her to jump in surprise.

He had been absent all week, visiting all the tenants on his estate, and his sudden appearance threw her heart into a spin. She burst into rapid speech to hide her excitement at his presence. "Not who. What. All of this." She waved her arms and twirled in a circle. "The Christmas ball will be the most elegant and magical ever held. I can see it in my head, and I want to dance until I drop. Oh, Oliver, this is perfection."

"I am pleased you think so." A strange look passed over his face before he bent to kiss the duchess's cheek. "Good afternoon, Mother."

"Oliver." Arabella patted his hand. "Have you finished with all the tenants?"

He straightened. "Yes, and I have come to offer my services for your ball."

A satisfied smile crossed the duchess's face. "Excellent. We require wreaths and lengths of greenery for the walls. Mistletoe, of course, is necessary, along with cranberries and plenty of red velvet ribbon to twist through the pine branches. If you direct the footman, we will have the ballroom all adorned in plenty of time for the party." Turning to Lavinia, she waved a hand. "Come along, my dear. We must turn our attention to the corridors and dining hall so the footmen can gather the proper number of branches for our holiday celebration."

Lavinia rose to her feet and accepted the duke's arm. "All of the invitations left this morning, and we are on schedule."

****

Oliver's mind lingered on the mention of mistletoe. The memory of Lavinia's husky voice begging him for more when he soothed her raging fever made him burn, as did the recollection of their kiss the day Victoria departed. He glanced at his mother. "I'm ecstatic."

She laughed at his dry tone of voice and patted his arm. "Make sure there is more mistletoe than normal. We must ensure this party is a resounding success.

Lavinia fell into step on the duchess's right. "I do not know how any party you host could be anything but successful, Madam. You think of everything."

He had to agree. Often, he cursed his mother for her ability to plan for every contingency, but in this endeavor, part of him hoped she would fail. For winning meant losing Lavinia. A thought he refused to entertain. And if she married local nobility, he would be forced to see her with another man as a regular occurrence. "I forgot something important I must address, Mother. I will send Cecil to your aid with instructions as soon as I see you settled in your salon."

She raised an eyebrow in his direction. "Your errand must be quite tragic, for you are frowning as though someone shot your favorite stallion. Really. Oliver. How can anything be more important than this? I am disappointed. Two minutes ago, you agreed to help, and now you make excuses to leave. I had hoped you would assist me in deciding how much greenery we require. You know I am not good at estimating lengths."

Oliver blew out a deep sigh. He could endure Lavinia's proximity for one afternoon if he put his mind to it, for his mother's sake. "Then I shall stay. And you are correct, Mother. This ball takes precedence over every other thing. I shall not stop until all is arranged to your satisfaction."

His mother gave a nod of approval and patted his arm. "Thank you."

Keeping his gaze forward, he ignored the enchanting presence beside them. Even from this distance, he could smell the delicate rose scent of her skin and hair. Heat flooded his veins, and his stomach tightened when Lavinia leaned forward and gave him her sweet smile. "Yes, thank you. We need all the help you can give."

God, why did she have to sound so intoxicating?

Shoving his arousal aside, he considered every man of quality in the area. "Who did you invite, Mother?"

"Lord Baltimore, for one. He has a considerable amount of land to the northwest and possesses a well-lined pocket. Any lady would be well provided for with him. He is an excellent catch."

Oliver disagreed. "He is too short and stubby. No woman wants to tower over her husband."

Arabella smiled. "The Earl of Dunhaven is six feet at least, has an excellent eye for horses, and possesses quite a charismatic personality. Many of the ladies in the area swoon at the mere mention of the man's name."

The duke shook his head. "He may have stature, but he is archaic in his farming methods and would not be a suitable match."

The duchess's lips twitched.

Oliver paused outside the salon door. "Did you invite Lord Greenwell?"

His mother shot him a surprised glance. "I thought you two were at odds over the proper use of farmland. If I recall your disagreement correctly, you believe rotating crops aids the soil while Lord Greenwell prefers the old methods."

She had a point. Could he allow his mother's goddaughter to marry such an idiot? Everyone knew selective breeding and proper crop rotations were the way of the future.

"You are correct. Do not invite the man. I would hate to ruin your evening with a heated debate over breeding practices."

The duchess chuckled. "I shall ban every man who mentions such a topic at my Christmas Ball. You included."

He had no doubt she would keep her word and nodded as she sank into the satin settee before the fire. "Let me send a footman for Cecil, and we can get the measurements for the lengths of greenery underway. I shall return in a few minutes."

As he retraced his steps and gave his command to the footman waiting outside the salon door, he considered Baron Downham. Tall, intelligent, and an excellent shot, he would keep the jackals at bay and Lavinia safe. But would she be happy living with Downham's aged mother and five younger sisters?

Shaking his head at the mental picture of Lavinia on the baron's arm, he frowned and returned to the salon. Nay. He would never do. Downham didn't have the stamina or patience Lavinia's husband would require.

Which left...him.

Oliver stood still in the middle of the sumptuous blue salon. Shooting a glance at his mother, he frowned, hoping her keen gaze missed his hesitation. Losing her husband almost killed her, and he knew enough about life to know Lavinia had the power to destroy him.

If he let her get too close.

Thank God Cecil interrupted his maudlin frame of mind before he dwelt too long on the thought of Lavinia, warm and luscious beside him in the large featherbed of the master chamber.

"We twisted five hundred feet of boughs last year, and the castle walls are the same this year as they were last. I sent the men after the same number of trees and such." Cecil planted indignant hands on his hips when they all shook their heads. "Why are ye all staring at me like that?"

"We require more than we had last year. Especially the mistletoe." The duchess lifted Princess into her lap and met Cecil's flushed face. "We must provide ample opportunity for stolen kisses if we are to succeed."

Oliver caught the sympathetic glance Lavina shot him. She didn't know the duchess wanted the mistletoe for her and not for him. His gut twisted.

"How many women have you invited?" Lavinia's soft voice filled the silence as she worried her bottom lip with her teeth and shot him another anxious glance.

Arabella smiled. "One or two. Most of the guests this Christmas will be men. You see, my dear, I cannot afford to have Oliver in a temper during the festivities. He would ruin my Christmas Ball, and I would never forgive him. Goodness knows he roared loud enough to wake my grandparents from their graves last year." She gave a small shudder as if the thought made her skin crawl. "One tiny little indiscretion and he turned into a wounded lion. In keeping with the situation, we shall be outnumbered by men this year, my dear."

Oliver snorted. "One tiny indiscretion, Mother? You drugged me with opium and thought to trick me into signing a marriage contract. I wouldn't call such underhanded methods an indiscretion. What you did was outright manipulation and an insult to my intelligence."

The duchess snorted this time. "And yet you remain

single. No harm was done."

He wanted to throttle his mother with his bare hands and turned away to stare out the window. "Just to the trust between us. I have my food sampled now, before I put it in my mouth."

"And Cecil's son makes good money doing so. Why do you complain?" The duchess arched a brow. "All is well, Oliver." Turning, his mother smiled at her goddaughter. "I shall be forthright, Lavinia, and confess this party is for you. I refuse to hand you over to the troll who fathered you or the strutting rooster you left in the cathedral without a fight. I invited every eligible man of my acquaintance within traveling distance with the hope one of them would appeal. The earl cannot force you to marry if you are already wed."

Lavinia froze and shot a glance at Oliver. "How kind of you both. Thank you."

Oliver shoved his hands into his trouser pockets and gave her a small smile. "With any luck, the mistletoe will work its magic, and you will find a husband."

Mrs. Whittle carried in yards of red velvet ribbon for the women to make bows and rescued him from the awkward conversation.

With a wave of his hand, he made his excuses and fled. Where in the hell did Cecil go? He required a sound, logical conversation from someone uninterested in his marital status before he lost his mind. God, the duchess, could try his soul.

The memory of the pain in Lavinia's eyes when his mother mentioned marriage burned his chest, and he shifted to ease his discomfort. He participated in finding her a mate for the very thing he fought to avoid. Picking up his pace, he called for his stallion and an axe. The best place for him and his frustration would be the forest, swinging his axe until his anger dissipated.

****

The guests trickled in a few at a time over the next few days, and Lavinia met fresh faces every morning at breakfast. The duchess must have reconsidered her decision about the uneven number of male guests, as more females appeared around the glossy wooden table as well.

The Earl of Dunhaven approached her in the corridor on the second day of his arrival and invited her to go on a sleigh ride.

Six feet tall with dark hair and laughing brown eyes, the man grinned down at her and bowed from the waist. His manner might have swept her off her feet if she were not so attracted to Oliver, but she agreed anyway.

Most of the women at the castle angled to get a moment alone with the handsome lord, and Lavinia wondered if he sought a bit of quiet. Since she had not drawn him into conversation or followed him around like a lovesick puppy, she would be the obvious choice for a peaceful afternoon.

Tom had the duke's gilded sleigh waiting for them the moment they stepped out the front door. Gleaming white with intricate golden detail and sleek runners, the vehicle boasted plush red velvet seats and a high curved back. Rows of golden sleigh bells hung from red leather strips draped along the sides, chiming melodiously with every step the horses took.

Lavinia sighed with pleasure as she accepted Maurice's helping hand and sank down beside the earl. "The sleigh is perfect and makes me think of Christmas. Thank you for inviting me."

"Of course. But the pleasure is all mine." The earl tucked thick buffalo rugs around her as soon as she took her seat beside him.

She smiled in response. "How kind of you to say so." All noblemen were not made by the same tailor, she mused. Why couldn't Hudson be as charming and gallant as the earl? If he had a quarter of the earl's charisma, she wouldn't be in this predicament. But then, neither would she experience the enchantment of Chauncy Castle for the holidays or know the wonder of the duke's kisses and the pleasure of his touch. Lavinia frowned and leaned back in her seat, lost in contemplation.

As she did so, the earl leaned closer, and she caught whiffs of his clean, masculine scent. Pursing her lips, she found it odd she did not experience any of the breathless tummy-twisting weakness she felt when sitting close to the duke. If *he* were with her now, instead of the earl, she would be incoherent with delight at his closeness.

The earl fussed over her, tucking in the buffalo rug while his face hovered mere inches above hers. Yet, despite his closeness, she felt nothing, not even curiosity.

With a final pat on the buffalo rug, the earl picked up the reins. "Well, off we go now." Whistling through his teeth to the two prancing horses, the sled whisked them out of the castle courtyard and onto the open road leading away from the castle.

Closing her eyes, she allowed the chilly air to rush over her face until she couldn't feel her nose. Then she tucked her chin behind her heavy woolen scarf and wrapped the ends over her cheeks, leaving her eyes and nose exposed. Staring at the endless horizon of white she marveled at how simple everything seemed from this angle. Freedom whipped against her face, sending chills down her back and freezing her feet beneath the heavy rug. And God, how she loved every minute. Papa, Hudson, and scandals were so far away they were almost nonexistent. Almost.

They drove for an hour over the glistening, sparkling snow before the earl drew to a stop and turned to give her a wide grin. "Are you ready to go back?"

She shook her head and got a glimpse of two footmen riding black stallions several feet behind them. "We have an escort?" Had they been trailing them the whole time?

He shot her a surprised glance. "Of course. Reputations can be ruined even in the far north, Lady Lavinia."

Ah, but she ruined her own weeks ago, and somehow, the fact he didn't know pleased her. "I would like to ride some more if you do not mind. I am enjoying this a great deal."

The earl's grin widened. "Then we shall go north for a bit and circle around."

Which they did to her utter delight.

Four hours later, they drew to a stop in front of the castle steps. Two footmen approached and caught the horses' bridle to hold them still.

The earl turned and gave her a wide smile as he handed the reins to the groom. "Thank you for a delightful afternoon, Lady Lavinia. I hope we can do this again soon?"

If only. With Christmas so close, who knew how much time she had before the disaster struck? And she had no escape plan. "I would like that."

The earl's gaze darkened and dropped to her lips. "Until then, Lady Lavinia."

Did he fancy her? She couldn't be sure, and just when she thought of a polite way to let him down and offer friendship instead, Tom and Maurice both appeared at her side.

Lifting the rug away so she could climb out, Tom offered Lavinia an arm. "His Grace asked for you, my lady. He waits for you in his study."

Chapter Fifteen

All the fear, anxiety, and dread of her past life returned like a cloud of black smoke settling over her and making it difficult to breathe. Her serene, peaceful afternoon dissipated like sunshine before a thunderstorm. "Of course. Let me take my cloak to my chamber, and I will be right there."

Ten minutes later, she gave a tentative knock and stepped into the duke's study when he called for her to enter.

He stood before the hearth, holding a glass of brandy with a frown etched on his face. "Good afternoon, Lavinia. Please close the door behind you. I do not wish for the whole castle to hear our conversation."

She shut the door with a soft click and turned to face him.

He waved a hand at the leather armchair to his right without sparing her a glance. "Please sit."

She perched on the edge of her seat and lifted her gaze. "Is something wrong, Your Grace?" She cast an anxious glance at his stiff form and waited.

Navy breeches clung to his muscled thighs, and tall black boots encased his long legs. He wore a gold embroidered vest over a white linen shirt, rolled up to his elbows, exposing the tanned length of his forearms. His black wavy hair gleamed in the afternoon sunlight and the scent of his cologne drifted over her as she sank back against the buttery soft leather chair.

She swallowed against the dryness of her mouth, her heart pounding a hard, rapid rhythm in her throat. "What is it? What has happened?"

He swirled the amber liquid in his glass and turned to stare at her flushed face. Anger stained his high cheekbones, a dark red, and fire flashed in his eyes. "This will not be easy for you to hear, but I have received word from my solicitor that the man you planned to marry, Viscount Becker, hired someone to find you. He goes by the name of Marlboro. He is an assassin and extremely dangerous."

Her heart rate quickened. "You know about Viscount Becker?" Biting her lower lip, she searched his face for any sign he planned to toss her out of the castle.

But his expression remained bland.

"Yes." If words could drip ice, this one would make the Arctic appear tropical.

Of all the things she expected to hear, this one took her by surprise.

Casting her gaze at the window to see how much sunlight she had to make her escape, she slid to the edge of her seat. She would need a few minutes to pack a change of clothes.

"There is no need to bother the guards with my trivial problem, Your Grace. I will not burden you further with my presence. I understand how a scandal the size of mine could be awkward for you and the duchess. But if you allow me a few minutes, I will be gone before anyone is the wiser." Lavinia rose and hurried to the door. She would save him the effort to toss her out and leave with her dignity intact. His next words stopped her in her satin slippers.

"I do not wish for you to leave. Quite the opposite. I called you in here to reprimand you for being so careless. You were gone for four hours without the protection I wish you to have. Do you have any idea what could have happened?" Warm hands settled on her shoulders, turning her to face him. His piercing blue eyes pinned her to the floor. "The man is ruthless. And Dunhaven would be no match for him. Even with two guards."

She glanced up at him in surprise. He knew about Hudson, *and he wanted her to stay?* Understanding dawned. "Ah. That explains the extra escort on my ride today." She murmured the observation, noting how his expression darkened to thunderous proportions. If he didn't release some of his fury, he would erupt.

"I have given my staff strict orders. You are not to leave the castle without an armed guard. I had no idea you left with the Earl of Dunhaven this afternoon, or I would have forbidden you to go." Accusation flared in his eyes.

She heard two words. Forbidden and guard.

Worried about her safety? Gaping, she twisted the side seams of her day gown and shifted her feet. "I was quite safe."

His gaze dropped to her mouth. "Were you? Although you are returned in good health and no assassin attacked while you were out riding, thank God, there is another concern I wish to address. You were alone with Dunhaven for hours." His gaze sharpened on her face. "I must know if he acted the part of a gentleman. Did he kiss you?" Fire flashed in his brilliant blue eyes as he drew her a step closer to the heat of his body. Leaning closer, he cupped her chin, lifting her mouth an inch from his.

Lavinia forgot to breathe.

"Did he put his mouth against yours, like so?" Brushing his warm lips over her cold ones, he dropped his right hand to the small of her back and drew her against his hardness.

Her knees trembled, and fluttering wings tugged at her belly as his masculine scent enveloped her in a world of sensuality.

"Or did he give you a proper kiss? Like this." She couldn't have answered if she wanted to because he settled his lips over hers and cupped the back of her neck to hold her still for his heated invasion. He devoured her lips with his, drinking deep from the sweet recesses of her mouth like a thirsty man with his first taste of cool, soothing water.

"Open for me." His breath fanned across her cheek as he wrapped an arm around her waist and clamped her to him, chest to chest, hip to hip, and knee to knee.

Awareness and excitement raced through her bloodstream as he slipped his tongue between her lips and stroked along the length of hers.

She gasped into his mouth and sank against his hardness, melting into the planes of his body. God, he made her crazy with desire.

Lavinia lost all sense of time and reason as she drowned in a pool of sensual, molten kisses that drugged her senses. There was only him, his scent, his heat, and his knowing roaming hands.

When he cupped the curve of her bottom and held her against the length of his arousal, she gasped into his mouth. Liquid desire pooled between her legs, and she squirmed against him. "Oliver."

He groaned and dropped his mouth to her neck to run hot kisses from her ear to her collarbone. One hand rose to cup her breast through the fabric of her gown. She wanted more and arced against him, wrapping her arms around his neck and leaning back so he could cup her other breast.

His lips slid to the frantic pulse at the base of her neck. "You drive me crazy with want."

Moaning, she nodded her agreement. He made her crazy for him in a way she never knew before. His wicked tongue and lips erased all reason and left her swimming in a world of sensation. She knew only the magic of his lips on hers, the excitement of his hands moving over her body, and the heat dragging at her insides, making her delirious for more of his touch.

A knock broke them apart.

She stepped away with a sigh of regret and clasped her trembling hands together.

"Your Grace, guests have arrived, and Her Grace asked me to invite you to join her in her salon." Cecil's droll voice penetrated the heavy oak door of the study, and his presence on the other side cooled Lavinia's ardor.

She risked a glance at Oliver and noted his frown.

"Inform my mother I will be there in a moment." His gaze met hers as the butler retreated. "We are not finished with this conversation, Lavinia. I will have your word you will not leave the castle without my permission again."

She hesitated and swallowed her rebellion before speaking. "All right. I consent. But courting during this Christmas house party and finding a husband shall be an interesting experience if I am to inform Your Grace when a man wishes to kiss me out on the balcony. Do you not agree? Unless, of course, you plan to accompany me."

She knew she got under his skin when his eyes flashed blue fire, and his lips tightened.

"There will be no clandestine meetings or kisses. And you will inform me before you step outside this castle as you agreed. Including the balcony."

She gave him her sweetest smile as he swung the study door open and stepped out into the corridor. "Then how am I to catch a man if I cannot kiss him? The duchess ordered extra mistletoe for that very activity."

He growled as he stomped down the corridor and disappeared down the stairs.

Lavinia stared after him. Anyone could be forgiven for thinking that thoughts of her with another man irritated him.

If only.

She knew his views on marriage and love. With a sad smile, she turned and walked away to her bedchamber. She didn't care to kiss anyone, *but Oliver* and the thought of him planning a party to prod her into another marriage made her stomach queasy. Yet, returning to her parents and Viscount Becker made her nauseous on a different level. The opportunity for a happy future, security, and love sailed away with her brother to France, to be replaced with Viscount Becker, fear, and humiliation on his return.

She had two weeks at most to come up with a solution before darkness and despair arrived with her parents' carriage. And her villainous fiancé.

For the rest of the week, Lavinia saw little of the duke. Arabella kept her busy handwriting place cards and twisting garlands until she wanted to scream in frustration. Maurice alone kept her sane with his soothing words and willingness to fetch tea.

The guests arrived a few at a time until the breakfast table was filled with handsome, titled gentlemen and a few older married women. The duke would make an obligatory appearance and then disappear to his study for the rest of the day.

Every time a gentleman asked to take her on a sleigh ride, she dipped a curtsy to the duke at breakfast and asked permission to go in the same tone of voice she used to drive the Mother Superior to drink.

Oliver's gaze narrowed every time before he gave a slight nod and signaled for Cecil. "The men will be ready." He left as he tossed the words over his shoulder.

If a gentleman invited her onto the balcony or the terrace following dinner, she smiled at the duke down the length of the glimmering table and asked if he cared to join them.

His gaze flashed fire before he gave a grim shake of his head.

Her godmother took delight in the exchange, for her smile grew wider with each passing day. Until the night the Earl of Dunhaven caught her by the hand and slipped out onto the terrace to take her in his arms.

He took her by surprise, and as she opened her mouth to protest, he covered her lips with his own. "My darling, I think of nothing but you and how you feel in my arms."

His tongue stroked the inside of her mouth, and although pleasant, the earth did not quake as it did when Oliver kissed her. For long moments, the earl's lips moved against hers as he held her against him.

She stood still in the center of his embrace and

contemplated marriage to the handsome man. His touch would be bland, but acceptable. Not earth moving or universe shifting, but bearable. If she put her mind to the task, she might even stir up enough emotion to like him. And she would be free of Hudson.

A shiver ran down her spine, and she stiffened in the earl's arms.

"How careless of me, darling. You are cold, and all I can think about is making you mine. I must ask the duke's permission to court you, and dare I hope you think of me enough to accept a proposal?" His dark chocolate eye burned into her with hopefulness, and Lavinia's heart bumped in her chest. How could she agree? But then, how could she not?

Biting her lip in consternation, she glanced up. "May I have the night to think it over?"

He smiled and stroked her cheek in a gentle caress. "Of course, darling. One night and then I must know if you will accept my suit. I will count the hours until I have your answer."

The door swung open behind them, and Lavinia didn't need to turn around to know who stood behind her.

"Come inside, Lavinia, before you are discovered. We will speak of this in my study after I have a word with Dunhaven."

"Of course." She gave the earl a small smile and lifted the skirt of her green taffeta gown. "I shall be in my chamber, Your Grace." With her head high, she brushed past him and made her way up the stairs.

Perspective seemed such a dreary word. Yet, it was all she had. Without the prospect of the love she yearned for, she could find peace of mind. Mediocrity and security with Dunhaven offered a refuge from the fear and humiliation her ruthless fiancé—or her father could inflict upon her. She harbored no doubts that Hudson planned to retaliate for leaving him at the altar and for evading his hired abductor. No one could accuse her of lacking in spunk or determination. And she had plenty of both.

Sitting alone in her chamber and staring into the flames, dancing and snapping on her hearth, she made her decision. She would accept the Earl of Dunhaven's proposal on condition they marry with all possible haste. Her parents could arrive at any moment, and she would be worse off than before she escaped with Victoria.

The knock on her door startled her to her feet. "Who is there?"

"His Grace requests your presence in his study, m'lady."

Cecil.

Lavinia smoothed her skirts and patted her hair. "I will be right there." She walked down the corridor to his study in a daze, aware with every passing moment, her freedom could vanish like the mist before the rays of the sun.

"Close the door behind you." Oliver's clipped voice made her glance up in surprise.

Somehow, she made the entire trek down the stairs and corridor without being aware of her surroundings. Complying with his request, she sank into the leather chair he indicated.

Turning away to stare out the large paned window, he folded his hands behind him. "Dunhaven asked permission to make you his wife." His deep, masculine voice gave no indication of his thoughts. "Do you love him?"

Tilting her head so she could study the back of his windswept hair, she frowned. What an odd question when one considers how many of the nobility married for convenience rather than emotion.

"I…no." Licking her dry lips, she hurried on. "But he could be the solution to my problem. We…get on well. His kisses are…pleasant, and he will keep me safe." She would never have the marriage she dreamed about during the dark hours of the night, but she would be out of her father's and Hudson's reach. That had to count for something. And Dunhaven would treat her with respect. If he took a mistress, he would never allow his indiscretion to be public knowledge or affect their relationship. Neither her sisters nor her mother found such consideration in their marriages.

Taking a deep breath, she sealed her fate. "I accept."

The silence in the room grew so heavy Lavinia worried she would suffocate.

"I see." Oliver did not turn around, but the hands behind him turned to fists. "I will make the necessary arrangements and inform my mother of your decision. You may have chaperoned visits to the balcony until you are wed. Shall we set the date for Christmas day?"

She swallowed hard. "Yes. The sooner we are wed, the better chance I have to escape my father and Hudson."

He stood so rigid; he could have passed for a stone statue. "That is all. You may go."

Lavinia hesitated as she rose to her feet. Did he care nothing for the fact he just agreed to see her wed another in little more than a week's time? She choked back the desire to run to him and shake some sense into him. Couldn't he see how much she wanted *him*? How she longed to marry *him*?

His words echoed in her memory. *Will you join me in a toast to our mutual decision to remain unwed? To freedom.*

Stiffening her spine, she turned to the door. "Good night, Oliver."

Chapter Sixteen

Oliver stared into the darkness and replaying the moment in his study when Lavinia agreed to wed Dunhaven. His stomach twisted and his heart throbbed with an unpleasant mix of emotions. Why did her swift acceptance bother him so much? Marrying Dunhaven solved all their problems and yet his future stretched before him, bleak and barren tinged with a sense of loss.

He rolled to his side and stacked his hands under his head. The guest chamber two doors down from Lavinia's had seemed the perfect retreat following their conversation. Delving into his gut reaction over her acceptance of Dunhaven's proposal shouldn't be this difficult or this painful. Why did he care? The earl had offered a solution on bended knee, babbling nonsensical words as he begged for Lavinia's hand in matrimony.

Oliver's stomach lurched, and he rolled to his other side. This chamber possessed a deuced uncomfortable bed. He would have a word with Cecil about acquiring a new mattress tomorrow. For now, he would have to make do with the lumpy thing. Pounding the pillow and rearranging the bedclothes, he stretched out on his back.

God, he remembered the first time he laid eyes on her. His mind replayed the scene in his chamber when she stripped off her clothes and slipped into his bed.

His mouth grew dry, and his member sprang to life. He could still see the long, slender length of her legs and her perky breasts pressing against the thin silk of her chemise. Taut pink buds ripe for sucking pressed against his bare chest when he held her in his arms. Oliver groaned. Memories of the honeyed sweetness of her mouth clinging to his when he kissed her made him flip to his other side with a curse. His mother would be overjoyed at his discomfort if she knew, and he wondered how she would take the news of Lavinia's marriage to Dunhaven.

Marriage.

They would share the same bed. Dunhaven would caress her silken skin and father children with her.

"Damn it to hell." The thought of another man taking her while he remained true to his vow of bachelorhood gnawed at him. Could he bear to see Lavinia grow round with another man's child?

"Bloody bollocks." Oliver took a deep breath and stared up at the ceiling. For all his distaste at the thought, the man would treat her well and keep her in the manner she deserved. And she would be free of worry regarding her father and Viscount Becker. That had to amount to something, didn't it?

A commotion erupted in the corridor, and Cecil's voice boomed in response.

"Keep him there. I will fetch His Grace."

Raised voices and clattering boots in the corridor had him rolling from the bed and tugging on his discarded breeches.

A heavy knock announced Cecil's presence. "The men found a Scot lurking in the tree line. When the guards detained him, he demanded to see Lady Lavinia."

Oliver turned to stone. Heat surged through his veins, and his vision turned red. He wanted to smash his fist into the man's face and then run him through. But violence wouldn't resolve Lavinia's predicament.

And he did tell her to find the man and invite him to the Christmas Ball. But why did he come early and lurk in the tree line?

"I shall be right there." He tossed on a shirt, tugged on his boots, and slammed the door of the chamber behind him. Two minutes later, he strode into the foyer to face a Scot as tall and formidable as he. Brawny and muscular, this man wouldn't be an easy opponent. Unlike the other noblemen in the castle, this one matched Oliver in physical stature and, from the look of him, in strength.

Steel blue eyes met his. "I wish to speak to Lady Lavinia."

Oliver narrowed his gaze. "Whatever you have to say to her, you can say to me." Curiosity about their afternoon alone together made him furious, and as his gaze roamed over what some ladies might call a handsome face, his rage mounted. Had she been kissing this Scot, too?

The Scot's keen blue eyes took his measure. "Lady Lavinia agreed to help me find Clarice. She has, and I came to keep my end of our bargain. But yer men attacked me before I could meet with her as we planned."

Oliver's blood froze in his veins. She agreed to wed Dunhaven this very night, and now *this* Scotsman stood in his foyer announcing her plans to run away with him?

He couldn't endure much more of this. Turning to Cecil, he dropped his voice to an undertone. "Find Lady Lavinia and escort her to me."

****

Lavinia shifted in the saddle, her gaze piercing the

darkness of the forest. If Wallace didn't hurry up, the chances of Oliver's soldiers finding them increased by the minute.

Saddling Grace alone and by the flickering lantern hanging from the stable wall had been an ordeal she hoped never to repeat. Grace did her part without a fuss, but the cold made Lavinia's fingers stiff, and she fumbled everything. Climbing into the cold, stiff saddle without aid had been a challenge. How did one keep the sound of labored breathing quiet?

The night enveloped her in solitude, and she shivered in the cold. Her breath hung like a cloud in the frigid air as Grace shifted her feet. Even the fresh scent of the trees riding on the arctic air did little to ease her nervousness.

"Whoa. Easy girl." She patted the mare's side and froze when five castle guards thundered toward her, their hooves pounding the frozen ground. She would never evade them at the rate they raced toward her, so she nudged Grace into motion to meet them.

"His Grace requests your presence, my lady. He is waiting in his study." Tom's steady gaze made her cheeks burn. He knew she planned to meet Wallace here!

His four companions wore grim expressions and took position on either side of her, with two bringing up the rear.

"The Scot is with him." Censure dripped from Tom's voice. He said nothing more until they stopped before the front entrance. "I will take Grace, my lady, while these men escort you to the duke."

"Very well." Lavinia unhooked her knee and allowed Tom to help her dismount. Holding her head high, she ascended the castle steps, traversed the corridors, and climbed up another flight of stairs to Oliver's office.

Cecil ushered her inside, and the chill in the air made her hesitate.

Her gaze skidded to a stop when she spotted Wallace standing beside the hearth with his hands bound.

"Wallace!" Dashing across the floor, she threw her arms around his neck for a brief hug before withdrawing to tug at his binding. "I am so sorry. Let me help you. No wonder you didn't come to meet me. I waited for some time and worried you changed your mind." The heavy silence made her glance up.

Wallace and the duke both wore hostile expressions and glared at her.

"Close the door and wait outside." The duke's clipped voice sent her escorts scurrying to comply.

Glancing from one to the other, she squared her shoulders for the battle ahead.

Wallace's gaze could ignite a tree from ten paces. Heat rolled off him in waves, and she wilted beneath the rage in his eyes.

In contrast, the duke's icy demeanor and impassive stance behind his desk sent chills down her spine, freezing her to the core.

Wallace spoke first. "Ye said to meet ye in the forest, and we could leave from there. Ye said the duke wouldn'a mind, and ye promised I wouldn'a be attacked" He held up his bound hands and glared. "And yet here I am."

Lavinia took a deep breath. "Yes. I did promise." Licking her lips, she swallowed the lump in her throat. She had to keep Wallace from going back on his promise, and her mind raced with worry. Although she agreed to marry Dunhaven, she hoped to find the path through the forest as a backup plan in case things didn't go as expected.

Nurse's miracles never got mixed up like this. "I did think it best to leave from there. As for the duke..." She cast him a glance, but his expression gave nothing away. In fact, he appeared quite bored with their conversation. "I didn't plan on him finding out before it was too late." She sucked in a deep breath when Wallace uttered an oath.

"Ye ken the Scottish and the English dinna like each other, lass? Why wouldn'a the duke care that I crossed his land and fled with an English lass under his protection? I would kill an Englishman for less. Ye will get me hanged or worse. And I dinna ken if I want to help ye now." Wallace frowned and shot a glance of distaste toward the duke. "Let me go. I havn'a done anything wrong."

Oliver lifted his gaze and studied his captive. "Where did you plan to take Lavinia, and what did you intend to do with her?"

Wallace's eyes flashed. "The lass asked me to show her the path through the forest to Scotland, and I agreed."

Oliver glanced at Lavinia before refocusing on Wallace. "Then you didn't intend to carry her off to the highlands and fulfill all her fantasies?"

Lavinia let out a gasp and rushed to Wallace's defense. "He came to show me the trail, as he says. Nothing more." Folding her arms, she glared at them both. "And I don't have fantasies. Not about Scotland."

Something flashed in the duke's eyes before he leaned back and studied them both. A heavy silence filled the room, and she resisted the urge to fidget.

At last, the duke spoke. "Tell me about the afternoon you two spent alone in the forest."

Her eyes closed for the briefest second as she prayed for strength. "Fine." With short, precise sentences, she explained their time together in the woods.

"You're saying nothing happened?" Oliver didn't sound like he believed her, and Wallace shook his head.

"If I planned to be indiscreet with a lass, she wouldn'a be English." His tone suggested they were both touched if they believed he would do such a thing, and the duke nodded.

Rising to his feet, he retrieved a knife from his desk drawer and cut the binding around Wallace's hands. "I apologize for this misunderstanding. You are free to go. I am happy you found your sister, but I must insist you stay away from Chauncy land in future."

"With pleasure. The lass is daft, but I do owe her my gratitude." Wallace rubbed his wrists and turned to Lavinia. "My mother sends a gift to show her gratitude for finding Clarice. A favor for a favor. Ye ken? If ye have need of assistance, show this to any of my clansmen, and they will help ye." He removed a medallion from around his neck and handed it to her. Made of hammered silver, the round object had a hawk with outstretched talons in the center.

"It is beautiful. Please convey my gratitude to your mother." Lavinia slipped the silver chain over her head and let the medallion fall between her breasts. The weight of the gift against her heart made her smile.

"I will." He nodded at the duke and opened the door.

"Escort our guest to the edge of the forest and let him go. He is not to blame for this situation."

"Aye, Your Grace." Cecil's brows rose when he

glanced at Lavinia. "And her ladyship?"

"She will remain here for a few more minutes. I wish to speak with her." His tone gave nothing away.

But her heart sped up just the same. Would he take her in his arms and kiss her like he did when he caught the Earl of Dunhaven kissing her?

The door closed behind Cecil, and Oliver sank into the seat behind his desk without making a move toward her.

Lavinia frowned. "I cannot think what you are upset about. You did tell me to invite Wallace to the ball."

"To the ball, yes. But not on some clandestine ride through the forest alone."

When his gaze met hers, her heart sank to her belly. She had never seen Oliver this furious before.

"What were the words you used? Oh yes. You didn't plan for me to find out." The muscle in his jaw clenched.

Mother Superior's voice rose an octave when she gave this kind of talk. Oliver's dropped silky soft, and it scared the life out of her.

"This is my castle and my forest. Why wouldn't I find out? The men are loyal to me and me alone." His steepled fingers and bored expression sent a chill down her spine.

Swallowing hard, she mustered her courage, "Wallace is…was…my escape plan. Surely, you can understand my reluctance to wed Hudson. I did what I thought best under the circumstances." She licked her dry lips. "Wallace knows the path through the forest to Scotland. And if my parents come before I wed the earl, I must have an escape strategy. I cannot and will not become some man's servant."

"And yet I have discovered you kissing and coercing

two different men since you arrived here. Swaying their will with the sweet promise of your lips. Who is a servant to whom? I ask you. Thank God I have the fortitude to withstand your…charms. I shudder to think what might happen if I were to fall under your spell. When Dunhaven hears of this clandestine midnight ride, the engagement will be off, and all my mother's plans will come to naught. I do believe you have the power to break her heart, something I will never allow. The way I see it, Becker made a lucky escape."

The world spun around making her dizzy, and she gasped as his words pierced her heart. "I did not kiss Wallace. And the earl kissed me. There is a difference." Years of dealing with her father came to her rescue, and her chin rose. She could cry later when she lay alone in the dark. "No matter what you think of me, I have done nothing wrong. Your mother knows I love her and will do anything for her. I could never hurt her. And I will never marry Hudson or any other so-called gentleman. You may convey my rejection to the earl tonight if you so desire. I will break it off first and spare him the trouble. Do not worry. I will leave your castle at my earliest convenience. Good night, Your Grace."

Turning, she bolted for the door and fled to her chamber as if the hounds of hell nipped at her feet.

The tears didn't come until she blew out the candle and drew the coverlet over her head. And then she wept until she could cry no more. For hours, she let her grief, her embarrassment, her frustration, and her fear spill out of her eyes and dampen her pillow.

She fell into a fitful sleep as the first rays of the sun burst over the top of the vast forest.

Chapter Seventeen

Lavinia sent a note to the village with a footman when she woke, summoning Victoria.

Although Annie brought her a tray of breakfast and helped her dress, she stayed in her chamber, ignoring every knock on her door until Cecil insisted she join the duchess in her salon. "She bade me ask you please, my lady." His tone suggested the duchess didn't say the word often, and with a sigh, she straightened her skirt and opened the door.

"Very well." Following Cecil's stiff form through the long corridors did nothing for her temperament, and her gaze darted side to side in case the duke strolled into view. But he didn't, and then she stood before the duchess, awaiting her judgment.

"Bring us a tray of tea, Cecil, and see we are not disturbed."

Princess sat on Arabella's lap, purring while the duchess stroked her fur. "Have a seat, child."

Lavinia sank onto the settee opposite her hostess and dipped her chin. She suspected Oliver briefed his mother on her situation, and now Arabella wished to discuss the whole affair.

"I did not kiss Wallace, and I planned to meet him last night to find an alternative path into Scotland in case my parents arrive before I wed the earl." She sounded like a rebellious child caught in a lie and cringed.

"Of course, dear. You did the right thing, and I must say from the description I received of your Scotsman, you showed remarkable restraint. If he is half as handsome as the staff says, I might have been tempted to be indiscreet." A smile hovered around her thin lips, and a gleam entered her eye. "To think you were alone with him for hours."

Lavinia's mouth fell open. "But nothing happened."

Arabella smiled. "Of course, it didn't. I never believed otherwise."

"But Oliver made it sound like—"

The duchess interrupted her. "For such an intelligent man, Oliver can be quite obtuse. I'm sure he said a lot of things in his anger, but he did not mean them. I know my son, and he will come to regret the entire conversation."

"Did he say so?" Her chin came up, and she stared at the duchess in surprise.

"No, but he will." Arabella sounded convinced, but Lavinia shook her head.

"You do not know what he said." Her heart dropped as she recited the conversation in her head.

"I can imagine." The duchess's dry tone lured a ghost of a smile to her lips.

A knock came at the door, and Cecil entered with a tea tray. Placing the tea on the table at their knees, he gave Lavinia what she guessed could pass for a smile. "Keep yer chin up, my lady. All is not lost."

Had the entire world turned upside down in the night? Perhaps the servants slipped something into her tea to make her hallucinate. Her godmother never begged, and Cecil never smiled. To encounter both events in the same hour took her breath away.

Arabella cleared her throat and waved Cecil from

the room. "I asked you here to have a serious conversation about your future."

Lavinia's hand trembled when she took the teacup from her godmother's hand. "According to Oliver, I do not have one."

The duchess snorted. "Nonsense, my dear. You can have whatever you wish if you want it enough. Take the Earl of Dunhaven, for example. Do you love him?" Sharp blue eyes, very like her son's, stared at her over the delicate rim of her teacup as she blew on the steaming liquid inside.

"Nay." Frowning, she cleared her throat and answered in a stronger voice. "He is pleasant enough and not too uncomfortable to be with. He would make a good match, and I would be free of Hudson." *And my father*.

"Cake?" Arabella's expression remained placid.

Lavinia shook her head. Only the duchess could have a serious talk and ask if she cared for a piece of cake in the next breath.

"How is he at kissing?" Arabella placed a piece of lemon cake on a delicate plate and picked up a fork.

Caught off guard, she swallowed. "Uh. He is pleasant."

Arabella chuckled. "The earl's kisses don't make you breathless or your heart race?"

"No." No one could have convinced her she would have this intimate conversation with the Duchess of Chauncy if they had offered her a million pounds.

"And what about my son?"

Lavinia choked on her tea and set her teacup down before her trembling hand spilled the hot liquid on her lap. She stared at the tea tray, hoping a witty response would fall from her lips and save her this embarrassment.

"Come now, my dear. Be honest. If not with me, with your own heart. If Oliver makes you breathless, sets your heart pounding, and blinds you to all other men but him, then he is worth fighting for. Do not give up so easily."

When Lavinia glanced up in surprise, Arabella placed her frantic note to Victoria on the table before her.

"I intercepted your cry for help because I do not believe you mean it."

When Lavinia opened her mouth to protest, the duchess held up her hand. "Look me in the eyes and tell me you do not care for my son, and I will send my footman to deliver the note with all possible speed."

Lavinia dropped her gaze. "Am I so transparent?"

A soft sigh filled the space between them. "To me, yes. But not to anyone else here at the castle, especially not my son. Your friend Victoria would take one look at your face and guess. "

"Then, the answer is yes."

The duchess did not answer. "We have less than a week to convince my son he cannot live without you. I asked you here to give you my permission to do what you must."

Lavinia's gaze darted to the duchess. "Are you suggesting I…that is…I cannot manipulate him into marrying me." She had a clear mental picture of Lady Elspeth in her undergarments parading around the duke's bedchamber and shook her head with vigor. "He might not take my…er…coercion the way you think he will."

"Nonsense. He is a man. And I can attest to their lack of mental acuity when an unclad female is present." The duchess took a sip of her tea while Lavinia gaped in disbelief.

Her godmother must have lost her ever-loving mind.

"I could not. And even if he did propose, he would come to resent me for trapping him." She knew because she would do the same under similar circumstances.

A small smile tilted the duchess's lips upward. "You love him, and he loves you. Although neither one of you is brave enough to admit it. The one thing I know for certain is true love is worth fighting for."

True love. Love and respect.

Lavinia tasted the words and sighed. "For once, Madam, your spectacles deceive you. I can assure you that your son does not harbor tender feelings for me." She remembered his arctic gaze from the previous evening and shivered. "I gave him my word I would leave the castle and summoned Victoria." She glanced at the cream parchment sitting beside the teapot and sighed. "I promised to be gone before the ball. Lady Beaumont will come for me."

"And where will you go?" Arabella sat her cup down with a stern look. 'What will you do? At least here, you are protected from the heathen your viscount sent to find you."

Lavinia dropped her chin. "Please send my note. I have no wish to be here any longer than I must." Seeing Oliver every day and knowing how he despised her would be her undoing. "I have no wish to see your son again."

"Then it is unfortunate that I agree with my mother. You will stay here for your own protection." The duke's deep voice carried as he entered the room. "I may not condone your behavior, but I cannot allow you to leave when an assassin is hunting for you. No, my dear, I am afraid you have no choice but to stay."

Lavinia's heart sank, and she swallowed hard. How much of their conversation did he hear? Glancing up, she met his cool, glittering eyes with heated cheeks. She would never stoop to the levels other women did and lifted her chin. With her escape route to Scotland crushed and her one offer of marriage rescinded, she needed time to consider her options before her parents arrived at the castle gates.

"I want your word you will remain within these walls until I deem it safe for you to leave." His gaze sharpened to a dagger point and pinned her in place.

Swallowing her pride, she nodded. "Of course. Please excuse me, Your Graces." With a quick curtsy. Lavinia rushed to the door and hurried to her chamber.

God, what a mess.

Wandering to her window, she stared out over the frozen ground with unseeing eyes. True love may be worth dying for, but unrequited affection wasn't worth being crucified over. Never again did she hope to see the cold, icy stare Oliver delivered the night before. Her heart couldn't take it. Self-preservation demanded she stay out of his immediate vicinity and figure out another way to leave before her parents, Hudson, or his sinister associate caught up with her. Somehow, she must find the elusive trail through the forest. Cousin Gwen and Scotland were the only options she had left. Perhaps if she rode back to where she met Wallace, she could find the trail on her own. His men had, so it couldn't be too difficult. But first, she must escape the castle walls and her extra guards.

Less than an hour after she gave her word to Oliver, she stared through wistful eyes as the duke cantered toward the village on his stallion to visit his tenants.

He would be gone until time for dinner. She knew from timing his previous rides. The duke liked order and kept a tight schedule, so she had ample time to ride north before anyone asked questions or initiated a search party. As for her promise to the duke to remain inside the castle walls, her survival took precedence, even over honor. And didn't she prove as much when she ran away and left Hudson waiting like a fool at the altar?

Slipping from her room with her heavy black cloak, she motioned for Maurice to join her.

He readied a horse for her and saddled his own. One other man rode with them, although the duke ordered a minimum of four riders if she left the castle walls. When she quirked an inquiring brow at Maurice, he shrugged and grinned.

Whatever influence he used worked, and she smiled in response. Once they rode out of view of the stable, Lavinia raced for the forest with Maurice on her heels.

An hour later, she smiled with satisfaction as she maneuvered through the trees, confident she was traveling in the right direction. Pleased with her successful escape from the castle walls and her escorts, she failed to notice Maurice emerge from the forest to her right, alone.

Riding closer, he breached protocol and drew in alongside her.

Frowning, she turned to confront him and gasped when he tugged her reins from her surprised grasp.

"What *are* you doing?" Thinking they might be under attack, she didn't struggle.

"Who is chasing us?" Searching over his shoulder for any sign of the enemy, she didn't consider her position or his true purpose until he drew a knife from his belt, and she read murderous intent in his expression.

"Where is the guard, and why do you have a knife?" A horrible suspicion formed in the back of her mind, and she swallowed.

This couldn't be real. Maurice was her friend. The one who stayed by her side, ensuring her every wish came to pass.

"He met with an unfortunate accident back there, and I have plans for ye. Yer future husband sends his regards. Ye and yer dowry are going to make me a wealthy man." He grinned, sending a chill down her spine.

"Many have supposed they could manipulate me, only to be disappointed. You will be no different. I have no intention of going anywhere with you, and the last thing I will do is make you wealthy." Wishing she kept her word to the duke and trying not to dwell on her foolhardy mistake in leaving the castle, she swallowed. One guard lost his life because of her foolishness, and she didn't plan to join him. There had to be a way out of this situation. One where she lived and maintained her freedom.

"Well, none of the other people in yer life were me. And that's why the viscount hired me. He knows yer trouble."

"Do you intend to kill me in the middle of the forest?" She must know his plans to gauge her chances of escape.

"If I did, ye'd be dead. I'm not one for idle chatter." Her captor turned his horse east and kicked his stallion in the flanks, drawing her and Grace along with him. "I almost wished ye put up more of a fight. Becker told me ye were a wildcat, and I'm a bit disappointed. I enjoy a good tussle."

No doubt he did. And if he wanted a good fight, she'd give him one. She figured they would intersect the main road north to Scotland within the hour, and the closer they were, the more hope she had of being found.

Forcing her terror down to avoid panicking, she held her voice steady. "If killing me isn't the plan, where are you taking me?"

Maurice chuckled, and this time, she couldn't hide her tremor of fear.

His laughter held a sinister edge that made her skin crawl. "Where do ye think? Back to Viscount Becker. He's paying good money to get ye back. Coins from yer dowry."

Ice broke out on her forehead and trickled down her spine. She could scream, but who would hear? *Think hard, Lavinia, and fast. We don't have much time.*

He didn't tie her, and she could slip from the saddle and run. But without a horse, he would catch her. And she didn't want to make him change his mind about letting her breathe. Unexpected behavior produced unexpected results. Her gaze caught on a low branch a few feet in front of them, and a plan formed in her head.

With her heart thundering in her ears, she swallowed to ease her dry throat and put her plan into motion. He had to take the bait.

And he did.

Slipping to the ground, she dashed past Maurice straight for the tree, hoping her legs didn't fail her.

"What in blazes are you doing?" he roared, spurring his horse into action and letting Grace's reins drop to the ground. "God damn ye, get back here!"

Racing through the trees, she dodged bushes and

trees with Marlboro's thundering hooves half a breath behind her. At the last second, Lavinia dodged to the side beneath the low limb and, pivoting around the tree, gave her all in a bid to catch Grace.

Whack. Crash.

Her would-be abductor crashed to the ground with a string of curses. In his haste to catch her, Marlboro paid no attention to his surroundings, just as she planned.

His mount reared and whinnied, frightened by the sudden chaos, and tossing his head, he raced away.

Lavinia thanked the giver of Christmas miracles her plan worked. Slowing to a walk when she approached Grace, she ignored the cursing man several hundred feet behind her and climbed on the mare's back. Looping her leg over the pommel, she lifted her reins and glanced behind her.

Marlboro pushed to his knees, swearing, and made a furious attempt to give chase, but Lavinia urged Grace into motion.

"Tell the viscount he will never lay hands on me or my gold. And make sure you use all the colorful words you're so fond of so he understands my feelings."

"Take another step, and I'll kill ye with my knife. I may not know how to ride like ye, but I can throw a blade with fatal accuracy." He didn't have to yell. The words sliced through her like an ax.

In answer, she kicked Grace in the flanks and fled. Darting left and then right, she maneuvered the mare through the thick underbrush. One couldn't throw knives with accuracy unless the target cooperated by staying in a straight line of view. And she had no plan to oblige the bastard.

A split second later, the whistle of the blade sliced

through the air and struck the tree behind her with a sickening, bone-jarring thud. Urging Grace into a full gallop once she returned to the main road, she raced back to the castle. With any luck, she would arrive before the duke, and he would be none the wiser.

But her luck abandoned her a few minutes later when she glimpsed Oliver and twenty soldiers charging toward her.

Lavinia grimaced. Her hour of reckoning arrived sooner than she anticipated. Oliver would be furious with her for disobeying him.

As she pondered the many possible outcomes of her disobedience, she conceded that, this time, Oliver might have been right.

Chapter Eighteen

Lavinia did her best to avoid Oliver since her near abduction the previous day. The duke spent two solid hours berating her over her deceit, and she agreed with everything he said until he issued the decree she must always be accompanied by a guard.

No exceptions.

She argued and pled until he turned his steel gray eyes in her direction and asked, "What would you have done if the branch failed to unseat him? Thank God the viscount ordered you to be delivered alive, or I would have the unpleasant task of giving your parents the sad news. Even now, Marlboro could be plotting his next abduction. He has a reputation to maintain, and failure is not in his vocabulary. And knowing firsthand how devious you are, he will be better prepared next time. For God's sake, Lavinia, what were you thinking?"

She had no answer for him and left his study with her head held high, avoiding him whenever possible. Awkward, stiff, and formal, she skirted around him when they met and dispersed to the opposite side of the castle. With no suitor or viable options for her future, she resented the men who shadowed her and the duke even more for ordering them to be there.

'Tis the season of miracles if you believe."

Her nurse's saying kept her sane while she helped the duchess prepare for the Christmas Ball. A miracle,

Lavinia mused, would be the chance to escape one more time, allowing her to ride north until she found Cousin Gwen and begged for amnesty.

Convinced of the futility of such wistful thinking, she failed to account for fate intervening once more.

For on the night before the Christmas Ball, a miracle appeared in the strangest and most frightening manner.

Lavinia retired to bed early and ordered her dinner brought to her chamber on a tray. She dined alone and bade Annie assist her with her night rail before the maid departed for her own supper.

The bustle of the castle enveloped Lavinia as she stared up at the gilded ceiling of her room, wishing a miracle would descend from heaven in her hour of need.

The Earl of Dunhaven left the morning after her ill-fated escapade with Wallace, and several other gentlemen in attendance followed suit. Lavinia had no stomach for the knowing eyes of the guests, now an uneven number of unattached women, and avoided them as much as possible.

The duchess proved more difficult to evade, and after a solid hour of Cecil knocking on her door, Lavinia relented and wandered downstairs to join Arabella for tea. They spent a quiet hour together until two women guests asked to speak to the duchess, and Lavinia left them alone.

She cared nothing for small talk or gossip and had no desire to be the subject of their next conversation, so she feigned a headache and withdrew.

Boots clumped down the corridor outside her door, and the servants' hushed voices filtered through the walls. The flickering candle beside her bed cast uncertain shadows as she lay staring at the flame. Repeating the words for her Christmas miracle, she rolled onto her side and stared at the hearth. Never had any person in all of England's history needed a miracle as much as she did now. And every night, Lavinia told the north star as much as she closed her eyes and made her wish.

A log settled in the fireplace, making her jump. The heat of the fire made her drowsy as the boots stopped and the corridor grew quiet. As she drifted to sleep, a sixth sense jolted her awake, warning her of impending doom. She sat up, clutching the bedclothes to her chest.

Thump. Thump. Thump.

Lavinia slid from her bed on trembling limbs and crept toward her door. She knew the sound of those feet and squeezed her eyes shut in denial.

No!

Her heart lodged in her throat as she cracked her door open a sliver and waited with bated breath.

The sound echoed again, the most terrifying baritone she could imagine.

Papa's voice.

"My lord, you cannot simply go barging through the castle, opening chamber doors. If you return to the blue salon, I will inform Lady Lavinia of your arrival." Cecil's voice rose in volume as the clatter of boots thumped toward them.

They were here! Her parents were here!

"I remember where her chamber is. Get out of my way, idiot." Her father's voice pierced the air, spurring Lavinia into action like a skittish colt at the crack of a pistol. She didn't bother with a dressing gown or slippers. Flying out of her room, she dashed down the corridor and rounded the corner as her parents' voices approached.

Pressing her back to the wall, she swallowed the lump in her throat.

Where should she go? What should she do? Glancing down at her night rail and bare feet, she bit her lip in consternation. She would hide until she could sneak back to her chamber and dress. Forgetting about everything, including the duke's mandate to take a guard with her whenever she ventured outside, she focused on evading the more pressing problem. Papa.

Her heart beat a fast staccato, threatening to bounce from her chest in a frantic bid for freedom. Her lips were dry, and her entire body trembled with fear. They arrived early, catching her unprepared.

Her father's enraged expression, Hudson's sneer of contempt, and fear of their retribution sent her into a panic. Scanning her immediate surroundings for possible hiding places, her frantic gaze settled on the door to her right like a portal to her salvation.

Careful not to give her position away, she inched open the door and stepped inside, turning her back to the interior of the chamber. Leaving a sliver of space to peer out, she bit her lip. She would never concede to her father's matrimonial plans. If he found her, he could force her to marry the very devil if he so desired, and she could do nothing. Compliance, humility, subservience. The words made her stomach heave. They were everything society expected of a woman and something she would never give. Not to any man. Ever. And least of all, her father or Hudson.

The voices in the corridor grew louder, accompanied by the increasing rhythm of more boots on the polished wooden floors. They were coming! Oh God!

As she turned, her eyes caught on the blazing hearth,

casting flickering light across the chamber. Her gaze swung to the overstuffed velvet chair as the memory of her first night in the castle enveloped her.

The duke!

He had mistaken her intentions once before, believing she sought to ensnare him, and tossed her out on her ear. He would never believe a second time was anything other than deliberate.

And she knew well his thoughts on marriage.

The velvet chair sat alone before the blaze, to her great relief. Wiping hysteria from her brow, she ventured further into the room searching for a clever place to hide. Glancing at the heavy velvet drapes covering the long paned windows, she hurried over.

It never occurred to her to wonder why a fire blazed on the hearth in an unoccupied chamber until the door flung open and hit the opposite wall with a bang.

Startled, she gasped and turned as the added light from the hall flooded in, revealing the duke rising from the bed, naked from the waist up. The light danced along the ridges and valleys of his abdomen and chest, making her eyes grow wide. Long, lean, and sculpted to perfection, his muscle and sinew rolled beneath warm caramel skin as he tossed the bedclothes aside and slid to his feet. She gasped in alarm and then with relief when she discovered he wore a pair of buckskin-colored breeches.

Her gaze dropped in embarrassment. God, even his bare feet made her breathless with desire.

Caught like a deer in a snare, she gaped at the man, unable to tear her gaze away from his masculine perfection, flexing in the light as it licked and danced over his body. Her breath caught, her heart raced, and she stood transfixed, captivated by his near-naked state.

His dark gaze tangled with hers for a moment before he straightened to face the intruders.

Nausea rose in her throat, and her face flamed. She knew how this must look and knew better than anyone what Oliver would think of her.

"What the bloody hell is going on here?"

Her father's bellow of outrage and her mother's horrified gasp reverberated through the warm bedchamber.

Lavinia wished the thick rug beneath her feet would open up and swallow her whole. Frozen in horror, she kept her gaze averted, dreading the inevitable wrath.

Oliver would think she orchestrated this entire event. And despise her for it.

Her stomach dropped like a stone to the bottom of her feet, and she shivered with apprehension. Why couldn't she have chosen a different chamber? Or fled weeks ago? What he must think of her!

He stood at her side before she realized he had moved. His warmth enveloped her frozen form, and his scent made her tremble anew. He smelled like her last chance for freedom.

His hard, hot length beside her made her belly flutter with awareness and her palms sweat. In a different time and place, she would turn to him. But not now. Not when he hated her for their current predicament.

A thick, awkward silence hung in the air, and she squeezed her eyes closed dreading what would come next. Hatred, judgment, accusations, demands, marriage, and subservience.

Choking back a sob, she stiffened her spine. Waiting for the icy condemnation that would catapult her out of the castle and his life forever, she didn't expect his soft words.

"Lavinia, my darling, will you do me the great honor of being my wife and my duchess." Oliver's warm hand enveloped hers as he swiveled and dropped to one knee. "This isn't how I planned to ask, but the moment is upon us. I find I cannot imagine life without you, and your acceptance will make me the happiest of men."

Her mouth dropped open, disbelief flooding her as she stared into his piercing blue eyes, searching for sincerity. Was he truly asking for her hand, or did he jest? The damage would be to her reputation, not his. Her parents stood mere feet away, eager to see her wed another. What did he hope to accomplish with his offer of marriage? Studying his impassive expression, she bit her lip with indecision.

"I beg your pardon?" Lavinia swayed, hoping he would enlighten her with his plan of action.

But he merely gazed at her with one eyebrow quirked. "I asked for your hand, my dear."

Lavinia licked her dry lips and wrung her hands. This could not be real. He must be up to something. No confirmed bachelor in his thirties, especially not a powerful duke, awoke one day and said, "I think I will propose to someone today."

Stiffening her spine, she swallowed and waited for the inevitable rejection. Any second now, he would give her the same look he gave the others right before he banished them forever and tell her he never wanted to set eyes on her again. Faint with anxiety, she shifted her weight.

Warm fingers squeezed hers. "Well, darling?" His deep voice sent tremors through her body, and still, she refused to meet his gaze. "Will you answer me?"

Cold sweat broke out on her brow. He sounded sincere, but after weeks of hearing his disdain for marriage, she didn't believe he meant to go through with it.

Her father snapped out of his stupor. "Lavinia cannot marry you when she is already wed. We witnessed her marriage by proxy in London a fortnight ago before we traveled north to collect her. How dare you take advantage of the viscount's bride while she seeks refuge beneath her godmother's roof! I thought you to be a man of honor, Oliver, but I made a fatal mistake in trusting you with my daughter. I demand satisfaction!" The earl's face flushed purple as he glared down his nose at Oliver with fisted hands.

Married by proxy? The blood drained from Lavinia's face, and she trembled in earnest. How could such a thing be true? Fear turned to anger, and rebellion took control of her senses. Over her kicking, screaming, fit-throwing, dead body, would she accept such a fate with Viscount Becker. Thoughts of Hudson claiming her loosed her tongue as nothing else could. She gave the devil free reign, and damn the consequences.

"Yes, Oliver. I will marry you. And only you. I love you like no other." And may God have mercy on her soul, for anything, even his disdain, would be more pleasant than being at Hudson Becker's mercy. Or in his bed.

She couldn't be sure, but she thought the duke let out a breath at her acceptance.

Shooting him a quick glance, she read nothing in his expression.

Rising to his feet, the duke turned to Papa, ignoring

the older man's outburst. "And there you have it. Your daughter's virtue and future are secured. You have done your duty as a father. Now leave my bedchamber. Lavinia and I have much to discuss in private."

Her breath lodged in her throat as Oliver returned stare for stare with her father.

Neither of her parents moved.

"Really, Lavinia. You cannot have two husbands, dear. Now let go of His Grace's hand and come with us." Her mother's soft censure tugged at her heart.

Glancing down in consternation, she discovered she clasped his hand in a death grip and sighed. If her mother truly cared, she would obey in a heartbeat. But Mama's heart cared for one thing: her own preservation.

"No, Mother. I cannot let go. He is my salvation." And now, let the battle begin. Lifting her chin in defiance, she studied her parents' expressions as they digested her proclamation.

"As you are mine." Oliver lifted her hand and brushed his lips across her knuckles, making her jump in alarm. His brilliant blue eyes gazed into hers as if searching for the answer to a vexing question. Cupping her chin, he tilted her face to his. A strong finger caressed the side of her cheek while his warm breath blew against her eyelids. "I am the luckiest of men," he murmured.

Her gaze met the heat in his as he bent toward her. Hot desire and a wicked promise danced in his incredible eyes, overcoming the denial hovering on her lips. How could he play the lover when he must hate her for what she forced upon him?

Sensual energy pulsed from his body, surrounding her in a tantalizing haze. Her stomach tightened as he leaned closer. God help her, if he didn't stop, she might start believing in miracles.

Her heart slammed against her ribs in a fast staccato, and her knees were as weak as figgy pudding as she anticipated how far he would take this charade.

Drawing her against his broad chest, he delivered a quick, hard kiss. His breath warmed her ear, sending a rush of heat through her frozen body. "We have now sealed our engagement with a kiss."

She blinked, hoping she hadn't somehow lost her mind. Did no one act normal during a full moon?

"Enough! Release my daughter before I summon the constable. You have no right to make advances on another man's wife," Papa's voice boomed behind her, and she jumped a foot.

Oliver's gaze narrowed. Tucking her into his side with gentle hands, he tilted his head to gaze at her father. "And yet you do so often. Lavinia is mine and will remain so. You owe her an apology. And if you ever raise your voice to her again, I will thrash you. As for your claim that she is the viscount's bride by proxy, provide me with the priest's name. Perhaps she didn't make her feelings clear when she left that pompous peacock at the altar. But make no mistake, Mortimer; my fiancée, resides beneath *my* roof and has *my* protection. As for satisfaction, I know you don't demand so on Lavinia's behalf. You're a lousy shot and worse with a blade. So why posture? We both know I would win blindfolded, with one hand tied behind my back."

He *defended* her. A slight breeze wafting through the corridor could have knocked her down. Lavinia's mouth dropped open, and she tilted her head to stare up at him, hoping to make sense of this surreal situation. She expected to be tossed out of doors, not held close against the duke's heated length as he defended her to her parents. His stony expression gave none of his thoughts away, and she chewed the inside of her cheek while she waited to see how her father would react.

It took no time at all.

The earl exploded in a fit of temper. "Release my daughter! Lavinia is married to Viscount Becker, and she's coming with me. Her husband will be here any minute, and he's a much better shot than I."

The earl lifted a hand to take her by the arm, but Oliver's silky, soft voice stopped him mid-air. "If you touch her, I will send Cecil for my sword and run you through. And if you do not keep a civil tongue in your head, I will call in all my markers."

Silence fell like a heavy curtain.

Markers? What in heaven's name did he mean? Tremors started in her chest and reverberated through her entire body until she couldn't breathe. Swallowing the lump in her throat, she shook her head, hoping to process it all.

Papa would do or say anything to get his hands on the hundred acres. Even lie. And what kind of markers did Oliver hold over Papa's head? They must be significant because the earl froze in midair.

Her father's jaw dropped. "By God, you jackanape. You inject such a topic into *this affair*?"

"I do." Oliver's eyes flashed in the firelight, locked in a battle of wills with her father.

She stared at Papa in disbelief as all the blood drained from his face. Glancing to the left and then to the right as if searching for a means of escape, he swallowed hard before speaking in a hoarse voice. "You are no gentleman, Oliver."

"At last, we agree." The duke's quiet answer whispered past her ear, stirring her hair.

"I...er...I...regret my words, Lavinia." The earl stammered as he dropped his hand and took a step back.

She gaped in stupefaction, unable to move a muscle as the shock of seeing her father retreat left her speechless. Lord, she had to sit down before her knees gave out.

Sagging against the duke, she shook her head to clear her thoughts.

His arm tightened around her, giving her strength while his gaze remained locked on the earl.

Lavinia glanced at her mother and resisted the urge to giggle. The countess's mouth hung open, and her eyes were twice their normal size.

A heavy silence settled over the room until the duchess's voice broke the tension from the doorway.

"I am awakened in the dead of night by my butler informing me we have guests, and when I rise to greet them, I find everyone congregating in my son's bedchamber with my goddaughter clad in nothing but a night rail. How...unexpected. And eventful. And to think, I could have slept through it all."

The dry comment made Lavinia smile. The duchess valued her sleep and woe unto those unfortunate souls who disturbed her. This situation, however, must be the exception.

"By the silence, I assume something profound has occurred other than my son being caught half-naked with his arm around my goddaughter."

Madelaine choked, and the earl grunted, his earlier anger returning and rushing to his ruddy cheeks.

"Tell me, Cecil. Or I shall perish with curiosity."

While the two held a whispered conversation, Lavinia met her mother's gaze and faltered. They were wide with fear and surprise.

She offered a weak smile and glanced at Papa. What had the servants put in her tea at dinner to cause such hallucinations? Whatever the concoction, she must have more. Papa *never* apologized.

Cecil finished whispering, and the duchess turned her gaze to the earl.

"I do not believe a word of it. Marriage by proxy, indeed. What proof have you, Mortimer?" Arabella stared down her nose at Papa, and for the first time, Lavinia witnessed her godmother as the rest of the world saw her: haughty, proud, and formidable. A dragon. "You offend us all with your deceit. Now, leave before I have you thrown out on your backside." Fire flashed in her godmother's eyes, and her nails extended like talons.

Lavinia's chest tightened in trepidation. Good Lord, no wonder Victoria hesitated before making her acquaintance.

Oliver must have sensed her agitation, for he massaged gentle circles on her back with his free hand. "Who performed the ceremony?" His light tone suggested they were at tea making small talk rather than in a bedchamber discussing her future.

Closing her eyes, she gave in to the delicious pleasure, hoping to draw some of his strength. Papa frightened the life out of her and had since the day she came home from the convent.

The earl harrumphed with indignation. "Father Flannegan. Not that it's any of your business."

"I disagree. Lavinia and everything pertaining to her *is* my business. If Father Flannigan of High Street is the clergy in question, the ceremony isn't valid. He lost his license over a year ago. I may live in the far north, Mortimer, but I *am* well informed."

She could hear her father's spine straighten and quiver in earnest. He wouldn't like Oliver calling his bluff and flinched when the earl lifted his hand in a gesture of unconcern. "I have the certificate in my hands and am prepared to take this before the House of Lords."

Oliver shot her a glance and frowned, tucking her tighter against his side. "Then it is worthless and fraudulent. Everyone in the House of Lords knows about Father Flannigan. If this wedding by proxy were valid, you wouldn't be standing in my bed chamber. You'd be on your country estate overseeing a new fence around your re-acquired hundred acres, and Viscount Becker would be in London spending Lavinia's generous dowry. Neither of you is here out of concern for Lavinia nor her feelings. Save your posturing and threats for someone else."

"But…You've destroyed any chance I have of regaining the land. I demand to be compensated." The earls' voice shook the rafters in the castle attic. "I've lost everything." His gaze swung to her, and Lavinia's blood drained to her soles.

More enraged than she'd ever seen him, he shouted his accusations. "This is *your* fault! You were not content with causing the scandal of the century by leaving Hudson at the altar. Now, you plot to keep my property from me."

"Enough! Cecil, see, the earl is escorted from the castle and my lands. He is no longer welcome here." Icy, cold eyes the color of thunder stared the older man down, and Lavinia shivered to the bottom of her bare feet. May

Oliver never stare at her with such cold contempt.

"You will never speak to Lavinia again unless she invites you to, and only then when I am present. Now leave before I give in to my anger and thrash you as I promised."

The earl hurried from the room, and the countess turned to follow.

"You, Madame, may stay so long as you are civil to my wife-to-be." Squeezing Lavinia's side, he waited for her mother to answer.

"Of course, Your Grace. And thank you." She gave her a smile and, in a brave moment, hurried over and kissed her cheek despite how close she had to get to the duke to do so. "Thank God you are safe. Good night, dear."

Lavinia's stomach swirled. "Good night, Mother."

With a wicked glint, the duchess took Madelaine's arm with a parting comment for her son. "What a fortuitous night. I am reunited with dear Madelaine, obtained the daughter-in-law I thought I would never have, *and* won our bet—all within hours. See, things are proper, will you, Cecil? Now come along, Madelaine. Let's have a nice cup of tea. You must be weary from your long drive."

Their voices floated off as they walked away and Cecil, with a raised eyebrow, stood in the door with his arms folded. "Ye may be affianced, but yer not married. Come with me, Lady Lavinia. You will see His Grace tomorrow."

Chapter Nineteen

Lavinia woke with a start and sat up as all the events of the previous night flooded back to her. What if Oliver regretted his proposal and tossed her from the castle? She knew his feelings on matrimony, and they were well and truly caught last night with her in her night rail and he in bed half-naked. Her belly sank as she traced the outline of a flower on the satin coverlet with her finger.

On the one hand, his offer solved her immediate problem of marrying Hudson. She would be a duchess, and in the northernmost region of England, the odds of encountering her parents or the viscount were slim. But at what cost? And could she endure the price of the duke's disdain, or did she trade a difficult situation for a worse one?

What did one call heaven and hell at once? Heaven because she would be with Oliver as his wife, but hell because she craved his approval, his touch, and his love. An emotional state she noted never crossed his lips the night before, even after her proclamation. While anger, resentment, and contempt for trapping him were the expected reaction.

Sinking back against the mound of feather pillows and tucking her silk bedclothes up to her chin, she re-lived Oliver's demand for Papa to apologize.

A satisfied smile carved her lips, and her chest filled with sweet, intoxicating solace as she remembered the way he stumbled through the words. Her father wouldn't like Oliver's demand and would concoct some plan to get revenge. But my, how delightful the memory.

Her thoughts were interrupted when Annie burst into her chamber. "Oh, my lady, the servants have been talking about yer romantic night all morning. I couldn't wait to come in and wish ye my best. I am so happy for ye! Ye will make a beautiful duchess, and His Grace is lucky to have ye."

Lavinia hoped with all her heart the duke felt the same way because she spoke the truth when she confessed her love for him. And vowed to never do so again.

Unrequited love was the most pathetic state a woman could entertain, and vulnerability did not sit well with her.

Smiling and nodding at Annie's chatter while she helped her dress, she took a deep breath of courage as she opened her chamber door and walked down the stairs to breakfast. With her heart in her throat and uncertainty dampening her brow, she swallowed her terror of facing her parents again. Pausing outside the breakfast room, she pinched her cheeks for color and squared her shoulders for battle.

"Good morning." Oliver's deep voice startled her from behind.

Unsure of how to respond, she sucked in a deep breath and turned to meet his dark gaze. "Good morning."

"I believe a morning kiss is in order. "

She opened her mouth to protest, but her words were silenced as he caught her to him and covered her lips with a lingering kiss. His hot mouth coaxed hers open so he could slide his tongue inside to mate with hers. Forgetting everything but the way he made her feel, she gave in to his tender assault.

Lemon, sage, and warm male surrounded her, and the touch of his hands sent her spiraling in an intoxicating sensual haze that turned her knees to molasses.

Hard, strong arms tightened around her, drawing her close to his heated length as he tilted her head to the side to deepen his kiss.

Languid desire warmed her blood to quicksilver, and she moaned with pleasure.

"Good heavens, Lavinia, what are you doing?" Mama's shocked voice spoke behind them, and she flinched in Oliver's arms.

"Such shocking behavior will tarnish your less than spotless reputation further. Do you want to be known as a lightskirt?"

"Be careful how you address my intended, Madame, or you will be sent to stay in the village with your husband." The duke released her and turned to stare at her mother.

Mama froze and cast a quick glance at the duke. Smoothing her disapproval into a mask of indifference, she cleared her throat. "I, er, apologize, Lavinia. I have no wish to stay in the village, Your Grace. I am content to remain here and keep my views silent."

"Then you may remain. Please, join us." The duke motioned for her mother to proceed as he tucked Lavinia's cold, trembling hand through the crook in his arm. "Shall we, my dear?"

Casting a quick assessing glance at his smiling face, she nodded as they strolled into the breakfast room, her legs wobbling the entire distance. Twice in as many days, he defended her to her parents and forced them to apologize. She stared straight ahead and focused on putting one foot in front of the other until he held her chair out with a small smile. "My dear."

"Thank you." Lavinia sank down with a breath of relief, uncertain how much longer her shaking legs could hold her. Smoothing her skirt, she kept her gaze down while she fought for control.

Today must not be the day he planned to banish her, which meant another day of freedom with the added benefit of his company. And for the moment, it was enough.

Breakfast passed in a blur, and more than once, she caught the duke's assessing gaze resting on her face.

Forcing a smile in return, she would take a sip of tea or ask for another helping of coddled eggs. Anything to keep her mind busy and her heart from reading too much into his attention.

Arabella invited them to her salon following breakfast to go over the final details for the Christmas Ball, and Oliver offered his arm with a slight bow.

Her hand trembled on his arm, and she tilted her chin up in false bravado, determined to get through this day with her emotions intact. Surreal and frightening, she never imagined a world where her parents apologized and Oliver acted the part of a lover.

And she had no idea how to respond to any of it.

She could handle her parents' disinterest and antagonism, but Oliver's affectionate behavior was a different matter altogether.

He played the doting fiancé better than he did in her midnight fantasies. If she did not proceed with extreme caution, her heart would believe his tender words and loving glances.

And then where would she be?

Several times, Lavinia pinched her side to see if she dreamed or if this impossible situation was real. Each time she turned to glance up at the duke, she found his gaze on her with an unreadable expression.

He never ventured far from her side all day, and she counted the hours as a condemned man counts his remaining time on earth with gratitude and with dread.

After they finished making plans with the duchess, Oliver invited her for a stroll out on the balcony, and she nodded, going tense.

"This is where he explains he has no plans to continue their engagement once the Christmas Ball ended and her parents returned to London." The voice in her head mocked her as she followed him out the double doors.

But instead of saying a word, he swept her into his arms for a thorough kiss. For long minutes, she gave into the pleasure of his touch until he lifted his head and tucked her face into the crook of his neck.

"I have been anticipating this moment all morning. Every time you glanced at me or gave me your beautiful smile, I envisioned escorting you out here and kissing your sweet lips until we were both breathless." His warm breath blew against her cheek, and she shivered with pleasure.

This had to stop before her heart threw off the chains of loneliness and believed in forever. Wiggling out of his embrace, she took a step back. "There is no audience here, Oliver. I know how you feel about matrimony, and I know how you must feel about being trapped." She took a deep breath. If he intended to break their engagement, she would rather know now before any more chains slipped off her heart. "I must know the real reason you asked for my hand. My reputation is in shreds by my own doing, and so your proposal cannot be for my sake. We both swore we'd never marry, and I require honesty. If you plan to dispose of me when my parents leave for London and the danger is over, I will have the truth now."

Oliver's lids dropped over his eyes, covering his expression. "Is it so hard for you to believe I asked for your hand because I wish you to be mine? You respond to my touch like strings on a musical instrument, and I yearn to immerse my body in yours. You will be my wife, Lavinia, on Christmas Day. Make no mistake."

She gaped in amazement. "But I trapped you, and I know how you feel about marriage. You've banished several young ladies for putting you in the same situation."

Or almost. None of them were caught in their night rails with the duke in bed half-dressed.

"Have I? Then you must know I plan to banish *us* to the master chamber for a solid week following the ceremony. I find the more I think about marriage, the more agreeable the topic becomes." His dark gaze dropped to the swell of her breasts visible above her tight neckline.

Heat filled her cheeks. "But you don't like women."

His lids lowered, shielding his expression. "You are mistaken, my dear. I like them very much, and you more than most. I will possess you, Lavinia. The desire to do so is a raging fire fueling my blood. We shall wed on Christmas Day."

Passion shivered down her spine at the images his words created. For the first time since her skirts dropped, she didn't feel unworthy. She felt alluring and enticing. Her breath came fast, and her heart pounded high in her chest. But reason whispered doubt as she struggled with the change in him from the previous day.

Oliver said nothing about love.

Her mind raced with worry and stopped as the rest of his speech penetrated the haze in her mind. She gaped. He planned to marry her on Christmas. Why so soon? Did he jest?

She must have asked the question aloud, for he answered in a deep voice. "No, my dear, I do not jest. Cecil has his instructions." Tilting her chin up, he gazed down at her with an impassive expression.

Not sure how to deal with the way her heart raced and her blood sang, she asked, "Does the duchess know you plan to wed on Christmas Day? Last night she acted as surprised by your proposal as my parents."

He gave a slight shake of his head. "I did not include her in my decision because I knew she would gloat when she won the bet, and I do have a little pride. Now she is aware of my proposal and your acceptance, she can add the finishing touches."

He used the words want, desire, and hunger, assuring her he would make her his. Her chin dropped as she sucked in a deep breath. Being his duchess and sharing his bed would be the pinnacle of her existence, for she had no doubt he would make the physical aspect of their union unforgettable. But without love, would his passion be enough to weather the storm? Or would she end up in a loveless union like her mother?

They were interrupted by Victoria's furious voice.

"I wish to see Lavinia."

Frustrated, she frowned at the closed doors leading into the salon. Did everyone travel to Falstone together? The road must have been quite congested.

Her mother's voice rang out. "How dare you come here and demand to see my daughter. I shall ring for the servants to throw you out before the duchess discovers your perfidy."

The click of heels on the stone floor of the corridor quickened as they came closer and then grew muffled as Victoria stepped onto the thick Persian rug covering the salon floor.

"Out of my way. My dearest friend is in danger, and she needs me. I shall not hesitate to use my force if needful."

"Get out of my sight, you strumpet." Her mother's furious voice rose several octaves from within the salon.

"Lavinia!" Victoria sounded frantic, and Lavinia called back.

"I'm here." She shot a glance at Oliver and dipped a curtsy. "Please excuse me. I must go before they come to blows."

"We will finish this conversation later." Taking her elbow, he led her back inside. "Allow me."

Lavinia flushed and stepped through the door the duke held open to face the brewing storm.

Victoria stood in the center of the salon with her hands on her hips. Her flushed cheeks and darting eyes spoke of frustration and anger.

Her mother stood in front of the hearth with a thunderous, indignant expression and one hand on the bell to ring for the servants.

The duchess strolled in the salon with Princess at her

heels and a hovering Cecil. "Lady Beaumont is my guest, Madelaine." The duchess's gaze glittered with icy censure as she approached the settee. Her tone held a hint of steel. "And she will be treated as such."

An awkward silence followed as Mama's gaze swung between the two women. Then, her shoulders drooped in defeat. "Of course, Arabella. If you will excuse me, I shall remain in my chambers." Dipping a stiff curtsy, the countess sniffed, replaced the bell on the mantle, and swept from the room.

No one challenged the duchess, not even Mama.

Victoria's gaze fell on the two of them before the double doors, and her eyes widened. Tilting her head, she grinned. "I thought you in mortal danger and rushed halfway across England to rescue you, only to find trouble of a different sort. Tell me, Lavinia. Do I slit him from nose to navel or retreat and unpack my formal gown I brought along for your wedding." Her eyes crinkled with laughter.

"Hello, Victoria." Running across the distance, separating them, she gave her friend a hug. And then drew back. "What danger? Have you word on Marlboro?" Her heart rate accelerated, and the room seemed to spin around her.

The duke's men were unable to find any trace of him following her adventure in the forest. And the thought of him alive, lurking in the shadows for another chance to abduct her, made her dizzy with terror.

Victoria shook her head. "I came to warn you about your parents and the viscount. But they beat me here by half a day. The half I would have made effective use of had the earl not accused me of thievery to the local magistrate. The constable refused to allow me to continue until I sorted out the matter of the true owner of my carriage." She lifted her chin, and fire danced beneath the surface of polite conversation. "Thank heavens Arthur had the foresight to make out a legal paper of ownership before he left for France."

"I am sorry, Victoria." Papa spent a good deal of time and effort making Victoria miserable. And Lavinia furious.

Her friend shook her head and squared her shoulders. "'Tis naught but an irritation." She was generous in her forgiveness, and they both knew why.

Arthur.

Victoria couldn't love him and not care for his parents despite their hostility. "In any event, Viscount Becker has a room at the inn in the village. You are rumored to be getting married in three days' time, and my investigator informs me Marlboro is in Falstone. I gave my word to deliver any news and came as soon as I could."

"I did not believe Hudson traveled north to Falstone when Papa said as much last night. He would do and say anything to gain the land. Thank you for coming, Victoria." She tucked her hands behind her back to hide their trembling. Hudson and Papa were both here, which meant one thing. They planned to force a marriage by any means necessary.

Cecil appeared at the open door. "May I have a word with you, Your Grace?" He shot a glance at Lavinia and tilted his head toward the duke's study.

"Of course." Oliver nodded. "If you ladies will excuse me?" With a slight inclination of his dark head, he left.

The duchess made polite conversation for a few

minutes, inviting Victoria to join her for tea and inquiring about her journey before she rose to her feet. "If you will excuse me, I must inform the staff we have another guest."

"Your Grace," They dipped curtsies as she swept from the room.

Silence fell as Arabella's slippers clicked on the stone floor and then disappeared around the corner of the corridor.

"What have you been doing all this time, I wonder?" Victoria's grin stretched from ear to ear. "I leave you for a couple of months and come back to find you out on the balcony enjoying a tete-a-tete with the duke. What happened to your aversion to marriage? Or did His Grace seduce you into compliance?"

"I wouldn't use the word seduce or compliance." Lavinia closed the salon door and filled Victoria in on all the happenings since her departure.

"And you let a handsome Scot slip through your fingers without so much as a kiss?" Clucking her tongue in disapproval, Victoria removed her gloves and placed them on the settee beside her. "I fear you are losing your taste for adventure."

Lavinia shrugged. "He refused to cooperate. But he did give me this as a token of his appreciation." She plucked the medallion from between her breasts and held it out for Victoria to see. "A favor for a favor, he said." Tucking the round metal object back under the neck of her day gown, she smiled at her friend. "Wallace is handsome all right, but he has a mind of his own. You should hear his voice when he says *English*. You'd think we invented the Black Plague, and associating with us would expose him to the disease."

Her friend nodded. "I've been worried about you. Liv. But I see I shouldn't have been. I hoped your mother's cousin would invite you across the border, but marrying the duke is a much better option."

"Yes." She fiddled with the lace edging the front of her gown. "Oliver doesn't wish to marry. I did the very thing he's avoided for years. I trapped him. Last night happened so fast I didn't have a chance to think. I said 'yes' to irritate Papa. Now, I'm worried Oliver will change his mind before Christmas and break off our engagement." Her heart clutched at the thought, and she shook her head in response. "I'm happy you're here. With Papa and Hudson close by, I may need a quick escape."

"Nonsense." Victoria rose to her feet and walked around to sit beside Lavinia. Taking her cold hand in her warmer ones, she smiled. "I saw your faces when you walked in from the balcony. You can fool everyone else but not me. You love him. And he loves you."

Lord, she hoped so. But then unicorns were never more than a figment of someone's vivid imagination, either. "How can you tell? He has not said the words."

Her friend gave a dainty shrug of her shoulders. "I see it in your eyes and hear it in your voice. He makes you breathless. Your heart pounds in your chest when he draws near, and your palms sweat. You want to touch him so much, your fingers tingle. Every second of every day, he fills your thoughts, and you cannot wait until you see him again. Do you have fluttering wings in your stomach when he kisses you?"

"Yes." She did whenever she thought about him and his kisses.

"There, you see? And he feels the same. His eyes

never leave you. When you smile, he does, too. I'm happy we brought you here for your and the duke's sake. But something must be done about the viscount and Marlboro."

The door opened, and Oliver strolled back inside. "I agree. I think it best if you stay inside until after we are wed, Lavinia. Extra guards will be posted in the corridor, at every entrance, and I've increased the number patrolling the grounds." Casting a glance at Victoria, he smiled. "I am relieved you are here and have a favor to ask. Would you be receptive to sleeping in Lavinia's chamber until the wedding so she is never alone?"

Her heart rose to her throat. "There has been a new threat?"

His gaze met hers, and she swallowed.

"Becker is here, just as Victoria said. He and the earl are boasting of marrying you Christmas Day. The two have been inseparable since your father left the castle." He paused. "I thought to cancel the Christmas Ball tonight, but Mother assures me it is far too late. Too many guests have arrived, with more to follow. Some have traveled all the way from London. I have agreed to allow the ball to continue on one condition. You must stay with either Victoria or me at all times. I want your word, Lavinia. And this time, you will keep it."

When she nodded, he glanced at Victoria. "I will have yours, too."

Her friend grinned. "We shall do as you instruct, Your Grace."

"Whatever they have planned, they will not succeed. And if you will excuse me once more, I must give orders to finalize the details for tonight."

She did not see Oliver again until much later when

she and Victoria gave their curtsies to the duchess in the grand ballroom.

Chapter Twenty

Lavinia sensed Oliver behind her a moment before his clean male scent enveloped her in a rush of excitement.

Ignoring her fluttering belly and shaking knees, she caught the skirt of her pink silk ballgown and dipped a curtsy to the duchess. With her chin down, she sucked in a calming breath to steady her nerves. Social occasions made her jittery, and amid the festive grandeur of Arabella's Christmas Ball, her tension heightened.

With Hudson and Papa mere miles away in the village and Marlboro unaccounted for, she had every reason to be on edge.

Victoria nudged her with an elbow and gave her a cheeky grin. "He's here." Her stage whisper carried further than she intended, drawing several curious glances their way.

"I know," Lavinia whispered back. Her over-sensitive nerves sent tingles through her body when the duke got within a hundred yards of her. "We...acknowledged each other when I entered the ballroom."

Arabella's eyebrow rose as she gave the girls a regal nod. "Is that what you did? I had to order a cool drink after seeing the two of you...greet each other. You look lovely tonight, Lavinia. And you as well, Victoria. Ah, Oliver, there you are. Why are you frowning? You appear as though someone stole your favorite horse. I do not pretend to know what put you in a foul mood already, but I will not tolerate you ruining my ball. Here stands Lady Lavinia, the loveliest woman present, and Lady Beaumont, a close second. And they both lack partners. Why don't you take them around and introduce them to the other lords in attendance before I am trampled with a bevy of bachelors anxious to make their acquaintance."

"No. Mother, I will not."

The duke's deep voice sent a shiver of awareness down her spine. But his quick denial made Lavinia flush, and for a moment, she wondered if Oliver had come to his senses.

Victoria read her expression and shook her head. "He's taking note of all the male attention you're receiving. Every man in the ballroom is staring at you."

Her face heated. "Are they?" Casting a quick glance to her left, she frowned when three gentlemen raised their glasses in greeting.

"Half the men are gaping and angling for an introduction. The other half are denying they do to their wives and sweethearts." Victoria's laughter made her wince. 'You are the belle of the ball, dearest."

"Me?" Lavinia stiffened when she glanced in the other direction, and more gentlemen nodded. How did one act in such a situation?

A low growl stirred the tendrils of hair caressing the back of her neck as the dukes' hands rose to cup her shoulders in a gesture of ownership. "Pay no attention to Lady Beaumont."

"Why not you? The gentlemen guests cannot take their eyes off you." Her friend's eyes danced with mischief as she shot a glance at the duke. "I think it must be the neckline of your gown. You look quite delectable, Liv. Don't you think so, Your Grace? The last time I wore a low square cut such as the one you have on, Arthur proposed."

"She would be irresistible," the duke drawled, "if she left off the Scot's damn trinket." His deep voice dripped with irritation.

Lavinia swallowed, ensuring the medallion stayed concealed beneath the neckline of her gown and the silver chain alone remained visible. "'Twas not my intention to, er, draw male attention. What shall I do?" Biting her lip, she folded her arms over her chest and took a step back in retreat.

"Not a thing, my dear." The duchess gave her a wide smile. "Men will be men, after all, and Oliver cannot control who looks at you and who doesn't."

"The hell I can't." He turned to glare at every man in sight. "I am the one she pledged her troth to."

The duchess's eyes twinkled, although her expression remained neutral. "Then make your announcement and be done with it. But I am disappointed. I hoped Lavinia could enjoy the ball for an hour or so before you made your claim. 'Tis such a shame to waste all this mistletoe."

"She shall enjoy the mistletoe with me. Let the gentlemen guests find their own partners." Blue fire shot from his gaze, and he motioned for Cecil.

The butler nodded and strolled toward the orchestra as if by a prearranged plan. The music stopped a moment later.

In an undertone, Oliver shot his mother an amused glance. "Are you never satisfied, Mother? First, you scheme to see me wed in the most outrageous fashion, and now you complain because my fiancée has not had a chance to kiss your gentlemen guests. She has accepted my proposal, and I see no reason to delay the inevitable. If my wishes were considered, we would be wed by now. Thereby eliminating the reason the viscount lingers in the north. I cannot abide the fop."

Of course. He proposed out of some chivalrous sense of duty and not because he wanted her. Opening her mouth to voice her thoughts, the duchess put a hand on her arm and nodded toward the glittering ballroom. "Later, my dear."

Cecil tapped his staff on the tile floor to get the guests' attention. "May I present your host, His Grace, the Duke of Chauncy."

With hooded eyes, Oliver stood tall and proud, gazing out at the sea of faces raised with expectation to his.

"My dear ladies and gentlemen." His voice carried with authority and warmth. "First, I extend a warm welcome to Chauncy Castle and bid you eat, drink, and make merry on this festive occasion. My mother delights in hosting lavish parties, and tonight holds a special significance for us." He turned with a slight smile, taking Lavinia's gloved hand in his and drawing her to his side.

Her heart slammed into her ribs as she felt the weight of countless eyes upon her. Her knees knocked together, and her breath caught in her throat.

Oliver's warm fingers squeezed her icy ones, and through the layers of cloth, she trembled at his touch.

"It is with immense pleasure that I announce my betrothal to Lady Lavinia Holbrook." Oliver's voice remained steady despite the stir in the crowd. " I invite you all now to share in the joy of this auspicious occasion with us. We are overwhelmed with happiness and extend our invitation to each of you to join us for our wedding ceremony, which shall take place at ten in the morning on Christmas Day at the village cathedral."

A murmur rippled through the crowd and several older ladies gasped. Two younger ladies burst into tears and ran from the room, one of them Lady Elspeth.

Lavinia sucked in a shaky breath and glanced at Victoria, who shrugged in response.

Her attention snapped back to the duke when he lifted her hand and unbuttoned her glove.

Her hand trembled, and her knees quaked at the intimate contact. "What are you doing?" Heat filled her cheeks as the crowd leaned forward, anxious to see more.

"This." The duke removed her glove one finger at a time, captivating their audience and increasing her embarrassment.

On bended knee, he retrieved a magnificent diamond ring from the pocket of his embroidered vest and slipped it over her third finger. Vivid blue eyes met hers, and something passed between them before he glanced away. "May I present Lady Lavinia Holbrook, soon to be the Duchess of Chauncy, and my wife." Raising her hand, he placed a warm, lingering kiss on her bare knuckle.

Her breath hitched in response, and her heart slammed into her ribs. Keeping her gaze on his dark hair, she focused on getting control of her body. Why play the lover before their vast audience? His every action bordered on indecent, and she flushed to the bottom of her glittering slippers.

Every eye in the ballroom rested on her face, and she licked her dry lips in response. If Oliver didn't cease taking liberties in public, they would all assume the worst. That he compromised her and thus they were forced into a hurried union.

Heat filled her cheeks, and she cast a helpless glance at Victoria, who stood three feet behind her, grinning like a fool. Shouldn't she be whisking her away and helping her get control of her feelings? Where were all her sensible words of wisdom?

Thank heavens Oliver took pity on her a moment later, and his mask of indifference returned.

The crowd murmured with approval when he rose to his feet and presented Lavinia's hand for their inspection. "She has made me the happiest of men, and I invite you all to celebrate our union. My mother has prepared a bevy of delights for this evening. I wish you all an enjoyable time, and once again, welcome."

Cecil nodded to the orchestra and waved his hands to disperse the guests. "Dinner will commence at half past eight in the dining hall. Enjoy!"

The guests turned away, murmuring with excitement and casting curious gazes back at their host.

Lavinia longed to sink into a chair and allow her shaking body a moment to recover.

But the duchess leaned forward and touched her arm. "Go dance with my son, Lavinia. He has the look of a predator ready to pounce, and I cannot risk him ruining my Christmas Ball."

The heat of his body beside her made her legs turn to jelly, and after the duchess's droll remark about predators, she refused to lift her gaze to his. When she turned to dip a curtsy to Madelaine at Arabella's right, a pang of concern gripped her.

Although draped in forest green velvet, with every

hair tucked in place, and wearing the duchess's emerald jewels, her mother sat perched on the edge of her satin seat as if poised for flight. A frown creased her brow, and she bit her lip as she gazed everywhere but at Lavinia.

"Mother." Her gaze dropped to the countess's lap, where she held a lace fan in a death grip.

Her greeting drew her mother's gaze. "Lavinia." She paled and turned her face away, scanning the crowd as if seeking someone.

How odd. Without Papa here charming the women hoping to find a new mistress, whom could she be seeking?

Victoria dipped a curtsy beside her. "Countess."

Her mother tilted her chin up and away with thinning lips, refusing to acknowledge Victoria. She may not like Victoria, but she would not say anything unkind while in Arabella's presence.

"My dear, shall we join the next set?" Oliver's deep voice sent shivers down her spine. The way he whispered endearments made her forget he performed an act to conceal the truth behind their engagement. Closing her eyes for a second, she allowed her heart one small Christmas wish that he meant the words and considered her his darling.

"Lavinia?"

His husky voice made her heart leap, and her eyes flew open.

"Of course." Giving him a winning smile, she placed her hand on his arm and allowed him to lead her to the floor, forgetting all about her mother's odd behavior.

No amount of magic in this realm or any other could compare with the wonder of being held close in Oliver's arms. As the music flowed around them, he slid his hand around her waist to rest against her lower back. His touch sent shivers through her, and her mouth went dry.

Lacing the fingers of his other hand with hers, he clasped her to his long, lean body, and Lavinia thought she might faint.

Releasing her hand, his long, lean fingers closed around the chain at her neck, withdrawing the medallion from between her breasts. With half-closed eyes, he leaned close to whisper in her ear. "When you are mine, the only jewels you will wear will be mine. The only kisses you will receive shall be mine, and the only man you dream of will be me." Tucking the medallion back beneath the tight neckline of her gown, his fingers brushed the swell of her breasts, causing her breath to hitch.

"Are we agreed?" Intent blue eyes searched her face.

No other man would ever stir her heart or thrill her body as he did.

"Yes." Her body vibrated with the urge to draw closer, and she sighed, unable to resist the pull in his gaze or the way his body called to hers. If this were all a performance for those in attendance, she would savor every moment.

Standing a head taller than any other man in the ballroom, he stood out in perfect masculine form. His black tailored evening jacket hugged his broad shoulders and tapered along the lean lines of his abdomen. Black linen trousers covered his muscular legs and polished, buckled shoes gleamed under the massive golden chandeliers overhead. A royal blue vest embroidered with gold mirrored the color of his eyes, drawing attention to his square jaw and firm lips. A lock of black hair fell on his broad forehead as he leaned close to whisper in her ear.

"I concur with my mother. You are the loveliest woman here."

Her lips parted as his warm breath blew against the side of her neck, and she shivered with awareness. The ballroom and all the guests faded away, leaving her enveloped by his intoxicating scent, his solid embrace, and the heat of his lean body.

Her breath quickened, and her heart raced as she surrendered to the sensual rhythm of their dance.

They joined the next three sets without pause, and Lord, did she relish every moment she spent in his arms.

Giving in to her growing desire to get closer, she leaned into his embrace and drowned in his deep blue eyes. Mere inches separated them, and her palms grew moist, tingling with the need to stroke his warm, hard flesh. Licking her dry lips, she dropped her gaze to his chest, recalling how he looked rising from the bed without his shirt on. So many ridges, planes, and dips begging for her to explore them in intimate detail.

A soft groan escaped her, and she flushed.

"If you do not stop undressing me with your eyes, I shall summon the priest and wed you this night. You hold the advantage, having glimpsed my bare chest, but you neglect to recall I've seen yours as well."

Her breath caught in her throat, and her feet quit moving. Shock held her still as her mind raced. "When?" As soon as the words left her lips, she knew. *He* was her ministering angel the night she fevered. Red-hot embarrassment surged up her neck, heating her cheeks. Dropping her chin, she focused on her feet, hoping a witty response would drop from the gilded ceiling and rescue her.

Oliver lifted her chin and smiled into her eyes. "You have nothing to be ashamed of. Your breasts captivate me and appear quite often in my dreams."

Clamping her mouth closed, she shook her head in denial. They were ordinary and too full for the current fashion. Hudson commented on the fact several times.

Glancing around with concern, she checked to see if anyone nearby had overheard their inappropriate conversation.

"Victoria and my mother are preoccupied, so they did not witness your lustful thoughts nor garner the nature of our conversation." Oliver chuckled when she gasped and whisked her out of harm's way as another couple twirled too close.

"I am sorry for staring at you in such a manner when you were…unclothed." The lie fell from her lips like cream from a tart.

His grin widened. "Don't be, my sweet. Soon, we shall be together day and night. And the nights…those I dream about, too. Soon, we shall know each other's bodies as we know our own." Dark hooded eyes, dropped to her lips and then back to hers with such intensity she tripped once more.

"I do not believe I can remember the steps if you keep making improper remarks. My head goes one way and my feet another. I know this is all an act to convince the crowd of our mutual affection, but you must show some restraint, or I shall end up in a heap on the floor." Deep blue eyes gazed into hers, heating her blood to liquid fire.

"You believe this to be an act?" He circled her around the floor and stopped a few feet in front of the balcony doors. "Shall we adjourn to the balcony? I require privacy to convince you of my sincerity." Leaning closer than acceptable, she trembled as he turned her toward the double doors.

Desire darkened his gaze and stained his cheeks as he whispered. "Your mouth is nectar to my soul, and I intend to savor every drop until you no longer doubt my passion for you."

Her breath quickened as she envisioned his lips moving over hers, and on trembling legs, she placed her hand in his.

"Your Grace, Her Grace requests your presence." Cecil's stoic voice interrupted their conversation, drawing their attention to the duchess seated on a white satin settee.

Oliver paused and glanced at his mother. "Of course." Squeezing Lavinia's fingers, he guided her back through the ballroom.

Suppressing her disappointment, Lavinia lowered her gaze and took a deep, shuddering breath to calm her racing heart.

"Soon." He whispered close to her ear, and his promise raced down her neck, sending a million wings fluttering in her belly.

As they approached, the duchess tilted her head, and a smile of satisfaction tugged at her lips. "I apologize for interrupting, Oliver. What *were* you two doing out there?" She gestured toward the ballroom floor with one eyebrow raised.

"We were dancing, Mother." Oliver stopped a foot away from where the duchess held court and waited.

"I see. Does anyone know the name of this mysterious dance where the gentleman holds the lady entirely too close, and they occupy the same square throughout the entire set? I do not think you did more than sway and stare into each other's eyes. In my day, you would have been challenged to a duel for being so intimate." A shimmer of approval danced in her eyes despite her speech. "And since her father is not here, and I am ten thousand pounds richer because of your fascination with Lavinia, I shall remain quiet."

The duke tilted his head in acknowledgment. "*Touché,* Mother. Now, why did you summon me? My fiancée and I have a pressing engagement."

She sighed and indicated Lavinia's mother who slumped in her chair. "Which will have to wait. Madelaine is not feeling well and refuses any help other than Lavinia's. She wishes to retire."

"Ah." Oliver nodded. His gaze swung to the countess, and he sighed. "I will allow my fiancée to accompany her mother under two conditions. First, she must respect Lavinia's position in this castle, and second, she must allow Victoria to accompany them. Either Victoria or I must be at Lavinia's side until the wedding."

Disappointment welled up Lavinia's chest. Of all the times her mother could have requested her help and didn't, why did she insist on it now?

"Well?" Arabella glanced at the countess. "Do you accept my son's terms? My offer to go with you still stands but if you prefer Lavinia, you must accept Victoria as well."

Madelaine nodded and extended her hand to Lavinia. "Forgive me, child. I have no choice but to retire."

Lavinia frowned at the odd choice of words, but her

mother's pale face and trembling hands took precedence. With a sigh of regret, she smiled at Oliver and slipped an arm around her mother's waist while Victoria did the same on her other side. For once, her mother accepted her friend without comment.

Together, they navigated the length of the ballroom, up the stairs, and down the long corridor to the stairs leading up to the guest chambers.

The countess stopped at the bottom and swayed. "Could you...take me to the salon? I am too weary to climb the stairs and must rest for a moment." Madelaine's voice trembled, and her knees buckled.

Both Victoria and Lavinia steadied her as they turned to enter the salon, crossing the room in slow steps, Madelaine gave a cry when they approached the settees.

"Of course. Fresh, cool air. Why didn't I think of it before? When my weakness attacked me as a child, my mother would take me for a stroll in the garden, and I would be better within minutes." She glanced at Lavinia with pleading eyes." Could you take me out into the duchess's garden for a few moments? I feel sure after a moment or two in the cold air, I will feel better and can retire without further assistance."

Lavinia frowned as she glanced from her mother's pale face to the double doors. "I didn't know you had such a weakness, Mama." She guided her mother forward and clasped the handle to the door.

"Oh yes, but I haven't had an episode in years. Your sisters used to help me then. You were too young to remember." Madelaine shifted her feet, and they exited the study onto the garden terrace.

"Help me to the bench, child." Her mother indicated a curved metal seat twenty feet away.

Victoria said nothing, but her gaze swung around to Lavinia's with alarm. "Where are the guards?"

Awareness settled over Lavinia like a moonless night, dark, sinister, and very wrong. "I don't know."

"Something is wrong, Mama. We must go back inside." She never had a chance to say more, for Marlboro's face appeared before her terrified eyes.

He wore Oliver's colors.

Speechless with horror, she turned to her mother, but he caught her arm and jerked her up against him until inches separated their faces.

Grinning, his eyes snapped with evil satisfaction as he spat on the ground at her feet. "Ye didn't expect to see so soon, did ye?"

She opened her mouth to tell Victoria to run but dropped like a sack of stones to the ground, with her mother's pleading voice fading into blackness. "You promised not to hurt her."

Chapter Twenty-One

Consciousness hovered above her like a painful nightmare. Her body ached from all the jarring and bouncing. Lavinia blinked, trying to recall why she rode in a fast-moving carriage. Blurry spots danced before her eyes, and then she caught sight of Victoria's red hair.

"Victoria?" Pain sliced through her head when she lifted it, forcing her eyes to focus. "Where are we?"

The wheels rumbled over ruts and dips at a breakneck pace. She groaned as her arm slipped, and she fell back against the hard leather seat.

Her friend moaned and turned toward her, looking pale and bedraggled. Her red hair fell in waves around her face, and her red velvet ball gown had ripped sleeves.

What in heaven's name happened to them? A flash of Marlboro's victorious smile slashed across her mind, and she struggled to sit up.

Oliver. The Christmas Ball. And her mother's betrayal hit her like a runaway sled.

When she managed to lift her head, she discovered she lay on the unyielding seat of a carriage with her hands tied.

Victoria lay opposite with her hands bound, as well.

"Well, well. You're alive."

Lavinia's breath froze in her lungs. She would know Hudson Becker's whiny voice anywhere. Turning her gaze in slow motion to ease the pain in her head, she met her ex-fiancé's gloating expression and stiffened.

"Oliver will kill you when he discovers what you've done." Her chin lifted as she met Hudson's cold dislike.

"Spare me the speech, Lavinia. I have this well planned, and the earl will take care of the duke. When your meddling lover discovers you are gone, it will be too late. It's already too late. You see, my dear, I refuse to take any more chances with your lovely dowry. We are nearing the Scottish border, and in a few hours, you will be my wife."

The way he said the words sent a shiver of terror down her spine.

"Never." Her heart lodged in her throat, and she swallowed to ease the discomfort.

He chuckled. "You can scream all you like. No one will hear you, and no one will care. I plan to wed you, bed you here in this carriage, and take you back to Becker Estate, where you will stay until you bear me a son. I imagine you shall have a great deal to scream about because I don't plan to be gentle."

"You bastard." Victoria's quiet comment had all the subtlety of a rapier, and Lavinia turned her head to see her friend upright and boiling with rage.

"Which brings us back to you." Hudson folded his hands over his belly and chuckled. "I came to collect one hellcat and found two. I considered your value to me while you two slept and decided I shall keep you. For a time." His gaze slid over her and came to rest on her chest.

Lavinia's fury erupted, and she launched her body at him with her claws out.

He fell from his seat when she slammed into him, and together, they landed in a heap on the floor.

Lavinia held nothing back and struck him as hard as her bound hands would allow.

"Bloody bitch." He slapped her so hard; she tasted blood and spots appeared. She thought she might faint until Victoria's bound hands caught one of hers and tugged her upright.

Lavinia stood up and fell against her friend with a groan, both of them turning in alarm as Hudson clamored to his feet.

Shaking a fist at them, he shouted a steady stream of curses until the carriage lurched, causing him to land with a thump on the opposite seat. "If you want to live to see tomorrow, you will never strike me again. Once I have your dowry, I can breed with any woman I desire and tell society the child is legitimate. They will be told you are a recluse, and after a brief time, the Ton will learn of your tragic death." His grin made her skin crawl. "I do not, in all truth, require you to live until after we are wed and the marriage is witnessed." His gaze darkened. "I shall take great delight in breaking you."

Victoria narrowed her eyes. "Aren't you forgetting the duke?"

Hudson chortled. "He will not want you once I am finished." Resting his white, lace-covered hands on his knee, he tilted his head. "If you think your wit will get you out of this, you are mistaken. Your father and I planned this event with great care. No one will come for you because no one knows anything more than you left to go on a carriage ride with your mother and two guards for security."

At the back of her mind, she remembered Marlboro holding her arm and helping her into the carriage with her mother right behind her.

"What have you done with my mother?"

His smile widened. "The earl sent her south in case she had second thoughts. We cannot have anyone giving away our plans, can we? The duke won't know you are absent until your maid comes to dress you this morning." Flipping open the gold watch he retrieved from his vest pocket, he grinned. "I would imagine he is getting the news soon. It is nine in the morning, and we are an hour away from Gretna Green. By the time he rallies his soldiers, we will be wed, and you will be satisfying my…urges."

She heaved all over the floor while Victoria gripped her hands.

Disgust and annoyance flashed across Hudson's face as he rapped on the roof with his cane to get the driver to stop. Gagging and cursing, he stumbled out the door of the carriage and threw up on the ground.

Marlboro's head appeared in the door and then disappeared. "I told ye she was trouble."

"Shut up, you fool, or I will order you to ride with them. Lavinia attacked me earlier and bloodied my cheek with her nails." His voice paused, and their footsteps walked closer. "How far to Scotland?"

A voice she didn't recognize spoke from the top of the carriage. "Another mile, and we are there, my lord."

Her heart inched higher in her throat, and she cast a worried glance at Victoria. "What are we going to do?"

Her friend grinned. Gagging and choking, she made all the sounds of someone tossing their cookies but not doing so.

Hudson's snort of disgust came seconds before the door slammed shut, leaving them alone. "Don't try to get away. Marlboro will shoot you before you make it two feet."

The carriage swayed as he joined the other two men on top, and the carriage started moving.

Lavinia giggled, before casting a glance at the small wet puddle on the floor of the coach. She grimaced. "I'm sorry I made such a mess."

Victoria laughed as she ripped a piece of her petticoat off and tossed it across the puddle. "Don't apologize. You had nothing in your stomach to worry about. This fabric will contain the mess and the smell. You heard the driver. We have a mile to think up a plan, and your being sick gave us the chance to talk in private."

Different scenarios were discussed and discarded as improbable, too dangerous, or too foolish until the carriage drew to a stop.

Both ladies stared at the closed carriage door and waited. The conveyance rocked as someone climbed down and then another.

The door swung open, revealing Hudson's sneering face. "Don't make a sound. I am going to collect the blacksmith and get this marriage done." He narrowed his gaze at Lavinia. "And don't be difficult or Marlboro will slit Lady Victoria's throat. We've been talking, and your friend will be useful after all, even if nothing more than make you do as you're told." His laugh rippled with evil delight. "I pay attention, too. And I've taken note of how you two care for each other."

Lavinia had a quick impression of an open square with several shops and a few houses before the door slammed behind him with a bang.

Two sets of boots thumped across the ground, standing on either side of the coach doors.

They were trapped, and they both knew it.

Lavinia swallowed. "We need a plan now."

Victoria's wide eyes and thin lips made her stomach clench. "What do you suggest? Shall we scream for help?"

Men's voices, heavy with a Scottish brogue, drifted across the open square.

Lavinia fiddled with the chain around her neck, and she shrugged, remembering how Wallace said the word *English*.

"They won't help two English ladies." The medallion fell into her open hand, and she smiled as she thought of a plan.

"But they might help two Scottish lasses abducted by the English." Wallace's words flashed through her mind. *Ye ken the Scottish and the English dinna like each other, lass?*

"Rock the carriage and scream in your best Scottish accent." Lavinia stood up and threw her body onto the other bench, yelling, "Dinna touch me, ye English pig!"

Victoria grinned and followed suit. "I want me da! Let me go!"

Five minutes of shouting and rocking the carriage later, angry male voices rose around them, and boots approached from several directions. "Who do ye have in there, Englishman?"

"None of yer damn business, Scot. Now off with ye." Marlboro's surly nature did not win him any friends, and more boots approached. "Ye keep quiet in there, or ye'll get my fist."

"Open the door, English, unless ye want to feel *our* fists." The deep voice didn't sound amused by Marlboro's bluster, and Lavinia cried louder.

"I want my da!"

Someone groaned in pain, and scuffling boots trampled the ground around them. Someone cursed, and two bodies dropped to the ground with a thud.

Lavinia braced as the door swung open, and several pairs of furious male eyes peered inside.

One man with red hair and a beard grunted in disgust. "Ye aren't Scottish lasses. What trick is this?"

"No trick." Stepping from the carriage and over the inert body of Marlboro at her feet, she held up her medallion. "We are ladies in trouble. Yes, we are English, but I have a promise from Wallace Armstrong. A favor for a favor, and I never needed a favor as much as now."

Gazing at the group of ten men surrounding them with their arms folded over their broad chests, she prayed for a miracle.

The red-haired man stepped close and turned the medallion over in his hand. "'Tis the Armstrong symbol." He glanced at his companions and then back at her. "Ye shall have the favor."

Lavinia could have wept with relief. "These men abducted me and my friend from Chauncy Castle. There is another man with them who is searching for the blacksmith to force me to marry him. But I love another and must escape. The favor I ask is to borrow two fast horses. Once I am safe, I can have them returned. The castle is a good day's ride from here."

"Did these fine English gentlemen give ye the bruise on yer cheek?" The giant man in front of her withdrew a knife from his belt.

"Yes." Light-headed and filled with dread, she held her breath as he approached. But instead of hurting her as she feared, he slid the point of the blade under the binding and released her hands.

"English or Scottish, we dinna like men who raise their hand to a lass. I am the blacksmith, and the Armstrongs are family. Ye shall have yer horses." Turning, he spoke in Gaelic to the men surrounding them.

Glancing back at Lavinia and Victoria he tilted his head toward an older lady clad in coarse linen and wiping her hands on a towel hanging from her skirt. "Go with Gretta. She will help ye while the men and I take care of yer friends."

Stepping close to Victoria, he cut her binding and slipped his knife back into his belt.

Hudson appeared on the other side of the square and yelled. "Get away from my carriage, you heathens."

The blacksmith pushed Lavinia and Victoria behind his back as the other men lined up on either side, blocking Hudson's view of them. "Get ye gone, and don't worry about the horses. Return them when ye can. We thank ye for luring these fine gentlemen to Gretna Green this morning. The lads and I havna' had a good brawl in a while."

The men grunted their approval and turned to face the furious viscount.

"If ye will come with me, lasses." Gretta's smile revealed several missing teeth, her green eyes snapping with approval. "Hurry."

She waddled away to the south with Victoria and Lavinia hurrying along behind.

"I will be honest. I did not think we would get out of that situation." Her friend swirled her wrists to get the blood flowing as she kept pace with Lavinia.

"Me either." Glancing over her shoulder, she picked

up her pace as Gretta led them into a cottage and into the back room.

"Ye canna ride in yer fancy dresses, ye ken? I have some of my own lass's skirts here, and ye are welcome to them. But ye must hurry. The lads will keep yer gentleman busy long enough for ye to get away."

They needed no further encouragement. Ten minutes later, they mounted spirited mares and raced back the way they came.

Two miles down the road, they veered off the main road and stopped beside a stream to let the animals drink before continuing their journey.

They kept conversation to a minimum and paused every few miles to care for the mares. Later, as they approached a fork in the road and turned southwest toward Falstone, they rounded a bend and discovered the path blocked by a carriage and four outriders, all wearing *her father's* colors!

Lavinia drew on her reins and turned the mare's head around, hoping to escape this obvious trap, but a bullet hit the ground in front of her, causing the mare to rear and whinny in fright.

Victoria's mare almost bumped her haunches in her haste to stop, tossing her head in protest.

"Stop, Lavinia, or the next one is for Arthur's whore." The earl's deep voice halted her mid-flight. His tone indicated he would follow through without hesitation. He stood on the ground beside the carriage with a revolver aimed at Victoria's head.

The girls exchanged a glance as the outriders approached, and despair tightened around Lavinia's chest.

"Tie them to the saddle." The earl fixed his gaze on

the road behind them. "I knew you would escape Hudson. He didn't think you were clever enough, but I know of your cunning. I give it less than an hour before he catches up to you."

"And then what, Papa? You know I will fight for my freedom to the last breath. How can you be certain I will not escape you, too? We are here in the middle of nowhere. Where will you find a priest willing to perform the ceremony? The closest one is in Chauncy village, loyal to Oliver. The duke will come for me, and you will lose everything." She held her father's cold stare without blinking, willing her words to come to pass.

He nodded. "Yes. Everything you say is true except one thing." He gestured toward the carriage. "Come out, Father Brown, and meet my daughter."

Lavinia's hope drained away like sand in a sieve as a thin, pale man wearing clerical robes emerged from the carriage.

From the priest's expression, she knew he wanted to be there as much as she did.

To add to her dismay. Three riders thundered around the bend in the road, their faces twisted with rage. Hudson, Marlboro, and the viscount's coachmen.

"You owe me a hundred pounds, Becker. And as you can see, I was right. My daughter eluded you only to fall into my trap as I predicted."

Hudson slipped from the saddle and stalked over to Lavinia's mare. "I'm not here to exchange pleasantries, Holbrook. You will get the money once I wed your bitch of a daughter." He glared up at her. "Get off the horse."

She glanced at her friend, her mind racing with the desperate need to find another way out of this dire situation.

"We will find a way." Victoria's gaze wavered, but she smiled with determination. "Somehow, I will find you, whatever happens."

Lavinia nodded as Hudson cut her binding and yanked her off the mare. Twisting her arm tight behind her back, he marched her over to stand before her father. "Now, Holbrook, no more delays. Let me show you how to handle your daughter. Drag the other woman over and put a gun to her head so this one does as she's told."

The four outriders took strategic positions around the little party as Hudson pinned Lavinia between him and the earl.

"Father Brown, proceed with the ceremony." He plucked a revolver from one of the outriders and held it against Lavinia's head while her father aimed his at Victoria.

"Wait. I have a better idea. Put Lady Victoria in the carriage and station an outrider in front of the door. I cannot have my bride distracted when I claim her, and together, these two are hellcats."

"Agreed." The earl gave a nod of his head, and one of the men freed Victoria, lifting her from the saddle. It took three of them to wrestle her screaming, kicking body into the carriage and secure the doors with guards on either side.

"Now, Father Brown." Hudson's voice dripped with malice, and Lavinia's stomach churned. Squeezed between her father and Hudson, she could hardly breathe.

"Dearly beloved, we are gathered here…"

The priest's shaking voice droned on in the background as Lavinia closed her eyes and pictured Oliver's face, longing for his presence and the hope he represented. Death would be preferable to what Hudson had in store, and she sighed. Who knew what these devils planned to do to Victoria once they no longer needed her to keep Lavinia in line? Choking back a sob, she straightened her shoulders and searched for a means of escape or a weapon...

Chapter Twenty-Two

Hours earlier, Oliver stood on the raised dais opposite the stairs, engrossed in conversation with an old acquaintance of his father's, when Lavinia and Victoria entered the ballroom.

His breath caught in his throat as the vision in pale pink silk paused at the top of the stairs and lifted her gaze to his. Her golden hair shimmered under the crystal chandeliers, giving her an ethereal glow. Gossamer silk clung to her luscious curves like a new lover's touch, and he couldn't tear his gaze away. Her shining lavender eyes sparkled with joy, and her pink lips curved in a Cupid's bow, making him want to take her in his arms and kiss her. His gaze traced the graceful line of her swanlike neck and lingered on the soft skin of her shoulders revealed by the gown's daring cut.

The tantalizing glimpse of cleavage pushed up by her corset left him speechless. Soon, he would take her to his chamber and explore every inch of her. His hands itched to caress her satin skin, and his lips yearned to taste her secrets.

She looked like a Christmas gift waiting to be unwrapped and savored. The thought made his mouth dry with anticipation.

He drank in the sight of her tiny waist and the gentle flare of her hips before her full skirt cascaded to the floor, adorned with diamonds and seed pearls. Oliver swallowed and shifted position. God, she enticed him as no other.

When he glanced back at her heart-shaped face, his breath rushed from his lungs, for she gave him the same heated inspection he gave her.

When their gazes tangled, he recognized the heat of desire in her eyes and tightened his grip on the champagne flute in his hand. God, how he wanted her. In two long days, they would be wed, and the anticipation was almost unbearable.

"Who is the young lady you are staring at with such interest?" Lord Dolby nudged him, drawing his attention.

"She is my fiancée, Lady Lavinia Holbrook." He grinned. "Tell me I'm not the luckiest man alive."

"Holbrook. Isn't she the lady who left Viscount Becker at the altar?" Lord Dolby chuckled as if pleased with the whole affair. "I laughed for days. Blown off, Becker didn't come to White's for weeks after she disappeared because he didn't have the stones to deal with the scandal. No one thought she would get another proposal after such a fiasco. But what about you, Oliver? What if she leaves you hanging as well?"

The duke dismissed the doubt with a wave of his hand and raised his glass in a toast to Lavinia. "She left Becker for me. You see, my dear Lord Dolby, she is not only beautiful but also quite clever."

"And I cannot argue with that." Lord Dolby paused and took a long swallow of his drink. "Who is the ravishing creature beside your Lady Lavinia? I do not believe I've had the pleasure of meeting her before. Such exotic beauty, I would remember."

Oliver's grin widened. "Would you? Allow me to

present Lady Victoria Beaumont, Lavinia's closest friend and confidante until now."

Lord Dolby choked in surprise and then shouted with laughter. "Only you, dear boy, could host the two most notorious women in the Ton and come out unscathed. I must confess to a twinge of jealousy. Marriage to Lady Lavinia will not be boring, especially with Lady Victoria Beaumont in the picture. I hear even the Mother Superior at their convent had her hands full with those two troublemakers as students."

Oliver turned his head to assess the two women one more time and shook his head. "I do not doubt the truth of it for a moment. I shall have to get Lavinia to tell me the tale one day." He couldn't tear his gaze away from the two.

Victoria Beaumont stood tall and elegant beside Lavinia. Dressed in a red velvet gown with a plunging neckline and daring drape, her red hair swept high on her head and sparkling with diamonds. She possessed the allure of an exotic flower, lush and ripe, waiting for the right man to tame her, while beside her, Lavinia embodied the typical English rose, sweet, untried, and innocent. Together, the two women drew every male head in the room, to Oliver's dismay and Lord Dolby's amusement.

"Steady on, old boy. If she loves you, she'll be true to you, and no other man will do." Lord Dolby clapped him on the shoulder and nodded at the duchess who held court with the other influential women of the Ton who braved the cold to attend. "I believe I will sit with Arabella for a spell. She is more to my taste and temperament."

"And still in love with my father." Oliver couldn't

resist teasing, noting his mother's reluctance for male companionship, even Lord Dolby's.

In answer, the older gentleman raised a hand as he strolled away. "I can hope. With persistence, I may persuade her to reconsider."

Oliver fell silent as he studied his mother. Her white hair framed her face, coiffed in the latest updo, drawing attention to her long neck. A handsome woman, she wore a pale blue silk gown complimenting her bright blue all-seeing- eyes, a faint smile playing on her lips as Lord Dolby approached. Whatever he said made her blush and extend her hand for his greeting.

Oliver frowned. He may have been hasty warning Lord Dolby away, for his mother never blushed or flirted. And now she did both.

Turning his attention back to the ballroom and his guests, he swept the area for any sign of trouble. Ten of his men were stationed at the tavern to keep an eye on Viscount Becker and the earl. Two squads of men surrounded the castle, and extra guards were posted at every door.

If he couldn't cancel the festivities, he could damn well keep Lavinia safe. And what better way than holding her in his arms and dancing the night away?

Around midnight, Oliver went in search of Mrs. Whittle. Lavinia had not returned, and his anxiety mounted with each passing second. Three hours elapsed since the countess demanded Lavinia's attention, and although he knew little of women's ailments, he couldn't imagine it would require so much time.

When Mrs. Whittle informed him neither Lady Lavinia, Lady Victoria nor the countess were in their chambers, he sent for Cecil and Tom.

Two hours later, he growled in frustration. The last time his love or Lady Victoria were seen, they entered a carriage along with the countess and two men dressed as his guards, who he now knew were imposters.

The real guards came to, and after questioning them, he discovered the countess lured the men into the stable under false pretenses, where they were ambushed, beaten, and left unconscious in their small clothes. After the men gave their description of the villains, he swore. Marlboro and another unknown accomplice, no doubt in the viscount's employ, abducted the two younger women with the help of the countess.

Sending a rider to the village, Oliver discovered that a single coach left the inn around midnight with two passengers, both posing as priests.

Viscount Becker, dressed in holy robes, would make even the devil uncomfortable.

Fueled with fury over Lavinia's mother's betrayal, his inability to protect his fiancée, and his fear of losing her forever, he ordered his stallion and rushed to his room to change.

His mind raced with worry. Where would they take her? The marriage had to be legal for Becker to claim Lavinia's gold and for Holbrook to secure his title.

The closest place would be Gretna Green unless the other man in the carriage truly was a priest.

His stomach clenched, and his fury mounted. Racing down the stairs, he stepped into his mother's salon to deliver the news.

"Bring her back, Oliver. She is good for both of us." The duchess's blue eyes glittered with concern and grief.

Nodding, he strode away to divide his men into groups and dispatch them to every known place of worship within a day's ride, demanding immediate reports.

Weary, determined, and furious, he thundered along the northern road to Scotland with his heart hammering in his chest. What a fool he'd been not to declare his love and his need to hold her close. For weeks, she'd been within arm's reach, and he ignored her, avoided her, and refused to acknowledge his need for her in his life. Glancing up at the morning sky, he pleaded for one more chance to be with her.

****

"…is there anyone who can give just cause why this man and this woman should not be joined together in Holy Matrimony? Let him speak now or forever hold his peace."

"I take grave issue with the matter." A male voice shattered the tense silence to Lavinia's right, and her eyes flew open.

Turning, she gaped at the man beside her with a wicked blade pressed against Hudson's neck. *"Arthur?"*

Her father's men straightened in surprise to stare at the newcomer.

Arthur turned his head to smile at her, and his expression darkened to thunderous proportions as they skidded over her bruised cheek. "Who did this to you?"

Lavinia's gaze shifted to Hudson, and her brother uttered several colorful swear words she had never heard before.

"Release my sister, you foul miscreant, or I will slice you from ear to ear with the same knife you left in my back." Her brother stood behind her, more furious than she thought possible.

Hudson choked, and on her other side, the earl

stiffened, turning his head in slow motion.

"Arthur?" All the blood drained from his face, and his eyes widened in shock.

"Hello, Father. We will have a talk after I deal with this lying, back-stabbing, treacherous piece of scum you're attempting to marry my sister to."

The older outrider gasped out loud. "Master Arthur?"

Victoria's white face appeared in the window, and she burst into tears. "Arthur!"

The world spun around Lavinia, making her dizzy. Perhaps she died, after all, and her brother came to rescue her from hell. Mother Superior had warned her this would be her fate if she didn't repent. And here she was.

Her brother's hair was the same shade of brown as she remembered, and his eyes, although angry, sparkled like they did when they were young.

Lavinia choked back a sob as a year of loneliness and grief washed over her. "I missed you, Brother. And if ever I needed you, I do now more than ever."

"I know, and I'm here." Arthur kept his gaze on Hudson. "Becker, recount in full the events of our last meeting, or you shall face dire circumstances."

The earl collapsed beside her, holding his chest and sputtering. His weapon clattered to the ground beside him, his mouth agape and eyes glazed with shock.

Marlboro frowned, glanced around at his preoccupied companions, and then hurried over to the mares Lavinia and Victoria borrowed from the Scots.

Lavinia couldn't decide if she should stop Marlboro or rescue a howling Victoria, but Oliver and a platoon of his soldiers made the choice for her.

Later, she couldn't remember what happened first.

Once the men at arms recognized Arthur, they dropped their weapons at his command.

Victoria burst from the carriage and raced over to throw her body into Arthur's waiting arms with a cry of disbelief.

The duke's soldiers surrounded Marlboro and the nasty carriage driver. Apprehending them, they were bound, gagged, and locked inside the earl's carriage for the long journey back to London, where they would face trial for abduction, murder, and attempted murder.

A whining, blubbering Hudson dropped to his knees before Arthur, who had one arm around Victoria and the other gripping the knife.

He confessed to stabbing Arthur in the back and leaving him for dead.

Oliver hurried to Lavinia's side, enfolding her in his arms, his gaze locking onto her bruised cheek where Hudson struck her. "Bloody hell. The bastard hit you."

Lavinia gazed up at the duke, and a gasp escaped her lips as she met the fiery rage burning in his eyes.

Without a word, Oliver seared the viscount with a murderous expression. In one swift movement, he turned to the whimpering man and drew his sword.

Lavinia swallowed, her knees knocking together a rapid staccato.

The sword flashed, and Hudson's scream pierced the air. Blood streamed from a deep slash across his cheek from ear to chin.

Oliver sheathed his weapon with a regretful shake of his head, staring down at the writhing man. "I promised Arthur I wouldn't kill you, or you would be breathing your last for touching Lavinia." His gaze flickered to Arthur. "He's yours. If I touch him again, I will kill him."

The knife in Arthur's hand flashed.

Hudson let out another shriek of terror, clutching his other cheek where Arthur sliced an identical path from ear to chin.

"That is for striking my sister." The blade flashed once more, slashing Hudson's shirt open to his waist, leaving a bloody trail across his chest. "And that is for stabbing me in the back." Arthur's gaze narrowed, cold and resolute. "While we only inflict mere flesh wounds today, true retribution will come as every lady you encounter recoils in horror at your appearance and every nobleman learns of your treachery. You shall be forever branded as an outcast, your reputation and good name forever tarnished."

Hudson's screams could wake the dead, and Lavinia trembled anew.

Arthur glanced at the constables waiting nearby on their horses. "He's all yours. We agreed to let him face the humiliation of court rather than kill him here for his crimes. Take him away before I or the duke change our minds."

Several constables rode forward to arrest Hudson and take him to Newgate, where he would await trial in the House of Lords.

The next thing Lavinia knew, Oliver had her in his arms, kissing her with such passionate, frenzied urgency she couldn't breathe.

"Thank God we arrived in time, and you are safe. I have been out of my mind with worry, and I deeply regret not carrying you off to my chamber the night of the ball as I desired. If I had, none of this would have happened." He expelled a long sigh and shook his head. "I'm grateful for a second chance to say what I should have said weeks ago. I love you, my darling, with all my heart and soul. No woman has ever been or will ever be as perfect for me as you are. I have known the truth for weeks and fought against it with every fiber of my being." Kissing her nose, he stroked her cheek. "But I could not escape you or the way my heart swells when you are near. I will never let you out of my sight again. You have no idea of the agony I suffered when I discovered you were missing. I fancied I would go mad at the thought of what Becker planned to do to you. I've never wanted to kill a man as much as I do him. God, when I think of what could have happened, I go a little crazy." Pausing to give her another lingering kiss, he continued. "But this is the season of miracles and dreams come true. Not only did we arrive on time, but we brought a miracle with us.

"Imagine my surprise when I raced down the stairs to rescue you and discovered your brother having tea with Arabella. I have so many questions, and we have much to discuss. But first, I must get you home and warm."

She had never felt so cherished, so worthy. With every kiss, her heart threw off the chains of the past, her insecurities, and her fear of the future. She wanted to shout with joy over the love she read in his eyes, the desire she felt in his touch, and the passion she tasted in his kisses. "I am warm. You heat me with your love until I cannot contain my delight. I love you too, Oliver."

Tenderness shimmered in his incredible eyes as he leaned closer.

The last of her words were smothered by his lingering sensual lips, kissing her into a state of blissful oblivion.

She never imagined she could be this happy or this loved.

"Forgive me, my darling, for not realizing your importance in my life until now. I have been so wrong about so many things. I thought if I allowed my heart to care for you, I would lose my strength and become another blabbering idiot spouting sonnets. But now I know your love makes me stronger. Every time I thought of you leaving or marrying another man, a stone settled in my stomach, and I lost interest in everything around me. My mother once told me true love makes life so much more *livable*.

"And she is right. With you in my life, everything is sharper, clearer, and far more enticing than anything I believed possible before. You are mine, Lavinia. Promise me you will never leave me again." Placing a gentle kiss on her temple, he continued. "I didn't like the time you spent with Dunhaven and wanted to run him through for daring to touch you. I detested your Scot even more. I went a little crazy when you spoke of leaving with him. The sight of his chain around your neck filled me with fury. But it wasn't until I discovered you were missing that I accepted the truth. You hold my heart in your hands, my darling, and I cannot live without you."

Tightening his hold around her, he whispered into her hair. "Tomorrow cannot come fast enough for me. For on the morrow, I make you mine forever."

Heat filled her cheeks as he stared down at her, and she resisted the urge to rest her head on his chest. God, it felt good to be held and cherished. With him, she had value, worth, and, most of all, love. Tears of joy filled her eyes, spilling down her cheeks as her heart overflowed with happiness.

Cradling Lavinia's chin with his hand, he brushed away a tear with the pad of his thumb. "Don't cry, my love. I am here and will never let you go."

Trembling with the aftermath of the last twelve hours, she took a deep breath. Who would have thought such a strong man could be so tender? "I know."

"But we must discuss something before we return to the castle."

When she glanced up at him, she discovered his gaze resting on Arthur and Victoria, a few feet away, sharing a passionate kiss.

"How do you feel about sharing our wedding day with your brother?" His lop-sided smile sent thrills through her, and she discovered, to her surprise, that she could love him even more.

"I am thrilled and delighted to share our wedding day with them."

"Then it's settled."

Her heart almost burst with joy, and she tugged loose to throw her arms around Arthur and Victoria.

Startled, they broke apart with a laugh.

"We have something to ask you, Brother, dear." Tucking her arm in Oliver's, she smiled and asked. "Will you wed with us tomorrow at the cathedral in Chauncy village? Nothing would make me happier than sharing my special day with the two people who mean more to me than anyone except Oliver. Please say yes."

They exchanged glances, and Arthur cleared his throat. "I have not asked if you still want to—"

"Yes! A thousand times, yes!" Victoria's smile rivaled the sun as she beamed at her beloved.

"Then, I suggest we return to the castle to prepare

for tomorrow." Oliver tucked her into his side and turned to motion to his men.

One of the captains approached and nodded toward the earl, now lying on his side. "Your Grace, what should we do with him?"

All four turned, and Arthur walked over to touch the side of his neck. "He's alive."

In the excitement, she forgot all about her father. "What should we do?"

She didn't want her father anywhere near her wedding and waited for Arthur's suggestion.

"He can go to the village, and we will send for the doctor. If he is fit enough to travel, we will have him transported to Holbrook Estate." Arthur smiled at her. "I know Papa gave you a hard time, and there are explanations to make. I do not blame you for not wanting him at your wedding, and after the way he's treated Vicotria, I don't want him at mine, either."

Oliver nodded. "We are agreed." He ordered his men to escort the earl to the village and deliver a report once the doctor examined him.

Then, he swept Lavinia into his arms and rode back to the castle with her tucked beneath his heavy cloak and her head resting on his broad chest.

All the way, she thought about the last few weeks and how often she wished Oliver held her as he did now. With a sigh of satisfaction, she wrapped her arms around his waist and snuggled closer to his heat.

The next thing she knew, he shook her awake. "We are home, my darling." No five words ever sounded better than those, and she gave him a sleepy smile.

Chapter Twenty-Three

"Where have you been all this time? It's been over a year since you sailed for France." Lavinia sat on a satin settee beside Oliver as the yule log burned bright on the hearth in the duchess's salon. She had a soft woolen blanket tucked around her legs and Oliver's arm around her shoulders to keep her warm.

Arabella sat on her left, holding Princess on her lap and smiling.

On the opposite settee, Arthur and Victoria snuggled beneath another woolen blanket, his arm holding her tight against his side as she glowed with happiness.

Arthur cleared his throat. "The first time I met the man who held the title to the hundred acres belonging to Holbrook Estate, a ruffian ambushed me outside the tavern. I fought him off, thinking nothing of it. Later, after I collected the title, I stepped outside into the alley to return to my rooms in preparation for my journey back to England. I did not see Becker until his knife entered my back, and I fell to the cobblestones, hitting my head and losing consciousness.

"Later, I discovered a Sûreté found me, but a kind merchant carted me away before they came to collect my body. The merchant's wife, Giselle, had a healing touch and nursed me back to health. But she could not heal my mind.

"I struck my head when I fell from Becker's blow,

and when I woke, I could not remember my name, where I came from, or anything of my former life. Though she tried different herbs and techniques and even asked a Gypsy to restore my memory, nothing worked.

"For most of last year, I lived on the merchant's farm, helping him raise turkeys, pigeons, and hogs for sale in his market. They called me Pierre, and I never ventured into town except on the odd occasion when I delivered fresh meat for the merchant to sell.

"A month ago, I brought a delivery into the market, and a beautiful aristocrat, Lady Dubois, strolled in to order pheasant for a special dinner at her chateau. Her red hair glistened in the morning sun, blinding me. When she turned her head to laugh, a flash of intense pain dropped me to my knees, and I saw Victoria in my mind's eye. My memory returned in waves—sometimes an entire event all at once, other times just a word or a name until I remembered that night on the docks.

"Becker stabbed me, laughed in my face, and bragged about marrying my sister. He took the deed from my pocket and sauntered off, leaving me to die alone in a narrow alley with his knife in my back.

"I thank God daily for the kind merchant who found me and nursed me back to health. And I am grateful for Lady Dubois and her glorious red hair, which brought back the memory of my beautiful Victoria."

They sat quietly, deep in thought, as Arthur told his tale. "The doctor in the village marveled at my recovery and informed me that memory loss after a traumatic experience is oft times permanent. On rare occasions, the individuals regain their memory. I must have a saint praying for me or a vigilant guardian angel. Perhaps both." Kissing Victoria's hair, he shook his head. "Once

I returned to England. I visited my estate, and Victoria's butler caught me up on the family news. You will never know how the news of Lavinia's wedding to the very man who robbed me and left me for dead devastated me. I saddled a horse and rode for Falstone as fast as I could hoping to arrive in time." He gave her a smile. "Thank heavens I did." He frowned. "Although one mystery remains unsolved: my father's private account. His man informed me the earl was in debt to some gentleman for the sum of two hundred thousand pounds. My father has a racing problem he cannot control, and lack of funding is his excuse for harassing my Victoria. He could not stand to have her living in luxury while he squandered the family coffers and could not touch the rest of Holbrook's wealth because it is entailed."

The markers!

Understanding dawned. Glancing up at Oliver, Lavinia tilted her head to study him. "You held his markers and threatened to call them in if he didn't leave me alone."

The duke nodded. "Indeed. If I did so, he would be unable to pay and would end up in debtor's prison. We both knew the outcome, and that's why he dared not cross me further."

She sighed. "Thank you for being so wonderful."

His eyes darkened, and he leaned down to whisper in her ear. "I cannot wait until tomorrow night when I shall show *you* how wonderful you are to me."

Tingles spread through her body like wildfire, and she trembled beneath the heat of his gaze. "I cannot wait, either."

Oliver glanced at his mother. "Since tonight is a night for revealing secrets, why did you make your wager about my wedding? What scheme did you concoct to bring about my downfall? Though I took every precaution, here I am. I must know, Mother."

The duchess's eyes sparkled in the dancing flames of the fire as she gave him a wide smile and a delicate shrug of her shoulders. "Nothing."

Oliver scoffed. "I do not believe you. After all the plots you've put into motion over the last three years, I do not think you would give up without a fight."

Her laughter filled the salon. "That is the beauty of the entire wager, Oliver. I challenged you with it after I watched you and Lavinia at breakfast the morning after her arrival. Any fool could see the two of you were meant to be together. All I had to do was wait and let things take their natural course. I made the wager to throw you off balance and keep you guessing about my activities. I also wanted to make a little money as consolation for making me wait so long to welcome your bride."

The duke shook his head. "You are more devious than any would suppose by your angelic, frail demeanor. Well played, Mother."

With a smug smile, the duchess cleared her throat. "Tomorrow will be here too soon if we do not get some rest. Shall we adjourn to our separate chambers?" She gave Oliver and Lavinia a pointed stare. "We must sleep if we are to be fresh and invigorated for the ceremony."

Oliver's mouth quirked. "Of course, Mother. But I shall escort Lavinia to her chamber before retiring to mine."

"No, Oliver. Cecil will do the honors, and Tom is here to escort Lady Victoria. We shall be proper for this one night, and then I shall not intrude in your private affairs again." Arabella rose to her feet and motioned for

Cecil and Tom to enter the salon.

"I wish I could believe you, Mother, but I wager the same ten thousand pounds that within a month, you shall badger me about producing a grandchild for you to hold, and I fear you will get involved in my private affairs once more. Although…" A thoughtful look crossed his face before his mouth turned up in a wicked grin. "If you are as creative about acquiring a grandchild as you were about acquiring a daughter-in-law, I may not mind the interference."

Lavinia's cheeks burned with heat, and she ducked her head in embarrassment while Arthur shouted with laughter.

Victoria rose with a wide grin and linked her arm to Lavinia's. "Come along, Liv. The sooner we sleep, the sooner tomorrow comes. And I, for one, am done with today."

Beside her, Lavinia shivered. "I agree. Good night, Your Grace." Dipping a curtsy to the duchess, she turned to Oliver.

He swooped down and kissed her hard before letting her go. "Good night, my love."

Thrills swept through her over the way his eyes darkened, and his voice deepened when he spoke.

Arthur caught her and hugged her tightly. "I love you, sister, and you have no idea how good it feels to tell you so."

Oh, but she did. However, that conversation could wait for another time and place.

Marveling at the way the day turned from one extreme to the other, the girls wandered off to bed, whispering about their coming wedding.

"I am so happy I could cry." Lavinia sighed as she

stopped outside her chamber door.

"I, as well. But think, Lavinia, tomorrow all our dreams will come true.

And she was right.

Christmas Day dawned in a brilliant display of orange, red, and pink. The sun emerged to warm the frozen ground and make diamond crystals in the snow.

Lavinia woke to Annie carrying in a tray of fresh fruit from the duke's hothouse, tea, and some of Cook's buttery soft biscuits.

"Good morning, my lady. Happy Christmas, and Happy Wedding Day." She placed the tea on the table beside the bed and propped pillows behind Lavinia so she could sit up to eat.

"Good morning. And Happy Christmas to you, too." Her heart swelled with happiness, and she sank back against the mound of feather pillows as Annie set the tray across her knees.

A sharp knock came at the door, and Annie frowned. "Who is there?"

"Cecil. His Grace sent me with a Christmas surprise for Lady Lavinia." The butler's voice boomed in the empty corridor as Annie hurried over to open the door.

A moment later, she returned with a dozen of the most beautiful red roses Lavinia had ever seen, tied with a white satin bow.

"I am to tell you His Grace counts the hours until you meet in church." Giggling, she set the bouquet on the vanity before the mirror. "His Grace is so romantic, and they will be stunning next to your white gown."

After a lavish bath with heated water and luxurious rose-scented soap, Lavinia sat before the fire in her satin dressing gown while Annie dried and styled her hair.

Curled high on her head, her maid threaded rubies through her thick curls.

Lavinia dropped her dressing gown and stood while Annie slipped a delicate silk chemise over her head, edged with dainty embroidery around the neck and hem. Silk pantalets came next, followed by silk stockings held in place with elaborate satin garters tied with tiny bows.

"Hold onto the bed, my lady, while I lace up your corset." Annie slipped the article under her arms and tightened the laces in the back until satisfied with the results. "You have a tiny waist, my lady. But I can say with certainty it will not last. The duchess is determined to have a grandchild by next Christmas."

Lavinia's face heated, and she stammered for an appropriate answer.

Annie chuckled. "Don't pay me any mind. I say what I think. I'm sure His Grace will consider your delicate feelings.

Oliver's child. She stared down at her flat abdomen, envisioning her belly protruding past her shoes, and sighed. Everything would be all right if she had Oliver by her side.

Next came the silk petticoats, followed by the satin underskirt stitched with tiny seed pearls and elaborate embroidery. The bodice emphasized her tiny waist and drew attention to her breasts pushed high by her corset. The low rounded neckline skimmed the top of her bosom, trimmed with more seed pearls and elaborate embroidery, all in white silk. Tight fitting sleeves hugged her arms to the elbows and then dropped in a cascade of lace.

Lavinia turned before the floor-length looking glass and sighed with pleasure over the tiny train trailing behind her. The embroidery halfway up the back of her skirt and along the lower edge gave the wedding gown an elaborate, elegant feel.

Slipping her feet into tiny satin slippers, she turned to stare at her reflection. Her cheeks were flushed pink with excitement, her lavender eyes brilliant with joy, and her lips curved with happiness.

The Chauncy family tiara lay on her bed beside her delicate lace veil, and she chuckled, remembering the last time she laced up a wedding gown.

Hudson Becker no longer worried her, and with Marlboro in prison, and her father in a deep sleep in the village, she had nothing to fear now.

Oliver loved her and wanted to spend the rest of his life with her.

Lavinia smiled and held out her arms as Annie carried in a length of red velvet ribbon. "I thought we could tie this around your waist to match the rubies in your hair. It is Christmas, and with the bouquet of roses His Grace sent, you will be the perfect Christmas bride."

A wedding and a duke for Christmas. Nurse's rhyme worked, after all.

An hour later, she walked into the cathedral holding the duchess's arm.

They argued over who would give whom away.

Arthur demanded the right to escort his sister down the aisle, but she protested.

"And leave your bride waiting alone? No, Arthur. I thank you for the offer, and though my heart swells with joy at your presence, this is your wedding day, too."

In the end, the duchess volunteered to do the honors for both girls at once.

"Chauncy women are not cowards. We do not mind

what the masses think of us. We do the right thing and hold our heads high while we do so."

Since neither had any other family present, they agreed and walked on either side of her down the aisle to their waiting grooms.

Lavinia's mouth went dry at the first sight of her handsome husband-to-be. Dressed in full formal attire, he took her breath away. Black windswept hair above piercing blue eyes, a square chin, and a straight nose. His pointed collars and starched white cravat gleamed in the sunlight pouring through the stained-glass windows of the cathedral. A black satin collar topped a black velvet jacket tailored to fit his body like a glove, highlighting broad shoulders, a narrow waist, and lean hips that led down to the high shine of his boots. Oliver wore a red vest embroidered with gold to honor Christmas, and a gleam sparkled in his dark eyes as he watched her walk toward him.

Victoria wore a red velvet gown adorned with white roses. She held a delicate spray of tiny white roses in her hand and wore the Holbrook tiara, which Arthur had tucked into his saddle bags before leaving Holbrook Manor on his way north.

Together, they created a stir as the crowd turned in their seats to see the Duchess of Chauncy, resplendent in a white and gold gown, leading the two brides to the altar.

Oliver's gaze could have melted ice in the middle of a blizzard as he took her trembling fingers in his and kissed her bare knuckles. "You take my breath away, my love."

"And you mine," she replied.

The ceremony felt like both an eternity and a

fleeting moment.

The next thing she knew, Oliver took her in his arms and kissed her before turning to present her to the crowd.

"My duchess and my love." His announcement sent thrills through her body as he beamed with pride and offered her his arm.

Arthur and Victoria stood beside them, glowing with love and happiness.

They returned to the castle for dinner and dancing following the ceremony, inviting the whole village to join the festivities.

Lavinia had no idea what she ate for dinner that night and sat beside Oliver in a golden bubble of bliss until he led her to the ballroom where the crowd gathered to continue the celebration.

More than one guest commented on the striking picture they made with her blonde hair against his black. Her white gown contrasted with his black suit, and her delicate frame compared to his muscular one.

Lavinia flushed with pleasure when he drew her into his arms for their first dance together as husband and wife.

"The red velvet bow on the waist of your gown is driving me insane, my love. I wish to take you back to my chamber and untie you to see my Christmas gift and give you mine."

Her heart swelled with happiness until she thought she would burst with joy.

"I already have yours, Oliver. You give me love, acceptance, and joy. I have everything I will ever need when you hold me in your arms. I am yours now and forever, and I wouldn't have it any other way."

Much later, as Lavinia and Victoria sat together

whispering as they waited for their new husbands to bid the guests good night, Victoria squeezed her hand.

"Do you ever wonder what the sisters would say if they could see us now?" Her smile widened as she took a sip of her wine.

Lavinia considered her question. "They would cluck their tongues and commend our husband's souls into God's hands for marrying us."

They both giggled at the thought.

"Did you ever suppose we would end up married and respectable?" Victoria flushed when Arthur tossed her a kiss.

"No. I didn't have much hope of anything when we drove north months ago. I figured I would end up an old maid in Scotland, living with Mama's cousin." She sighed and hugged her dearest friend. "I am so relieved things did not work out as I expected. Because here I am with everything I ever wanted and much more. I will never again doubt the power of Christmas or the miracle of the North Star again. I have you. I have Arthur, and I have Oliver. Together, we are a family."

And Victoria had to agree.

Arthur appeared at their side and whisked Victoria away with a smile and hug.

Lavinia sat alone, twirling her wine glass until Oliver appeared by her side. He plucked the glass from her hand and set it on a nearby table.

"Are you ready to retire, my beautiful new wife?" He kissed the side of her neck and drew her to her feet.

"Oh yes." She smiled and stroked the side of his face with the tips of her fingers still deep in thought.

"What are you thinking with such a serious expression?" Tucking her trembling arm through his, he led her toward the stairs leading to the master chamber.

"I have my miracle, for on this Christmas, I thee wed, and together we shall live happily ever after."

And they did.

Epilogue

The Earl of Holbrook never regained consciousness and died two weeks later. The doctor told them the earl had suffered a stroke. And whether caused by the shock of his son's return from the dead or from striking his head when he fell, he could not be certain.

Arthur had his father's body transported to Holbrook estate, where he laid him to rest on a hill overlooking the cherished hundred acres that caused them all so much turmoil.

Marlboro never faced trial. One of his fellow inmates took offense to his arrogance and slit his throat before he could be brought before the magistrate. The warden buried him in an unmarked grave where he spent eternity, alone and forgotten.

Hudson Becker's trial came up on the House of Lords docket a year later, but his health had deteriorated too much for him to attend. He succumbed to illness caused by the damp condition of the prison, refusing to eat or drink the rations provided. He died in a soiled set of clothes he wouldn't have been caught dead in when alive.

The Countess of Holbrook sought refuge with her oldest daughter until she learned of her husband's passing. The following week, she arrived on Arthur's doorstep, pleading for shelter, and spent the better part of an hour cajoling her son to forgive her for past grievances against Victoria. "You cannot hold me accountable for such paltry offenses. All is in the past now that you are both respectable."

But Arthur did not bend. "After the way you behaved toward my wife, I am surprised you ask. I could forgive your bitterness but not your betrayal. You aided Papa and Becker in abducting Victoria and Lavinia, the two who never lost faith in me or each other. For that, I cannot forgive you."

Tears filled her eyes and dripped down her cheeks. "Mortimer threatened to keep me from seeing Miryam and Anabel unless I delivered the girls to the garden."

"Then isn't it fitting you shall spend the rest of your days with them?" Arthur ordered her off Holbrook Estates, and the countess returned to her daughter Miryam's home to live out her remaining years.

Arthur and Victoria went on to have two children and enjoyed a long and joyful life together as husband and wife. Though they never forgot their first child, Charles, their days were filled with gratitude for their family.

Lavinia and Oliver were blessed with three children, one of whom later attended schooling at the same convent as Lavinia and Victoria.

When the older sisters learned the bright-eyed girl with the black hair, Mary, was Lavinia's daughter, the Mother Superior asked to be transferred to another region, leaving the younger unsuspecting sisters to care for her.

They soon regretted their impulsive decision and spent the next four years navigating through the various escapades of the precocious child.

Lavinia read every letter the sisters wrote and

laughed until she cried, empathizing with both sides of the anecdotes.

When Oliver commented on her amusement, she would tuck the letter away and smile. "There is nothing to worry about, my love. Our daughter is having the time of her life and will grow to be a very wise lady."

Lavinia spoke from experience because Mary, her daughter, mirrored her spirited nature at the same age.

But Mary possessed an additional charm. She was born a year to the day of their wedding.

"How can you be so sure?" Oliver teased, pulling her close and planting a tender kiss on her lips.

"Because Mary is our Christmas miracle, born on Christmas Day. What else could she be but extraordinary?"

And he had to agree.

A word about the author...

I knit, crochet, quilt, sew, and embroider. I love roses and the smell of gardenias. My happy place is sitting on the beach and watching the waves. They are very calming to me.

I occasionally bake when the mood strikes me. Mostly I consider cooking and baking necessary evils.

My husband of forty years is my greatest fan/critic and I don't know what I would do without him. My family is my greatest support and I love every minute I spend with them. Life is a journey and I can't wait to see where it leads me next!